There was a vulnerability about the princess that appealed to the hunter and the warrior in him.

Yet since he'd seized her at the castle, she hadn't made much of a fuss or begged to go home, or even shed a tear. No, he'd seen a defiant strength beneath her delicate exterior, but also a kindness when she'd tried to help that man at the settlement earlier today, and even himself. Brand was starting to wonder if she had a bad bone in her delectable body. Her only vice seemed to be her choice of husband and that she was a Saxon.

Her soldier comrades seemed to have taken the main track out of the forest, and he hoped if the two of them remained by the hedgerow, they could stay hidden and one step ahead.

"Is that the ocean?" Lady Anne said, her voice a whisper on the wind. It was the first time she'd spoken to him since the forest. Since he'd kissed her.

What had he been thinking? Damn him, he must not be put off course by her pretty face, no matter how tempting she was. He told himself it was a temporary lapse of judgment—faced with the reminder of how she'd saved him once, and was offering to do the same again, he'd weakened. But it must not, could not, happen again.

Author Note

Thank you so much for choosing to read
The Viking's Stolen Princess.

Brand, the hero, has been in my thoughts for a
while now. Strong yet compassionate, and with his
penetrating blue gaze and wicked grin, he is the
most fascinating man you could ever meet. He owes
Princess Anne a debt for saving his life, and when
he steals her away, he believes he is rescuing her
from the brutal hands of her future husband, as well
as seeking blood vengeance on the man who killed
his father.

Brand's fearsome reputation has been cultivated
through careful design on his part, and he keeps up
his fierce-warrior act with Anne initially, wary of how
her beauty makes him feel. He fights his enemies
along their journey, but the biggest battle he has to
face is over his feelings for this kind Saxon princess.

Beautiful and spirited, Anne has lived a repressed
life and is tired of being used as a shiny penny
to be bargained with to protect her father's lands
and power. When she is captured by Brand the
Barbarian, the adventure of her life begins. And I
so enjoyed going on this adventure with her.

I hope you enjoy being a part of Brand and Anne's
lives as much as I have.

Recycling programs for this product may not exist in your area.

ISBN-13: 978-1-335-40754-2

The Viking's Stolen Princess

Copyright © 2021 by Sarah Rodi

This edition published by arrangement with Harlequin Books S.A.

For questions and comments about the quality of this book, please contact us at CustomerService@Harlequin.com.

Harlequin Enterprises ULC
22 Adelaide St. West, 41st Floor
Toronto, Ontario M5H 4E3, Canada
www.Harlequin.com

Printed in U.S.A.

SARAH RODI

—

The Viking's
Stolen Princess

Sarah Rodi has always been a hopeless romantic. She grew up watching old romantic movies recommended by her grandad and devouring love stories from the local library. Sarah lives in the village of Cookham in Berkshire, UK, where she enjoys walking along the River Thames with her husband, her two daughters and their dog. She has been a magazine journalist for over twenty years, but it has been her lifelong dream to write romance for Harlequin. Sarah believes everyone deserves to find their happy-ever-after. You can contact her via @sarahrodiedits or sarahrodiedits@gmail.com

The Viking's Stolen Princess
is Sarah Rodi's debut title for Harlequin Historical.

Look out for more books from Sarah Rodi
coming soon.

Visit the Author Profile page
at Harlequin.com.

For Chris, Mya and Ayda

Chapter One

Termarth Castle, late spring, 821

Princess Anne ran along the ramparts of Termarth Castle like a hunted deer in desperate flight, her hair fluttering in the cool evening breeze. The battlements of the impressive fortress were meant to keep her safe from attack, yet in reality they had kept her prisoner her entire life. But it wasn't the place she despised, it was the man who held her hostage—her father, King Eallesborough.

He had shown her little kindness when she was growing up—it was male heirs he had wanted. But now it was as if Anne had blossomed into a shiny silver coin to be bargained with and he'd finally cashed in.

At the end of the north corner she came to a stop, gasping for breath and gripping onto the cold stone wall to steady herself. The sun was fading fast as she looked out over the sweeping countryside, where little fires from the tiny cottages were lighting up all over the land.

The people deserved better than her father to rule them, and so did she. Every day they heard more accounts about the Northmen and their devastating raids on defenceless villages, and even though she did everything she could to help—finding families shelter, sending out scraps from the kitchens and tending to the sick or wounded—it wasn't enough. Meanwhile, the King was only interested in safeguarding his lands and power.

Anne feared she was about to suffer the same lonely fate as her late mother, by being married off to a man she did not care for. She had been so dreadfully foolish to dare to dream of finding love. To want more. And her father had crushed those dreams just weeks before, when he'd informed Anne—and all his subjects in the Great Hall—that he'd brokered a deal for her to marry the Ealdorman Lord Crowe of Calhourn in exchange for an army of men.

Anne was distraught. Her happiness meant nothing to the King when weighed against him having soldiers to protect him from a possible invasion by the Danish warriors. She'd heard the attacks were drawing dangerously closer all the time. But it wasn't the Northmen's approach that had the walls of Anne's bedchamber closing in on her—it was learning that Lord Crowe had arrived at the castle to claim her as his wife the next day, so she had escaped to the battlement walkway to get some air.

She would never be ready to face him. She didn't want to lock eyes with the burly balding man who was twice her age.

The last warmth of the sun was beginning to ebb away, the vibrant amber streaks in the violet sky were gradually giving way to inky evening hues and the moon was starting to burn bright. Anne shuddered. Despite the unrest across the land, the kingdom was buzzing with excitement about her upcoming nuptials. There had been a constant stream of guests arriving, bringing ale, food, flowers and gifts into the city in celebration of a marriage she didn't want.

Her only solace was that the union would bring the people more security from the Northern clans. She had learned of some unfortunate Saxon women being offered in marriage to these Danish barbarians, to form alliances or in exchange for peace, so things could be worse. She would do her duty.

'*God kveld*, Highness.'

Startled, Anne whipped her head round to see who was there. She had been so wrapped up in her thoughts, she hadn't noticed anyone approach in the darkness. She struggled to see who the deep voice belonged to—she knew at once the man must be a stranger, for she did not recognise his silky tone. It was a voice from another world and certainly one that didn't belong here.

'Who's there?'

As he stepped into the moonlight, lowering the hood of his woollen cloak, Anne found herself staring across the passageway into the wild blue gaze of the most fearsome and fascinating man she had ever seen, and a jolt of awareness sent her blood soaring.

He was incredibly tall and very muscular, with long,

dark blond hair, braided and tied on top of his head, but shaven almost to his skin at the sides. He had a thick, well-groomed beard, secured with an iron band, and a deep scar ran from his forehead through his left eyebrow to his cheekbone.

This was the face of a man who had seen many battles. He epitomised the meaning of danger.

A shiver ran down her spine as it dawned on her; he had spoken in Danish tongue. A Northman had gained access to her private quarters.

'Highness,' he said again, with a slight inclination of his head and a knowing smile.

Anne reeled, the fierce need to protect her identity her immediate concern. 'I'm not Princess Anne. I'm afraid you are mistaken, sir.'

There had been many times in her life when she'd longed to be a normal village girl, with a loving family, true friends and freedom to do as she pleased, and now she could add this moment to the list.

'I think not. How could anyone fail to recognise the Royal Princess?'

Anne wasn't blind to the way his full lips curled slightly in disdain, nor unaware of the sudden erratic beating of her heart.

'You are as beautiful as people say, Highness, and you should not be out walking alone at night…'

She tilted up her chin in contempt. 'Well, it seems I am at a disadvantage. You appear to know all about me, yet I know nothing of you,' she said. 'Might I be enlightened as to who has interrupted my privacy before I call for the King's guards to arrest you?'

He grinned wolfishly, not even bothering to cast his eyes to the left and right, knowing there were no such soldiers. No one knew she was here, as she was supposed to be tucked up in bed, getting her beauty sleep for her wedding day.

'Your name, sir,' she pressed, lacing her voice with a confidence she did not feel.

'I am Brand Ivarsson of Kald, Highness,' he said, closing the distance between them.

One of her father's deadliest enemies. Here? No!

The shock of the realisation made her legs tremble. This couldn't be happening. She had heard stories of the warrior Brand Ivarsson. Everyone had. His reputation for being undefeated in battle had reached the kingdom of Termarth, as had rumours of his brutal raids on disarmed villages, his ransacking them for gold, and his ruthless sexual conquests.

'Brand the Barbarian'—that was what people called him.

Her pulse quickening, in a moment of determination Anne gathered up the layers of her silk nightgown and threw herself into one of the gaps in the castle wall. 'Don't come any closer,' she said, her entire body shaking.

The Northman stared at her for a moment, the dark warrior's kohl under his eyes making him look wild and formidable. His lips twisted in amusement. 'Don't be ridiculous! What are you doing, woman?'

'Step back,' Anne said bravely. 'I know who you are. I've heard all about you. You're a monster. You rape and pillage and have no care for anything or anyone. Now, step back, sir, or I'll jump.'

A muscle flickered in his jaw as he contemplated her threat. Thankfully, her words seemed to make an impact as he moved away slightly to peer over the next crenel in the wall.

Staring out at the dark, shimmering moat, almost sixty feet below, she realised it was a long way down. The faraway sound of laughter from the men in the mead halls, sitting around fires drinking, drifted up towards them. Would anyone hear her if she cried out?

'Don't do anything foolish, now,' the Barbarian said. 'It would be a terrible waste.'

She felt the slow ascent of his piercing gaze as he followed the points of her ankle boots up to her figure-hugging silk nightgown—and then, to her surprise, he frowned in disapproval.

'Come, get down from there. You have my word I mean you no harm.'

She shook her head vehemently. 'Then what are you doing here? What do you want?'

'To save you from making a grave mistake tomorrow, Highness,' he said, his face growing serious. 'I didn't come here to watch you jump to your death—it would certainly spoil my night.'

She sensed him edge closer again, like a black wolf silently stalking his prey. 'Well, I'm sorry to ruin your evening…'

'Give me your hand and I'll help you down.'

His eyes had turned surprisingly soft, penetrating, and his voice was gentle, but she knew it must be a trick. She had heard the Northmen were only ever cruel.

Anne gripped the wall even tighter. She dealt with ealdormen and knights all the time when they came to visit her father's castle. They weren't Danish warriors, and perhaps not as intimidating as the man who stood before her, and maybe she didn't have quite so much depending on those encounters as she did on this one, but she could handle this.

'Tell me what you want first,' she said.

'You, Highness,' he said simply, and her stomach flipped in response.

'Now it is you who is being ridiculous, sir. That will never happen.'

'You are to leave with me right now,' he said, crossing his arms over his broad chest, his eyes glinting in the moonlight.

The way her body was reacting to his ever-increasing nearness made her nervous, and she laughed, incredulous. 'And why would I do that?'

'For the good of your kingdom, Highness. You will leave with me quietly now, or my men—who have already infiltrated the castle walls—will begin to enjoy themselves however they see fit. They do so love a good wedding.'

She froze in horror. She'd heard of how these Northmen plundered villages, kidnapping people, making them slaves. But not before they'd had their fun. Fear chilled her to the marrow at the thought of what they might do to the women, the children...

'I'm not asking. I'm telling you,' he said, uncrossing his arms and taking a predatory step towards her.

She didn't have a choice, Anne thought bitterly. It was the bane of her existence.

And clinging on to the stone wall of the castle, in the now drizzling rain, with a sheer drop beneath her, seemed to be the most foolish choice of all. Just one wrong move and she would surely die. If she left with the Barbarian, she might just stand a chance—she hoped it wouldn't be long before her father and Lord Crowe would raise the alarm and come looking for her.

So she was still that frightened deer who had taken flight—it was just that now she was ensnared by a very different hunter. Was it her body or a ransom Brand Ivarsson was after? And just how much gold and silver would the Saxon lords have to pay?

Anne nodded. 'All right. Help me down.'

The Barbarian reached forward and took her hand in his, and the peculiar heat that rushed up her arm made her heart skitter. She faltered, losing her footing on the slippery surface—and screamed. Her stomach slammed against the cold, damp outer wall of the castle, her legs flailing, but two strong hands gripped her wrists.

She didn't dare look down, only up into his steady gaze, as he pulled her forwards—hard. With sheer strength the Barbarian dragged her over the top of the ledge and then her fall was broken by a broad, solid chest encased in smooth leather.

Anne was momentarily disorientated. She gripped

his upper arms to steady herself and his large muscles flexed under her fingers.

'What were you thinking?' he ground out, from where he lay beneath her on the floor.

She wasn't sure. She was shocked by what had just happened, and trembling with emotion. But those feelings were only heightened by the sensation of his warm, firm body pressing against hers, the invasion of her body space, and the stranger's spicy, musky scent wrapping around her.

She'd nearly fallen to her death but he'd saved her—which meant he couldn't want her dead. At least that was something. She must have some value, some use to him.

As she stared down into her enemy's brilliant blue eyes and felt his breath whisper across her face heat flooded her and she struggled off him, scrambling to stand. To occupy her shaking, tingling fingers, she ran the tips of them over her braids, which were becoming increasingly frizzy in the rain.

'*Helsike*, woman—you could have killed yourself!' he scolded, rising to his feet, his brow furrowed. He looked very angry. 'From this moment on you will do exactly as I say, unless you want yourself and others to get hurt. Here, put this on.'

He thrust a woollen cloak that matched his own into her hands and she didn't dare argue.

'We leave now. Keep the hood up and your head down. Follow me.'

'I have your word that if I leave with you now, no one will get hurt? Your men will stand down?' Everything she did was to protect her people. She wasn't about to change that now, even if she had to put herself at risk.

He levelled his gaze to hers. 'You have my word, Highness,' he said, before encouraging her to move with a firm grip to her elbow. 'Now, come.'

Anne knew she should be kicking and screaming. She should put up a fight and resist—pull away from his strong hold on her arm and run. But she couldn't bear it if innocent people were slaughtered because of her.

She nodded. She would go calmly. She would not fight him. Not yet.

His long, powerful strides were larger than hers, so she had to walk quickly down the narrow staircase to keep up with him. She felt as if she was being led down an unknown path, her sheltered, conventional life spiralling out of control. No one had heard her scream, and the realisation that no one was going to come to her aid—at least not tonight—slowly began to sink in.

Most of the royal household had stilled by the time Brand tugged the Princess down the endless stone steps, keeping within the shadows of the castle's keep so as not to draw any unwanted attention. They made it to the stables, where he had tied up his horse, and thankfully, disguised in their thick woollen travellers' cloaks, they were granted safe passage out of the gatehouse.

Once they'd crossed the drawbridge Brand gripped the reins of his faithful steed hard and applied his spurs to the horse's sides. His thighs tightened around the Princess's, and they began the long gallop towards Kald.

They continued over hills and ravines, putting as much distance between them and Termarth—and Princess Anne's impending nuptials—as possible.

Every now and again Brand allowed himself a furtive glance back at the castle, which was slowly shrinking on the horizon, to check that no one was following them. He knew they only had until morning, when the King would realise his daughter was gone and all hell would break loose. Crowe would soon come looking for her, wanting revenge—and that was exactly what Brand was counting on. Finally, blood vengeance would be his. For his father. And for his sister.

But for now they were free of the Saxon castle walls, and he finally allowed himself to relax his hold on Rebel's reins, and on his prisoner.

Heading for her chambers, but finding her on the ramparts, Brand had known it was Anne in a heartbeat. The epitome of elegance, he'd recognised her glossy dark brown hair, worn in two thick, long plaits, and her slender figure at a glance—she was unforgettably beautiful. He had been surprised to find her there, out on the castle walkway alone, and so late at night. And in her nightgown! Did she and her father have no regard for her safety? Where were the guards and her protection?

He had thought that when she saw him she might crumple and cry in fear—his scar and his imposing appearance, teamed with his reputation, had had that effect before. He'd expected dramatics—a possible fainting, perhaps. But in fact the opposite had been true. And the thrill that had flashed through him at her surprisingly stubborn highborn haughtiness had caught him off-guard. She was strong-willed, and he had enjoyed taunting her, provoking a reaction—until she'd almost got herself killed.

Skit! His blood had run cold. But even then she'd fought to keep control of her emotions, not giving anything away bar the trembling of her body.

He'd met her once before, a long time ago, when he'd been a teenage boy, and he'd shown no restraint tonight in stepping closer to take another look into those deep fern-green eyes that had once been tarnished with loneliness. She was still exquisite: a true English rose.

He remembered their first meeting as if it had been yesterday... He recalled the snarling of the bloodhounds and the shouts of the Saxon soldiers chasing him through the forest. And when they'd eventually caught him he had suffered the iron fists of the men over and over again, before they'd left him for dead.

He had been coughing and spluttering, gasping for air, with blood pouring from his nose and a limp arm hanging by his side, when a girl around the same age as himself, with two immaculate long braids, had tentatively approached him. She'd tasked herself with stopping the flow of blood, her hand to his face. Her kindness had calmed his fear, his rage—and his shame. And yet when the sound of fresh horses' hooves had drawn near, she had taken the ring his father had given him from his finger.

The wave of memories brought back the bitterness, the simmering anger that he'd been fighting to keep in check, and he gripped the reins hard once more.

It seemed the Princess didn't remember that boy, though she'd clearly heard rumours of the man he had become. He hadn't failed to notice her sharp intake of breath when he'd introduced himself—had expected it. So she knew the stories of his battles? *Good.* It was his intention to strike fear into the hearts of all Saxons, so they would stay away from his lands and his people. It was his duty to keep them safe.

Perhaps it was his reputation that was responsible for the Princess's demeanor now. She must be weary from travelling half the night, and the cold was beginning to seep through their clothes, but she still held her body stiffly away from him.

Instinctively, he pulled her against his chest. She felt warm and soft under his hands, and her long hair smelled of wildflowers and honey. As they hurried forward, through the dark, winding woods, jumping over gnarled roots and avoiding low, tangled branches, she struggled like a caged dove against his hold.

'Stop wriggling,' he barked. 'You don't want to fall again, do you? Next time it might not be such a soft landing!'

She stopped fighting him for a second, instead attempting to challenge him with words. 'Where are you taking me?' she demanded.

'The barbican on the bridge—your father's last line of defence. We'll rest there a while and regroup with my men.'

'Your men? The ones who were in Termarth?'

'Yes,' he said, and her relief that his warriors had left the castle was palpable. She almost sagged against him.

How strange, he thought, that she seemed to care more about the safety of her people than her own predicament.

'And then what?'

'Then we head to Kald. My fortress.'

'You mean a place you stole? A place you took from others by ending their lives?'

'You surprise me with your lack of knowledge, Highness. Kald was uninhabited when we arrived on these shores. We made it what it has become. Is it wrong to fight to defend our home?'

'This country will never be your home!' she bit out. 'You should go back to where you came from. Nobody wants you here.'

She was right. They'd hardly had a warm welcome from the Saxons. In fact, his people had suffered many attacks, and there had even been assaults on his clan's defenceless women and children when his men had been on a fishing expedition. Since then Brand had made everyone learn how to use a sword and shield— even the farmers and the very young.

'You wound me, Highness. But still, I think we'll stay. Perhaps you'll find you like our settlement too.'

She made every effort to free herself from his arms again.

'Stop it,' he said, with a voice full of cold fury. 'You'll just make it worse.'

For him, anyway. He was enjoying the feeling of her warm bottom nestled between his thighs a bit too much.

'I doubt I'll see much from the inside of a cage. I wonder…what is it that you plan to do with me when we get there? What is it that you want?'

Brand had the unsettling desire to reassure her, to tell her that he meant her no harm. He didn't want her to be afraid. But the less said the better. Now was not the time to be soft. She was his captive, and he must not forget himself. He must not lose sight of where her loyalties lay, who she was betrothed to. And yet, even knowing this, he felt his body disturbingly re-acting to hers.

A loud clamouring of horses' hooves approaching snatched his attention, sending his adrenalin soaring. Tossing his cloak over his right shoulder, he reached for the hilt of his sword. His steed, Rebel, nervously cantered from side to side, and suddenly they were surrounded by half a dozen men on horseback, their weapons drawn.

'Brand?'

'Kar! Torsten! *Heill ok sæll.* I am pleased to see you,' Brand said, as their faces came into focus in the darkness.

'And us you. We have taken the tower on the bridge,' Kar said. 'We are glad you made it out alive.'

'Are there many dead at the outpost?'

'The Saxon fools saw us coming and left, running scared!' Torsten laughed.

Brand felt Anne shiver in his arms. But it wouldn't

hurt her to know they were not to be trifled with, should she have any notion of trying to run.

'They will raise the alarm. We must be on guard.'

He spurred Rebel back into action and led the way, covering the rest of the ground quickly.

Arriving at the barbican, he surveyed the old building for the second time that day. It was little more than a ruin, with a crumbling lookout tower surrounded by a small fort on the water's edge. There wasn't much to it but at least it offered the advantage of height and a good view up and down the fast-flowing river.

It would do for tonight. And he'd worked out that from here they'd be able to see if the warning beacon was lit at Termarth Castle.

'We'll make do here for the rest of the night and continue on to Kald in the morning.'

On his command, the camp became a hive of activity, with his men collecting wood, starting a fire, and unpacking straw and animal skins to rest on.

'Brand, do show us what treasure you have stolen from the Saxon King.'

His burly redheaded friend, Torsten, smirked, and the group all sniggered, but Brand felt an uncomfortable, prickling sensation down his spine. Had he made a mistake in bringing the Princess here? Perhaps he should have left her out of it. But when his eyes had fallen upon her familiar lovely face all reasoning had been lost.

He hadn't thought ahead to how his men might react to having a Saxon in their midst—especially one of such beauty. That had been foolish of him. He, of all people, knew what animals men could be—he'd witnessed it first-hand. And yet still he'd been so consumed with stealing Anne away and the insult it would cause to her Saxon lord… Plus, he had his people to think of. She would earn them quite a ransom—enough to keep many mouths fed for a long time. They were depending on him.

He motioned to his prisoner. 'This is Princess Anne of Termarth.' Brand climbed down from his horse, relieved to be out of her intoxicating proximity for a while, and began to lead Rebel and his passenger to a small lonely oak tree in the centre of the courtyard, where he tied up the animal.

'Let us see if she is as beautiful as they say,' Torsten said, stepping closer. 'Or if it would be better to take her on her belly.'

Unrestrained laughter broke out across the group again, and Brand wanted to wipe that smile off Torsten's face with a quick blow to his jaw. If Svea had been here, he felt sure she would have castrated him with a flick of her sword for saying such a thing.

Brand took a steadying breath. He knew his friend was only jesting and yet a fist had clenched inside his stomach. Torsten had been one of his father's closest friends and fiercest fighters, but he had a mind of his own, and a thirst for Saxon blood and women. This situation would only serve to bring out the brute in him, making everything harder than it needed to be, and Brand was getting bored with having to keep him in check.

'She is of value and my prisoner. She is not to be touched.'

'Are you saying she is spoken for, Brand?' Torsten continued to jibe. 'Are you not going to share?'

Brand made a swift decision. It would be easier if they thought he wanted to bed her. He trusted his warriors with his life, and yet he knew every man had a weakness…

All those years ago, it had only been when the Royal Guard had snatched Anne up and headed in the direction of Termarth, leaving him rubbing the black bruises that had begun to appear on his face, that he'd realised the girl who'd helped him was the Princess.

He couldn't fathom why she had robbed him of his silver. And he'd never forgotten her beauty or her kindness when he had been at his weakest. It had brought him back from the brink of despair and it had lived long in his memory. But she had also taken something that was precious to him and he intended to take it back.

All these years he'd kept his distance. She had been forbidden but not forgotten. But when he'd heard that Anne was being married off to the one man he despised, he'd seen it as an opportunity to take revenge.

He stared at the Princess, still sitting atop his horse, her back rigid and her haughty but pretty nose in the air, acting all prim and proper. And yet her cloak was hanging open to reveal the outline of her delicate frame in that virginal nightgown and silly little boots, and her face had turned ashen at Torsten's words.

Not so high and mighty now, was she? But her vulnerability struck him with an unusual pang in his chest.

She glared at him with contempt and he made his decision. If his men thought she was his property, they would leave her alone.

'She's mine to do with as I please, and no man is to lay a hand on her.' His voice carried the threat of violence—and they knew it.

He turned to Anne to get her down, but she refused his help. 'You make me sick,' she said, snatching her arm away. 'I would rather die than have you touch me.'

He gripped her wrist anyway and aided her descent. Her cool, soft skin under his roughened palm sent a shot of heat through his body and he set her down onto a stone step. 'Rest yourself…catch your breath,' he commanded.

'I am not tired. And even if I were, I do not think I could sleep,' she said. 'Not surrounded by a pack of wild animals. And certainly not in these freezing conditions.'

The men all looked at each other and laughed in amusement, and Brand felt his annoyance spike. This was not the time for her to be speaking so freely. He admired her wilfulness, and the fact that she was putting on a brave face in the circumstances. But the last thing he needed was for her to raise a reaction from one of his men, ignite a flame she didn't intend to. The effect she'd had on him from the moment he'd seen her again was disturbing.

'The cold won't hurt you, Highness, but your tongue might.' He used another length of rope to tie her wrists together and fastened the end to the same tree as his horse. 'Don't run away, now, will you?' He winked.

She tilted her chin up, revealing to him that there was more to come. 'You know, it's not too late to change your mind. You could have me back at the castle by first light. Any one of you,' she said, looking around at the group, who were now tossing logs of wood into a pile to add to the fire.

Brand raised one eyebrow, yet remained silent for a long moment, his cool gaze assessing her. Thankfully, he knew his men were loyal—they would never go behind his back. 'And why would anyone do that?' he asked.

'Maybe you can realise you have made an error in judgement. Yes,' she said, as if she'd come up with a great idea. 'We could put it down to a momentary lapse of concentration... I'm sure the King would forgive that. If I asked him to. Whatever you ask for—silver, gold—I'll make sure it's yours.'

It was a tempting offer. As an occupying force here on this Saxon island, it would certainly help to secure their power in Kald. They could live like royalty, and in safety. But all in good time...

'And just how much are you worth, Highness?'

'To my father and Lord Crowe? Priceless, I'm sure.'

Something that felt strangely like possession darted like poison through Brand's blood at hearing her talk about her fiancé—which was ridiculous, given how she was the one woman in the world who could never be his. He rose to his feet, tossing another log onto the fire. He instantly felt its heat. He lifted his gaze and their eyes met over the dancing flames.

'Which is why they'll be coming after me at first light,' she said.

'I'm counting on it,' he said, his voice dark.

The way he saw it, he'd done the Princess a favour. She would be thanking him if she knew the type of man she was betrothed to. Or perhaps she knew and was prepared to go ahead with the marriage anyway. Brand was determined to find out.

'So it is a fight that you want?' she said. 'You really are all the things I have heard about you and more? Well, you'll get your fight—you can be sure of that. And no doubt my fiancé will kill you, sir.'

The men fell about laughing again, knowing their leader and his skill with sword and axe. But Brand's lips formed a thin, hard line. He'd waited years to avenge his father, and there was nothing funny about that.

He wanted Crowe to suffer as he had suffered. He wanted him to be humiliated as his sister, Svea, had been. He wanted Crowe to lose all that he held dear—and if that meant stealing Anne away, then so be it. And yet even though he had thought of nothing but revenge for years, even now as he was drawing nearer to getting what he'd longed for, he was distracted. *She* was distracting him.

Strands of her long hair were flying free from her braids in the cool breeze, and he watched as she tried to blow them aside because she didn't have the use of her hands. How dare she mock him, with fire in her emerald eyes, even while she sat there in bonds before him, her arms wrapped around knees that were tucked up to her chin?

'You have made a bad choice in husband, Highness. I fear Crowe is not the man you believe him to be.'

Anne shook her head to cast her braids back over her shoulders. 'It is a good match. I'm certain my father wouldn't make it without cause.'

Frustration rippled through him. So she cared for her future husband? So what? The fact had no right to bother him one bit. But it did. The idea of her with any man, let alone that one, made rage boil over in his stomach. He had the urge to claim her for himself, to rid her of thoughts of any other man. What was wrong with him? He was acting no better than Torsten and he chastised himself for it.

'Mind you don't confuse his interest with ambition, Highness. After all, you can ensure his succession to the throne should something untoward happen to your father. You might even be worth more to him dead once your wedding has taken place.'

Anne inhaled sharply. 'What do you mean?'

'He is using you, Highness.' He shrugged.

Her nose rose in the air once more. 'Women always have a use, sir. I believe that is why I'm still alive. What would *you* use me for, I wonder?'

He ignored the smirks of the men and instead tried to crush the vivid imagery that had entered his mind on hearing her last words.

'You are indeed a most valuable prize, Highness,' he said, rounding on her, with the slow burn of resentment blazing in his blistering blue eyes. He crouched down before her and took her chin in his hands, angling her face up towards his. 'And as for the matter of finding a use for you… I don't think you want to put those kinds of ideas into my head, do you? Isn't it time you started valuing yourself and your safety more highly?'

Chapter Two

Anne had tried to sleep, but it was impossible while sitting upright on a cold stone floor. When she opened her eyes and finally saw brilliant sunshine in the clear sky above her, she realised it was perfect weather for a royal wedding. It was the dawn of what should have been the most momentous, if most unwanted, day of her life—yet here she was, tied to a tree and miles away from home.

'Morning, Highness.'

She started at the low, deep voice. She hadn't realised the Barbarian was so close. Disturbingly close. He was crouching down near to the burning embers of the fire, his body like a coil of power, trying to get the last dregs of heat out of them. Had he been watching her?

'You're right—the morning is lacking the "good" part,' she said.

He grinned. 'Did you sleep well?'

'No, not well at all,' she said, surreptitiously taking

in her surroundings, which were now bathed in day-light, and checking for any possible escape routes. If she managed to get away from the men, could she find her way home from here?

'Well, what bride ever sleeps the night before her wedding?' he mocked.

Anger heated her blood. How did he do that? How did he make her go from being calm to incensed within seconds? She squinted up at him. 'It wasn't the thought of the long walk down the aisle that was worrying me.'

'No?'

No…it definitely hadn't been thoughts of missing her wedding that had consumed her, or even bothered her. It had been her captors—especially Brand Ivars-son.

'She's mine to do with as I please.'

Did he mean it? She shivered, even as the warmth of the early-morning sun streamed down on her face. She tried to tame her unruly hair with her bound hands while looking at him, studying him properly. It was the first time she'd seen him in the light, and her mouth went dry as she drank him in.

He really did have no equal.

He had a taller, more formidable build than the rest of his men, and his hair, shaven at the sides, was more severe, with dark ink scrawled around his head. On one side there was a pattern that resembled a wheel of spikes, and on the other a curved ladder of symbols. But it was his eyes that made the biggest impact. There was something wild and reckless and yet vaguely familiar about them, but she couldn't quite put her finger on it.

She couldn't have met him before—she certainly would have remembered a man with such defined, carved features and a deep scar such as his. It was the scar of a warrior, and she found herself wondering what other scars lay hidden—scars that had made him the monster everyone believed him to be.

She searched the depths of her mind to find what she knew of him, what she'd overheard from her father and his witan talking. But, frustratingly, she came up with rumour and hearsay—no facts.

She had witnessed the injuries of the villagers who had suffered attacks by the Danes. Burned and bleeding, they had come into the grounds of Termarth Castle seeking sanctuary. Against her father's wishes, she had tried to help as many as she possibly could. She wanted to use her position to better the lives of her people—which was why she had reluctantly agreed to marry a man she didn't love or even like, having been convinced it would ensure their safety.

Was the man before her responsible for all that pain and anguish she had seen? He had the reputation of a barbarian, and yet he didn't frighten her as much as he should. Instead, she found herself fascinated... He reminded her of a magnificent dark bull standing in a field. His dominating presence made you want to give him a wide berth, and yet such was the power of his virility and strength you couldn't help but just stand there and watch. But if you took the risk and stayed, there was no telling at what point he might charge and destroy you.

'Here,' he said, tossing her an apple. 'Eat it slowly—we have a long ride ahead. But tonight we'll be feasting at my fortress. You should find it a lot more comfortable there than on those cold steps, anyhow.'

'Great,' she said sarcastically.

Did that mean a cell, or a cage, or worse? She shuddered. She had never done well in confined spaces, not since she was a little girl. But she would be careful not to mention that fact to the Barbarian, as he would no doubt use it against her.

She glanced around, trying to put those thoughts out of her mind. She admired the mature trees framing the sunlit ruins of the outpost and listened to the soothing sounds of the tumbling water. Her thoughts turned to how the Danes had fought off the guards last night, before she and the Barbarian had arrived.

'Your men...they were never in Termarth, were they? They were here waiting for you all the time.'

'Clever girl,' he said. 'We tend to stick out like a sore thumb among Saxons. I couldn't risk us all entering the castle walls.'

'You lied to me. Tricked me.' She winced, her eyes flaring.

He held up his hands in mock-defence. 'Guilty,' he said. 'But you wouldn't have come willingly otherwise.'

'I didn't come willingly anyway,' she bit out.

She shook her head. She had been a fool to believe him. She had given herself up so easily, believing it was best for her people. Perhaps he was right—she should take better care of herself, and not be so trusting when it came to Northmen and their word.

'So you still intend to go ahead with this insane plan of yours?'

'If you are so sure your betrothed will come to save you, you have nothing to fear,' he retorted menacingly. 'If you're lucky, he may even have you back at Termarth for your wedding night.'

He was trying to wound her with the mention of her ruined wedding, and yet she only felt relief flow through her as she digested his words and realised that the consummation of her marriage might not take place today. It was one small mercy.

She longed to make her own way in life—to marry a man of her own choosing. She hadn't even begun to live or to have any adventures of her own. She longed to see other places and meet new people, and when the time was right, to have a home to call her own and a husband and children to love.

But her status in life had ensured that was impossible. Her happiness was a small price to pay to consolidate the power of her father's kingdom. And this was the reason the King and Lord Crowe would come after her. And yet she couldn't be sure of it. The Barbarian might have picked the wrong Princess. Her father had always treated her coldly, keeping her out of sight and out of mind, and there was no love lost between her and her fiancé. It was a marriage of convenience on both sides, but she wasn't about to let the Barbarian know that.

'Fortunately, my father's price for my hand in marriage was an army. Ironically, the one that will now be used to rescue me and defeat you. What about you? Have you decided on your price for my freedom?' she snapped, suddenly angry.

She was sick of being a pawn in bitter men's lives. Her father was about to sell her off through marriage, as if she were an object, and now this stranger believed he had the right to put a price on her head too. Well, she was tired of being treated like a plaything, or as leverage, to help men get what they wanted, used as and when they needed her but cast aside the rest of the time.

So what he said next shocked her.

'No amount of treasure will do it, Highness. I want your Saxon lords to pay in blood, not gold. I'm afraid you will not be returning to Termarth until Crowe— or I—am dead.'

His brutal honesty took the strength from her readiness to fight him verbally. She had not been expecting that. In her mind, she had envisaged a rose-tinted scenario of her father emptying his chests of gold and silver and handing the treasure over to the Northmen in exchange for her freedom. She had thought the Barbarian a kind of pirate, wanting cold, hard money—not this… This sounded personal.

'I do not wish for any man to die on my account,' she whispered.

And it was true. She could not pretend to love or even like Lord Crowe, but she could never wish another man in the ground. And as for Brand Ivarsson… he was her captor, but did she want him dead?

'Sorry to disappoint you, Princess.'

Bristling at the injustice of it all, Anne tried to re-taliate, but when she glanced back up at him she re-alised he was no longer looking at her.

He picked up his wooden shield and began beating his sword against it. 'Wake up,' he barked at his men. 'The warning beacon has been lit. We leave now and we ride hard.'

The men were swift and efficient, but they'd only just mounted their horses, ready to leave, when a mael-strom of arrows came whistling over the barbican walls. The horses began to snort, agitated.

'It's the Saxon fools we scared off last night,' shouted the ruddy-faced redhead they called Torsten. 'They've come back for more!' he grinned.

Was this some kind of game to them? Anne won-dered, her heart pounding so hard she could feel its beat right through her body. The Barbarian had lifted her clear off the ground and onto his horse without giving her a moment's warning, and she was still smarting from the feel of his big hands cupping her back and the top of her thighs, her arm pressed into his chest. Her hands were still bound; she'd been unable to do a thing about it. And now he was pulling her against him again, in that firm but gentle and extremely disconcert-ing way he'd held her the evening before.

'They don't know the Princess and I are with you, so let's split up,' Brand yelled, readying his horse to gal-lop. 'Torsten, Kar, distract them and lead them along the main road. I will take the path through the forest. We will meet back at Kald by nightfall.'

* * *

They had been riding at quite a pace for a while, without a glimpse of the Saxon guards, when huge drops of rain began to lash down on them, obscuring their view. They hadn't seen a single person since the outpost and Anne was finding it increasingly unnerving being alone with the Barbarian again.

Last night, riding away from Termarth in the dark, she must have been in shock as they'd raced across the undulating landscape. But now she was aware of his every movement, of the taut muscles in his thighs gripping the steed, the warmth emanating from the solid chest that was rubbing against her back with every gallop, and her bottom shifting between his thighs. She had never been so close to a man before, let alone a Northman—and it was most definitely indecent! If her maids could see her right now they would have a fit.

She had been trying to concentrate on taking in the scenery of the meadows and the little brook, assigning it all to her memory so she could perhaps remember the way back. And she was trying to blot out the deafening silence between them and every curious and unsettling sensation, but her eyes kept returning to her captor's large, strong hands holding the reins. She was riveted.

It had been aeons and he hadn't said one word to her. Not one! And she was beginning to feel more and more agitated.

When she saw the straw rooftops of a farmstead on a hillock up ahead, she could have wept. At least she knew they weren't totally cut off from civilisation. But as they drew closer to the settlement Anne could tell that something was terribly wrong. The Barbarian slowed the horse as the acrid smell of smoke hit her, causing a bitter taste in her mouth. And then they came upon the heinous scene of homes destroyed and bodies of all ages strewn about.

'Look away, Highness,' the Barbarian ordered. 'Shut your eyes.'

She could not. Now that he was forbidding her from taking in the devastation, she had a morbid curiosity to see it. But as she glanced around she instantly regretted her decision, and realised he'd been trying to protect her from the horrors that lay before them.

She drew in a sharp breath as the desolation stormed her. 'Oh, my God. What has happened here?'

The Barbarian halted the horse and swung himself down. 'Stay here,' he commanded, as he quietly paced his way over to some of the bodies.

When was he going to learn that she didn't take orders from him? She slid down to the ground and watched as he went from corpse to corpse like a sleek, dark raven on the battlefield, moving stealthily. She was half expecting him to rob each one, but instead he surprised her by checking to see if anyone was breathing, running his hand over the women and children's faces, closing their eyes.

A sob began to rise in her throat. 'Did your men do this?' she choked.

He shot her a cold-eyed look. 'They didn't take this path, remember? And I thought I told you to stay put. It could be dangerous. Are you always this wilful?'

'Yes, actually.'

The inarticulate sound of someone groaning in pain distracted them, and Anne followed the Barbarian as he stalked over to where a man lay wounded on the ground.

'Stay back,' he warned her.

But she couldn't just do nothing. Instead, she quickly fetched a cup of water from one of the huts. Every task was made so much harder by the fact that her hands were still bound, the rough rope biting into her skin. But she knew the injured man must be a lot more uncomfortable than she was, so she hurried.

'What happened here?' the Barbarian was asking him, as Anne knelt down beside them and tipped the liquid into the man's parched mouth.

'Mercenaries…they passed through yesterday and ransacked the village.'

'What did they want? What cross did they bear?'

'Our food. Women. They wore black, with yellow markings on their shields…'

He coughed and spluttered, and then he lay back and shut his eyes. He was gone.

'Danes. Danes did this!' Anne exploded, violently jerking to her feet.

'You're wrong, Highness,' the Barbarian said coolly, standing to meet her anger. 'I'm not saying it's not something raiders from the North would do, but this is the work of Saxon soldiers. I've seen it before, and this man said so himself. Mercenaries. Men in uniform. These people were killed by their own kind— for loot, or for sport.'

She shook her head. 'I don't believe you. You've

come to our country and you are destroying it, ripping apart innocent villages. Just look at what you've done.'

His cool eyes considered her for a moment. 'Believe what you want, Highness. It makes no difference to me,' he said, walking back to his horse.

'Why would Saxons do such a thing? Why? They have no cause…' she vented, trying to keep up with his long strides.

'Because they can get away with it. Or maybe to blame us, to cause unrest and gain more power. Tell me, are more and more villagers who have lost their homes making their way to your father's kingdom?'

'Yes.'

'Then ask yourself what those once-farmers will do next? They'll make great soldiers, especially if they believe they have something to fight for, to take revenge upon. But perhaps they're being led down the wrong path.'

Anne gasped, and the Barbarian bent over to check something on the horse's side.

She couldn't believe it to be true. Yet why would he lie? After all, didn't the Northmen like to brag about their raids and conquests, wanting to strengthen their savage reputation? Why would he make up such a thing? Could it be possible? Surely her father wouldn't go to such lengths to create an army. No, she couldn't believe it.

'You should take off those wet clothes.'

'What?' she asked, her face swinging to his, horror-struck. Oh, my God, it was happening. All this talk of raids and unrest…and now he was going to attack her.

He looked her up and down, brushing his hand over his beard. 'There's another village up ahead and we don't want to raise any suspicions by having you parading around in wet nightclothes. You should change into something more appropriate. And dry.'

She looked at him, nonplussed. She'd always prided herself on her good sense, but he was messing with her composure, clouding her judgement. Her thoughts were a jumbled mess. Or perhaps she was just in shock from having seen what they'd discovered here. Yes, that must be it. She'd forgotten about the rain and her own drowned rat appearance. When they'd come upon the village, her own discomfort had paled into insignificance.

'You want me to steal someone's clothes?'

'I doubt they'll mind. I don't think they'll be needing them, do you?'

He strode off into a hut before coming back out and heading inside the next one. This time he came out carrying a long tunic and a pinafore.

'Here, go in there and put this on. And no arguing. You don't want to draw any unnecessary attention to yourself, do you?'

Anne hated to admit it, but he was right—she was cold and soaked through, and she had felt a bit foolish riding around in her nightgown. Plus, she really didn't want to turn up at the Danes' settlement wearing it— that was if they got that far. She'd be glad of something more substantial to wear.

The Barbarian took a knife from his belt and sliced the bonds that held her hands together. The abrasions from the rope were suddenly replaced with the gentle caress of his fingers circling her wrists, and for a moment time stood still.

'You didn't say they were hurting you.'

She snatched her hands back. 'Well, what did you expect?' she spat, yanking the clothes out of his arms and disappearing inside the hut, putting as much distance between herself and his soothing touch as possible.

She stepped out of her wet things and threw the clean and dry long-sleeved tunic dress over her head, but she couldn't fathom how to fasten the pinafore over the top. How did the straps work? She'd never worn such a thing and wasn't sure how to get the pinafore to stay up. She was becoming increasingly frustrated, her cheeks burning hot. What was she going to do?

'Everything all right in there, Princess?' the Barbarian called.

She had no choice; she'd have to ask for his help.

Cringing with embarrassment, she emerged a few moments later, still struggling with the straps. The Barbarian was busy tending to his horse, and when he saw her holding out the two long straps, looking perplexed and just a little bit flustered, he tutted. He stalked back into the hut and came out again, carrying two brooches. He came towards her and, stopping just a whisper away, put his big, beautiful hands to her chest. Then he set to deftly fastening the pins to hold the dress in place.

'I bet you've never dressed yourself before, have

you? Let me guess—you have servants to do that kind of thing for you,' he smirked.

How dare he mock her? Her silence spoke volumes before her chin tilted up in defiance again. 'If you must know, I've never seen such garments before. And I had no mother to take the time to show me how to fasten my clothes and wear my hair.'

He blanched, and when his face softened she realised his caring glances were much more dangerous to her than the mocking ones, so she babbled on.

'Anyway…how do you know how to fasten a dress? Had a lot of practice with women's clothes, have you?'

She had meant to be sarcastic, but when his full lips curved up into a wicked grin and she saw the amusement in his eyes, she felt the heat rise in her cheeks again. What was the matter with her?

She put her hands up. 'Wait, I don't want to know the answer to that.'

'There,' he said, stepping back to admire his handiwork. 'You look every bit the peasant girl. Now we just need to sort out your hair.'

'What's wrong with my hair?' She gasped, inching away from him, her hand coming up to curl over her braids. He reached for her again and her breath hitched. 'What are you doing?' she asked, panicked.

He tugged the bands from her two plaits, startling her, and raked his hands through her woven locks, releasing them. 'Peasants tend to wear their hair loose, like this,' he said, by way of explanation. 'That helps. Now you don't look quite so…lofty.'

Anne just nodded, mute. She was trying to come

to terms with the disturbing tiny tingles his fingers in her hair had sent erupting down her spine. She was glad when he turned his attention back to the animal.

'What's wrong with your horse? Rebel, is it?'

'I thought he was tiring quicker than usual. Seems he was hit by an arrow at the outpost earlier.'

'Oh, no, is he hurt?' she asked, coming up beside him.

She stroked the horse's muzzle while the Barbarian inspected the wound. 'It's just a graze.'

'Poor thing,' she said, and Rebel began nickering at his newfound friend.

'He'll be fine—he's had worse.' He inclined his head a little. 'I think he likes you.'

Anne was pleased. She loved animals.

'Come on, we're losing time and we don't want anyone to find us here.' He held out his hand to help her up into the saddle again, and before letting her go said, 'Whatever you might have heard about us Danes, Highness, my clan doesn't go about murdering innocent people.'

'No, you just go in for a little kidnapping here and there.'

He grinned again as he mounted the horse, and her stomach flipped.

'Let's get out of this place.'

It must have been mid-afternoon by the time the next settlement and the glowing amber light of a mead hall came into view. Anne was bone-achingly tired.

She had never ridden for this long before, plus she was starving—she hoped they were stopping.

As if he could read her thoughts, the Barbarian pulled the reins to guide Rebel into the stables at the back of the small building, and she instantly felt the loss of his protective body heat down her back.

Her eyes narrowed on him. 'Is this a good idea? Someone might notice me,' she said. And then she cursed herself. That would be a *good* thing, wouldn't it? She did *want* to be rescued, didn't she?

'Probably not. But we're a long way from Termarth, and you'll catch your death if we stay out in this rain all day. I imagine you're sore from being in that saddle so long, plus we both need something to eat. The journey is taking longer than I expected with Rebel being hurt—he could also do with a rest.'

Anne seized the chance to lower herself from the saddle while he tied up the horse—anything to avoid him helping her down and her having to touch him again… Every time he did so, a strange little ripple of heat shot up her arm.

Instead, the Barbarian's large hands came up to gently pull up her hood, startling her.

'Do you mind?' she said, snatching back the material.

'We don't want you being recognised. Keep your face covered and don't make a scene. Or there'll be trouble,' he warned.

'Do you know this place? Is it respectable?' she asked, taking in the exterior of the small drinking hall.

He smirked. 'You're miles away from home, having been taken hostage by me... Isn't that the least of your worries? It's mainly settlers, Danes... Most of them would probably love to get their hands on you, so don't draw attention to yourself.'

Anne nodded, suddenly nervous. She'd never been to an alehouse before. And as they made their way to the front entrance, she took a moment to compose herself before the Barbarian pushed open the door.

The noise of clinking tankards and the vile stench of men and ale reached out and hit her. If she stepped over this precipice and was recognised her reputation would be damaged for good. But she might also be able to signal to someone to send word to her father, although refusal to comply with the Barbarian's wishes would surely see her punished.

'Don't make eye contact with anyone,' he whispered, ushering her forward. 'We can't be too careful.'

He guided her to a table in a secluded corner by the fire, while she scoured the room for exits. She could try to make a run for it...

'Don't even think about it,' he said, as if he could read her thoughts. 'There's nowhere to go.'

Damn him, but he was so aggravating! She wanted to lash out at him, but she couldn't in such a public place.

'I'm going to see if I can find us some food. I won't be long,' he told her.

Scanning the bustling room, Anne cautiously took in a couple at a nearby table and men in chainmail and furs at the far end, seated around a long table, sipping from their full jars and joking with the serving girls.

But the goings-on in the buzzing room couldn't rid her of her tormented thoughts.

Would the Barbarian's plan last out the day? Or were Lord Crowe's men already out looking for her and hot on their tail? They couldn't be far behind.

Anne had lived such a reserved, sheltered life in the safety of the castle walls, and her loneliness had quickly turned to despair when her father had delivered his news about her upcoming marriage. Sickness swirled in her stomach. She hadn't even yet begun to live, and now she was to be handed over as a wife to a man she felt nothing for.

There had been moments when she'd thought life as an outcast, or taking the veil, would be better than even one night spent with Crowe as his bride. But her father had not heard her voice. And he'd played on her good nature and her desire to help their people in encouraging her to go ahead with the marriage.

If only there was another way… She didn't want or need any man. She was yet to meet one who would treat her as an equal, who would understand her thoughts and feelings—and who would offer her the freedom she sought. She bit her lip. Did such a man even exist?

She took a furtive glance across the room. She studied Brand Ivarsson, who was leaning against a post, in conversation with a lady. Even with his wet hair and sodden beard, his face streaked with mud, he was a striking, dangerous-looking man, all hard muscle. Did he have an even harder heart?

The buxom blonde obviously thought he was attractive, as two pink stains had appeared on her cheeks as the Barbarian spoke to her. He was talking in a deep, dulcet whisper that Anne found herself straining to hear, and she tried to curb her irritation as the woman giggled at whatever he'd said.

So what if he had impossibly broad shoulders and large, tanned hands, now braced on the wooden beam? Every now and again he would run them over his dishevelled hair, emphasising the muscles in his arms... She tutted blatantly, her frustration flaring. She was starving hungry—wasn't he? What was taking him so long?

He was the most masculine, intimidating man she had ever seen. He certainly lived up to his reputation. Yet so far he hadn't hurt her. And even though she couldn't believe her father's men were to blame, something made her believe that the Barbarian had had no part in those killings today.

She had been held tightly in his arms on horseback, and he had not once been rough with her as she'd thought he would. And he'd had every chance to drag her from the horse and attack her. Instead, he'd handled her with care—physically at least. But she knew he must have gained his nickname somehow. No one was called the Barbarian for nothing.

If she were to raise the alarm now, what would he do? She doubted anyone in the tavern would want to fight a man like him. And had he been telling the truth when he'd said most of the men in here would want to claim her for themselves? She tugged her cloak tighter around her and nudged up the hood.

When the blonde woman began talking animatedly again, and reached out to touch the Barbarian's arm, Anne's patience waned. She was annoyed with him—and with herself, for the peculiar feelings rushing through her.

One of the armoured men at the far end of the room put down his empty tankard, making her jump. He rose to his feet to signal for another, which confirmed she'd been waiting long enough, so she began tapping her foot in an impatient beat on the floor. Another shrill giggle escaped the blonde's lips and, feeling incensed, Anne added a cough for effect.

Finally, she saw the Barbarian's tall figure straighten before he turned and began to manoeuvre through the tables and benches, heading back towards her. As he came into the firelight, their eyes clashed, blue blazing into green.

'Is something wrong with your throat?' he asked.

'I do not appreciate being left alone in such a place,' she bit out.

He smirked and her heart skittered. 'If I didn't know better, I'd think you were starting to enjoy my company.'

She gave him a sour look. 'Definitely not. But one Dane is better than those five over there.'

Brand glanced over at the raucous men in the corner. Bringing Anne anywhere so public had not been part of his plan, and he was already kicking himself. They should have been almost home by now, but Rebel being hit had slowed them down, as had the driving rain.

He had been glad when they'd parted ways with

his men; he felt he could ensure her safety better on the journey on his own. But what he should have done was ignore his horse's injury, Anne's sodden clothes and his rumbling stomach. He should have thrown her over the back of his horse and ridden out at full gallop to Kald. Yet her whole body had been shivering, her soaking wet hair plastered to her face, and he'd become concerned—he still wasn't sure she'd make it without catching her death.

But her beauty was causing far too much interest in this hovel of a place. And he didn't like the way the men were trying to get a better look at her. In fact, a tall, balding man at the far end couldn't take his beady eyes off them. He didn't look like much of a threat, but Brand wanted to tear a piece off him anyway for ogling her.

But he couldn't cause a scene. The last thing he needed right now was for the Princess to be recognised.

He felt better when their steaming bowls of soup arrived. They ate in silence, and he avoided looking into Anne's accusatory emerald eyes, but that didn't mean he wasn't aware of her every movement. Every now and again her knee would brush against his under the table and she'd pull away sharply. Her wrists rested on the table, and it troubled him to see the faint red marks on her delicate skin where the rope ties had been.

That was his fault, he'd tied them too tight.

She kept wiping her palms on her dress. Was he making her nervous? He didn't know why, but the thought pleased him.

When he'd finished his food, he finally stole a look

at her face, and was glad to see the colour had come back into her cheeks and her new clothes were quickly drying out as they sat by the fire.

'How much further is it?' asked Anne quietly, as she mopped up the last of her food.

'It'll be a while longer, but we should still make it by nightfall if Rebel can keep up his pace.'

She nodded, and he was glad she hadn't fought him or cried out and sought rescue. Although he still wouldn't put it past her to try. She was spirited and courageous—he'd give her that. And she didn't seem to care about her own wellbeing, if her walking alone at night and squeezing herself between castle walls was anything to go by.

'What will your people make of me?'

He had been thinking the same thing. He wondered what Svea would make of her, and the rest of his clan. They would all be looking at him to set an example.

He shrugged. 'My people like Saxons about as much as you like us Danes.'

He thought he saw a slight tremble in Anne's fingers as she put down her spoon, and her wide green gaze swung to his in dismay. He relented. She had such a lovely, expressive face. He didn't want her to feel frightened.

'But you have my word you will not be misused or ill-treated.'

'The word of a Dane—can it be trusted? You've lied to me once already.'

The pulse beating fast in her throat intrigued him, and he had a strange desire to reach out and run his thumb gently over the base of her neck. But that would surely entice more scrutiny in the small mead hall, so he kept his hands to himself.

'About as much as a Saxon's, I'm sure. And I have no cause to lie about this.'

As they left the hall and Brand settled Anne back onto Rebel, he rolled his shoulders, letting out a long breath. They'd gone unnoticed, and now the rain had stopped they could finish their journey back to Kald—hopefully without incident. He'd be glad when he'd got his stolen Princess within the safety of Kald's fortress walls and she could warm up by the fire and get some sleep.

But just as they were joining the forest track, too late Brand noticed a tall figure jerking out into their path at a junction, taking them off-guard.

'Whoa!'

All at once, Rebel reared up, letting out a loud snorting sound from his nostrils, warning them of potential danger.

'Princess Anne?'

'Giraldus!' she gasped.

It was the balding man from the alehouse.

'Your Royal Highness! I thought it was you. Although I can hardly believe it. I thought my eyes were deceiving me. You can have no business being this far from home,' the man said to her. 'Where is your convoy? Is everything all right?'

Brand gripped her arms tight in warning, bringing the relief she must have felt at seeing someone she knew to a quick end. He reached for his sword and she tensed beneath him.

'Giraldus, my father has sent me on an important errand. I am afraid I require your absolute silence in this matter. I do hope I can trust you not to say anything?'

'Of course. Are you certain everything is all right?' Brand saw his eyes narrow as he tried to get a better look at the Princess's companion.

'Yes, I can assure you it is. We will pay you handsomely for your silence,' she added quickly.

Brand was furious with himself that he had not kept his hood up in the drinking hall, especially after demanding Anne did so. He had thought he was among other Danes. His shaven hair and ink markings would surely have given him away to a Saxon.

'There is no need for that. No need at all. Anything to keep you safe, Your Highness.'

'Thank you. I will see you very soon, I hope. Goodbye for now.'

As they cantered away, Brand released his grip on Anne and his sword. 'Who was that?' he asked.

'One of my father's loyal messengers. A good, kind man.'

'I admire your quick thinking.'

'Would you have killed him?'

'If I had to.'

'But he was just trying to help me!' she said, exasperated. 'He had done nothing wrong. You're despicable! Surely not everything needs to be settled with the sword?'

'Which is why I didn't. But I wouldn't be surprised

if he raises the alarm. He'll run straight to your father to say he saw you with a Northman. Now, let's get off this road.'

As they turned the corner, out of sight, Brand spurred Rebel into action. They made their way through the dense canopy of the forest, the afternoon sunlight dappling through the trees. Little primroses covered the ground in a vibrant yellow haze and Brand knew they would soon exit the woodland and hit the coast. Then he would breathe a little easier, as they could follow that familiar path all the way to Kald.

He hadn't slept in days, and longed to stretch out his muscles. He felt tense, and irritable, but not because he thought the enemy was on his tail—because he needed to get Anne out of his arms. She felt far too soft and perfect in his embrace, with her floral scent wrapping around his senses. With every gallop, her warm bottom was thrown backwards against his groin, and her small breasts kept rubbing against his arm that was wrapped tightly around her waist.

Talk about torture.

She must despise him, he thought. He'd snatched her from the safety and comfort of her home and deprived her of her wedding day. He promised himself he'd make amends for it later. And yet he couldn't fathom why he felt so protective of her when her acquaintances had deprived *him* of a family. Did she know what Crowe had done? What he was capable of?

They had travelled some distance from the mead hall when his heightened senses saw movement nearby. He had a clear line of sight through the sunlit forest corridor ahead, and right at the end he saw a swarm of Saxon soldiers, gathering in a clearing by a fallen tree. They were talking to Giraldus.

A sliver of anger sliced through him and he roughly gripped Anne's arms and pulled her back against his chest.

'What on—?' she gasped.

He wrapped his warm palm around her mouth, just in case she had the inclination to scream. '*Hold kjeft.* Quiet,' he bit out. 'Look! It seems the old man can't be trusted after all.'

Silently, he pulled the Princess down from Rebel and shoved the horse's hipbone, urging the animal to move forward without them. 'Go,' he said.

Although it pained him to let his faithful friend go, if they stayed with Rebel they would surely be seen. And he hadn't spent weeks planning all this to give Anne up now.

He tugged the Princess further into the undergrowth and gently released his hand from her mouth. 'Don't say a word.'

His hard hips pinned her against a tree, securing her to him, chest to chest, thigh to thigh, with his palms on the bark either side of her head. Her beautiful green eyes blazed up at him. *Skit*, up close she was even more stunning. Her skin was so pale and perfect, without even the smallest blemish, and her delicately arched eyebrows and long eyelashes looked as if they'd been spun with silk.

His eyes dipped to her full, lush mouth, which he realised he'd never seen curve into a smile. He *re-*

ally wanted to see that—to see her use those cherry-blossom-pink lips move in a display of warmth towards him. She had shown him kindness once, and he believed it was that which had stopped him from being entirely poisoned by his need for revenge.

As he continued to stare, his heart picked up pace.

'Your Royal Highness, it's Giraldus. Are you there?' the man called out into the forest.

Brand stilled.

He heard Rebel snort, and with a shift of annoyance realised his faithful steed was now in enemy hands. He vowed to himself he would get his animal back when the time was right. But that had been close—it could have been them. Now they would have to cover the rest of the ground to Kald on foot.

'Hand the Princess over, Dane, and you will not be harmed. There's nowhere to go.'

He needed to focus. To weigh up the situation. But he was finding it difficult to concentrate on anything but the nearness of Anne. Her breath was coming in bursts against his throat… He noticed her usually pale skin was flushed and her gorgeous big green eyes were dilated… The air surrounding them felt charged as he continued to stare down at her. His chest was almost pressing against hers… Was she as aware of him as he was of her?

'You should give me up,' she whispered. 'I will go to them and you can run. I won't tell them who you are or where you are going. I promise I won't let them hurt you…'

Brand's brow furrowed. Even now, at her most vulnerable as his prisoner, how could her thoughts be for him and not on escaping her situation? She was offering him freedom—despite the fact he'd kidnapped her. Well, she was a much better person than him—because there was no way he could let her go...not yet... He needed to see this through.

Brand felt her hand on his chest and stared down at her delicate fingers. It was the first time she'd touched him of her own accord, and his skin burned under her grip. He felt like a bull in silk chains. But his intuition, honed from years of fighting, told him she was about to push him away, as he'd done to his horse. She was about to make her location known to those men.

'Brand—'

No!

Instinctively, he lowered his head and covered her lips with his to stop her from making another sound. The moment his firm lips captured hers, his traitorous body gave up the battle it had been fighting since the moment he'd seen her again and all thoughts of the soldiers drifted away.

It was the little gasp that came from the back of her throat that did it—that allowed him to glide his tongue inside her mouth in a hot, silky, sensual tour. He waited for her to pull back, to struggle, but the hands that had been about to push him away instead splayed out against his chest, and the smouldering rage he'd felt when he'd realised she was about run to those men was transmuted into desire.

He drove his mouth down onto hers as his fingers twisted into the tangled mess of her hair. Her head tipped back into his hands and he angled her for better access, deepening the intensity of the kiss. He felt her whole body tremble as she surrendered with a backward sway, desperately clinging to his chainmail vest, and a spark of triumph shot through his body, right down to his groin.

The sound of galloping hooves leaving the forest and the feel of vibrations on the ground beneath their feet broke through the moment, helping him to recover his sanity. He stared down at her, his breathing ragged.

With fierce urgency she disentangled herself, finally pushing him away as she'd originally intended, dragging her hands over her face in flustered dismay.

'What was that? What on earth do you think you're doing?' she gasped. Her cheeks were a pretty shade of pink, her eyes wide with stunned alarm.

He shoved his tunic sleeves up his arms and ran a hand over his beard. 'I couldn't have you crying out to your father's servant, now, could I?' he said, backing away from her. 'It was the only way I could get you to be quiet.'

Her fingers flew up to her mouth as if he'd burned her. 'Never do that again!' she fumed, more than a little unsteady on her feet. She momentarily closed her eyes in what appeared to be an effort to keep calm and regain her composure.

Skit, he'd had no right to touch her. None! But he needed her to know he was a man who would do what was necessary, didn't he?

'No need to read anything into it, Highness,' he said, trying to shrug it off as if it was nothing. 'It was just a little kiss. Put it down as a mistake—one I won't be making again. And besides,' he added, 'we have bigger things to worry about. We're going to have to make the rest of the journey by foot. Can you walk, or do I need to throw you over my shoulder and carry you?'

'I'll walk!' she bit out, stumbling away from him. 'Just don't touch me! Don't ever touch me again!'

Brand was glad when he found the familiar wide track edged with mature hedgerows and the shoreline finally came into view. They walked in silence along the primrose-strewn path and he tried to focus his mind on the relentless roaring waves crashing onto the sand in the distance—not on the way Anne had felt in his arms.

He took in the wide stretch of beach surrounded by the dunes and heathland he knew so well, which had soothed his soul these past few years, when at times his only focus had been hate and revenge. But right now his thoughts were scattered—they kept returning to the taste of her lips against his...

He was such a brute! There was a vulnerability about the Princess that appealed to the hunter and the warrior in him, and yet since he'd seized her at the castle she hadn't made much of a fuss, nor begged to go home, nor even shed a tear. He'd seen a defiant strength beneath her delicate exterior, but also kindness when she'd tried to help the man at the settlement earlier today. She'd even tried to help *him*.

Brand was starting to wonder if she had a bad bone

in her delectable body. Her only vice seemed to be her choice of husband and the fact that she was a Saxon.

Her soldier comrades seemed to have taken the main track out of the forest, and he hoped if the two of them remained by the hedgerow they could stay hidden and one step ahead.

'Is that the ocean?' asked Anne, her voice a whisper on the wind.

It was the first time she'd spoken to him since the forest. Since he'd kissed her. What had he been thinking? He must not be sent off course by her pretty face, no matter how tempting she was. He'd told himself it was a temporary lapse of judgment—faced with the reminder of how she'd saved him once, and was offering to do the same again, he'd weakened. But it must not—could not—happen again.

When he'd threatened to throw her over his shoulder and carry her she'd looked appalled. She had charged on ahead, putting up a silent barrier between them by crossing her arms tightly across her body, as if protecting herself. Why had he acted like such a fool? The trouble was, she was making him act in all kinds of foolish ways.

'You have never seen the sea before?' He couldn't believe it. Didn't Saxon royalty tour their kingdoms and beyond?

'I have never been so far from home before.'

When he looked at her with disbelief in his eyes, she continued. 'My father forbade it. I've never left Termarth. So, no, I've never seen the sea. I have admired paintings of it, but it is so much bigger than I thought…so vast.'

Her gorgeous green eyes were wide with wonder and he understood it. Brand had always felt a connection to the ocean, since his mother and father had put him and his sister in a longboat and they'd all left Daneland, heading for new shores full of hope, in search of a better future.

There was no way his father would have left his woman or either child behind. And even when the sea had grown angry and fierce waves had crashed all about them, drenching them and tossing the boat around, taking his mother into its icy depths, he had felt in awe of it. It was loud and unapologetic. It was wild and untamed. And that was how Brand had gone on to live his life.

After losing his mother on their journey to this country, it had been even more important to his father that they found success here. So that she hadn't died in vain. They'd settled in Kald and tended to the land. They had built up a village and defended it over and over again from the Saxons with the loss of many lives.

They hadn't come here looking for a battle. Despite what the Princess thought, they were never the first to strike. They didn't have a thirst for blood like some clans. But, under witness of the gods, they would defend what was now theirs with whatever strength it took. And they'd been forced to do so many times.

After his father had been killed, the responsibility to protect their people had passed to Brand. He'd been young, and his father's closest friends, Kar and

Torsten, had helped him lead their people for a while. But since Brand had turned from a boy into a man he'd led *them* in building up the fortress palisades and the people had become self-sufficient—fishing and rearing their own animals and growing crops. But they'd recently suffered a particularly bad harvest, and an even harsher winter. And then the Saxons had slaughtered some of their livestock.

The people would need extra help this year, and they were looking to him for a solution. The responsibility lay heavy on his shoulders, but he'd vowed that his people would never go hungry. The gold he would fetch from a ransom for the Princess would certainly help...

'I'll take you down to the sea while you're in Kald. Just wait until you dip your toes into it,' he said in a conspiratorial tone, and was rewarded by her whipping her head round to face him, her long dark tresses cascading around her shoulders.

'I could not!' she said, her eyes wide. 'In our customs it is seen as scandalous for women to show their feet in public.'

He laughed freely at that. 'Then how do you wash, Highness?'

'In private, of course. We are not animals, like you.'

His smile grew wider. 'I think you need to be a bit more adventurous,' he said. 'What else have you never done?' He grinned, enjoying teasing her.

She strode on, her back rigid, her pretty little nose in the air, and a thought struck him.

He couldn't resist gripping her arm and tugging her

back gently. 'I know you're angry with me, for earlier... But it's not as if you've never been kissed before...'

She yanked herself away, as if she'd been burned by his touch, her chin in the air.

He walked faster to keep up with her.

'If you must know, I had never kissed anyone before you ruined it for me,' she threw at him. Only her voice didn't sound as if she completely meant it.

He stopped dead. 'That was your first kiss?' he asked, his blue eyes wide. 'I'm sorry...'

He was going to say if he'd known he would have been more gentle. He wouldn't have kissed her so hard. But he didn't think anything could have kept him from doing so, and he couldn't bring himself to regret it.

She charged on, but he kept pace with her. So she'd never kissed Crowe...there was hope for her yet.

He took a step towards her, stopping her in her tracks again, and cupped her face in his hand. 'It won't happen again. I promise. But...' He grinned. 'Was it really so bad?'

He knew she wouldn't answer, and a glimmer of anticipation sparked inside him.

He glanced up at the dark clouds looming above. 'After I have fed and watered you, I will show you how we bathe in Kald.' He winked. 'I think you'll like it.'

'I— You— You will not!' she said, as a brilliant crimson blush spread across her cheeks.

In that moment he knew she was truly innocent, and he felt a pang of guilt at his treatment of her. But the painful tightening in his groin was his instant punishment.

Chapter Three

Anne was struck by how far removed the longhouse at Kald was from her father's Great Hall at Termarth. It was more like a barn, packed full of people braying with laughter, who seemed genuinely interested in each other. Where she had come from, no one seemed interested at all.

The celebrations to mark the warriors' return were in full swing, and she had to admit the Barbarian's home was not what she'd been expecting.

It seemed to have none of the stifling traditions Termarth was renowned for, and the people were so free and at ease with one another. A little too free, if the Barbarian's earlier actions in the woods were anything to go by! But she would not think about that.

Oh, what she would give to have the freedom to come and go as she pleased back at home. Perhaps to train in the art of healing, or to go riding whenever she wished, to mingle and make friends with the other women in the kingdom…to make a proper life for herself.

She shrugged off her thoughts.

The buildings here were basic compared to the castle she had grown up in, but much more homely, and as for the views… The circular fort of Kald was set in a commanding position on chalk cliffs and heathland, overlooking the sea and a vast stretch of sand below. And the ocean was even more incredible than she could have imagined. Just looking at it, she felt so far away from her ordinary life. She only hoped she hadn't let her wonder show…

When the imposing wooden gates had opened late that afternoon, the people had rushed forward to greet Brand and welcome him home. Anne had envisaged any number of scenarios—including being dragged to a cell and tortured, whored to the Barbarian and his men, or thrown into a cage and starved—but none of those seemed to be her fate. Yet.

Instead, the Barbarian had embraced a young woman with a warmth she hadn't expected him to possess, before asking her to find Anne some food and water, and to fetch clean clothes. And then he'd given her one last, lingering look before he'd turned his back on her and walked away.

The woman—Svea—had done just as he'd asked. She'd given her a plain underdress and a blue apron-style pinafore to change into, and thankfully this time Anne knew what to do with them.

Now, as they entered the large hall, Anne followed Svea through the throng of revellers, keeping her head down, trying to make herself as small as possible. Having heard of these pagan men and their ways with women, she did not want to solicit their attention. She would much rather have stayed in the small farmstead adjacent to the hall.

The noise of the raucous Danes made her pulse race, and though no one laid a hand on her, many pairs of eyes in the room turned to look in her direction. She was used to men admiring her in Termarth—most likely due to her royal position, not her looks—but this was a totally different experience. Yet it was only the man they called Torsten, with his red braided hair, who sneered at her as they passed and made her skin crawl. He looked at her as if she was a lamb about to be slaughtered…as if she was a juicy piece of meat.

Her senses were on high alert, with the hairs on the back of her neck like little needles, standing on end.

She took in the hunting trophies on the walls and the dancing flames of the huge firepit, her rumbling stomach reacting to the smell of spices and salted fish in the air. She noticed the large wooden doors were thrown open, overlooking the square, should she need to attempt to make a run for it—although she knew the high wooden stake walls surrounding the fortress would make escape almost impossible.

But mainly, she was aware of the Barbarian, who was sitting in a large wooden chair on a raised platform in the centre of the hall. She could feel his close proximity from across the room. Men, women and children filled the cloying space, chatting and laughing, and Anne felt so out of place, so overwhelmed.

When Svea motioned for her to sit on a bench in a corner, relief flooded her.

She sat there stock-still for what seemed like an endless amount of time, going through the motions, being polite, answering the questions the young woman threw her way and raising her voice to be heard over the rumble of conversations.

Svea placed a meal of fish and vegetables before her, and although Anne was starving, and knew she should eat, she could barely bring herself to scoop up the food with a wooden spoon. Instead, she pushed it around on her plate. She was finding it hard to concentrate on anything but the Barbarian, sitting just a short space away. His commanding presence was surely felt by everyone in this hot, oppressive room, with his piercing gaze surveying the scene. And when he rose to mingle with his men he was easy to locate in the crowd. He was so tall he towered above everyone else—which at least meant she could try to avoid him.

Serving girls handed the men overflowing tankards, smiling provocatively at them and sitting on their laps—all except the Barbarian, who just acknowledged them with that slight nod of his head Anne had already grown used to. He had all-knowing eyes that seemed to see right through people, and the way he stroked his beard as if he was deep in thought was equally unnerving.

She noticed how the other women looked at him, as if he was their god Odin himself. But none of them seemed to dare approach him, and neither did he solicit their attention.

'She's mine to do with as I please...'

The words kept echoing in her mind. Now that they

were here, what did he intend to do with her? It had shocked and disturbed her when he'd kissed her earlier today. She had never expected her first kiss to be with a Northman. And she had never expected it to be like *that*.

His warm lips pressed against hers, his beard grazing her skin, had lit a flame in her belly, with the heat coiling downwards, stealing along a new and disturbing path. And as his fingers had burrowed into her unkempt hair to draw her head closer, deepening the kiss, her skin had erupted in goosebumps—and yet it was strange…she had still felt hot inside, not cold. She'd thought herself like that hunted deer again—only this time it wasn't running, it was wildly leaping. And then she'd pushed him away…

It hadn't exactly been horrible.

And afterwards he'd astounded her by apologising.

She didn't understand. No one had ever said sorry to her before. Certainly not a man. And yet this man, who was more male than any other she'd ever met, with his wild customs and reckless reputation, who had stolen her away from her home and had the strength to do what he liked to her, whether she was willing or not, had tried to make amends for a kiss…even gently teasing her to try to win her round.

She shook her head, confused. Just who exactly was this man they called the Barbarian?

'They were pleasant to you on your journey, I hope?' Svea asked, disrupting her thoughts.

The woman poured her a cup of ale and Anne took a tentative sip. She had heard that the Northmen supped from the skulls of the dead and was very glad to see that wasn't the case! She rarely drank alcohol in Termarth, but right now she needed all the courage she could get.

'As well as to be expected.'

She nodded. 'That is good. Brand would have made sure of it.'

Svea glanced over at him as she spoke, a soft smile on her lips, and Anne thought it uncanny that she knew where he was; was there anyone in the room who wasn't affected by the man's presence?

She felt wrong-footed. This was not what she had been expecting. What was happening here? Where was the humiliation, the degradation that slaves or prisoners of the Danes had spoken of? Were they simply lulling her into a false sense of security?

'You are his woman?' Anne asked, and then heat flooded her face at being so bold. It was none of her business.

But Svea just laughed at the seemingly ridiculous suggestion. 'No, he's my brother.'

Anne allowed the information to sink in, a peculiar feeling of what couldn't possibly be relief washing over her. But of course they were related. Looking at the beautiful woman before her now, she could see the similarities. She was Brand's equal in height and looks. They both had the same striking blue gaze and dark blonde hair.

'He is fond of you, I think. Perhaps he is not as hateful as he makes out,' Anne said.

Svea smiled. 'He is a good man.'

'A good man who kidnaps women?' Anne argued,

and then instantly regretted it. Her mouth was running away with her again.

'You were saying?'

A low, silky voice came from behind her. The Barbarian. Anne's spoon paused halfway to her mouth. She went completely still.

'Don't hold back now, Highness…'

She felt the warmth of his breath on her cheek and goosebumps erupted all over her body. How had he crossed the distance between them so quickly? Slowly, she turned to face him. And, damn him, the familiar, earthy scent of him gave her a rush. She had been in his proximity for no more than a day and a night, but it had felt like an eternity of being pressed up against his solid chest on horseback, caught between his strong thighs, and she was disturbed by the strange feelings that his nearness had stirred in her.

She had never spent so long in one person's company before—not even her father's. He'd always treated her as a child, who might sometimes be seen but never heard. It had been as if she was invisible. Yet with the Barbarian, when he'd looked at her with his deep blue gaze in the forest earlier today, it had been as if he was truly seeing her, and her body had become heavy and achy. She'd tried to put it down to the long, rigorous ride, but as she felt the whisper of his voice on her skin now, heat raced up her spine again.

Cool, guarded eyes studied her. They were painted with that dark kohl around the edges, and yet they crinkled when he smiled in that wicked way that stoked her pulse, and she was acutely aware that she had stopped breathing. Was it getting hotter in here?

'The lady believes I'm hateful, yet I think she provokes me,' he grinned at his sister.

'Well, try being nice, then,' Svea berated him, nudging him jovially. 'I'm going to leave you two to it. I need to see how we're getting on with serving more food to greedy men.'

'Did you hear that? She said you have to be nice to me,' Anne mocked, but instantly regretted it when thoughts of just how 'nice' he could be to her made her mouth go dry.

What was wrong with her tonight? And why did she keep putting these ideas in his head?

The Barbarian grinned a slow, seductive smile, as if he could read her thoughts, and her breath caught in her throat. Anne had to tilt her chin up to glare at him. He towered above her, looking relaxed, exuding a confidence that was both maddening and intriguing at the same time. He was dressed rather differently from when they'd been travelling earlier. He'd lost the leather and chainmail vest and was now wearing a casual dark tunic that hugged his muscled chest, fastened with a belt. Her eyes were drawn to the open neck that accentuated the tanned skin at the base of his throat and hinted at the ink swirling beneath.

'We could both give it a go.' He raised his cup in a mock salute. '*Skol!* A toast to you making it to Kald.'

'Forgive me, but I don't really feel like celebrating. After all, I am a prisoner.'

'I don't see any shackles or chains—or even a cage,' he said, his large palms upturned.

She swallowed. 'So am I free to go?'

'Sure!'

He laughed, and her breath halted. She could tell he felt more relaxed now they were here in his domain.

'If you can find your way home in the dark. Or you can stay the night and see how you feel in the morning.'

She scoffed. An impossible choice. Again. Only a fool would try to walk back to Termarth in the dark. She was stuck here and they both knew it. She took a sip of her drink while struggling to think of something to say. She didn't know this man, or his customs, and she knew she was very much at his mercy. Still, she could try to be polite. Perhaps it would help her cause. She had been brought up properly, and could exchange pleasantries with him for a few moments, even if she suddenly felt the strange need to crush her thighs together.

Damn the man—his presence was stifling.

'So,' he said, sitting down beside her on the bench and lounging back against the table, his long legs outstretched. 'Are you going to speak to me, or are we just going to sit here having a staring competition?'

'Actually, I was planning on ignoring you.' As if that was even possible!

He gave a short laugh, which magnified his generous mouth. 'Very mature...'

Despite herself, she bit back a smile. So much for being polite...

She watched as he lifted his tankard to his mouth,

saw the pulse throb in his neck as the liquid slipped down his throat, but he didn't break eye contact. He leaned forward, sliding a little closer to her on the bench. He was analysing her with those intense, penetrating eyes.

She snapped her gaze away to study the beads of condensation on her cup and stroked her fingers through them, making patterns with the droplets.

'Why don't you tell me about your life in Termarth?' he said. 'What is it like there?'

She gave him a cool look. 'You can't be serious? You can't expect us to share stories about our land with each other now? Not when every week more devastated villagers seek shelter within our walls after one of your attacks.'

She frowned. She was struggling with this forced conversation. And it didn't help that her eyes were drawn to the curve of his mouth, her body to the warmth radiating from his closeness.

He sighed, but she couldn't stop herself now. She'd noticed she couldn't help babbling when she was in his company. 'Did you bring me here to learn of my father's weaknesses and how many men he has at his command?'

'Not at all,' he said, not rising to the bait. 'I'm interested in your life, not your father's. And besides, I already know my way into his home and how to reach his most prized possessions, do I not? It is my opinion he should take better care of them. And I certainly wouldn't have chosen you as my prisoner if it was battle insights I was after.' He smirked. 'Anyway, we have our own land...we are merely farmers, despite what you might think. The raids you speak of have nothing to do with us.'

Some farmer, she thought. Leader of a fortress of warriors, whose fierce reputation had travelled the length and breadth of the country, he was more powerful than a mere farmer and he knew it. How had he garnered such a reputation if he hadn't done these despicable things? He was certainly not a man you'd want to provoke. So why was she trying to do just that?

Anne took a large sip of her drink, grateful for the cool liquid lining her stomach, which was helping to ease the knots of nerves that had formed there. Snatching a glance at his face, she wondered at the duty and responsibility he must feel in taking care of all these people. He clearly wanted to protect them and his lands. Were he and she so very different?

'So you don't want to talk about your home. What shall we talk about?' he said, 'What about your lover, Lord Crowe?'

She didn't like the vitriolic way he said his name, or the way his stunning eyes narrowed on her.

'What about him?' She was just about to reveal that she and Lord Crowe were practically strangers, and that he was the last person she wanted to think or talk about, but she bit her eager tongue. 'You seem to know more about him than I. Tell me, why do you despise him so?'

The Barbarian shrugged, as if it was nothing. 'He's a Saxon, isn't he?'

'As am I. Do you profess to have a general ha-

tred of our kind? Well, the feeling is mutual…' Anne
smoothed down her dress with her clammy palms and
took a deep breath. 'It's getting late. If you don't mind,
I'd like to go to bed,' she said, rising and attempting
to step past him. 'If you could just show me where I'll
be sleeping—?'

He gripped her arm. 'Wait!'

She flinched. The touch of his skin sent a wave of
heat through her body right down to between her legs,
and her lips parted on a tiny gasp.

'Let go of me.'

She was shocked by his sudden touch, and even
more distraught to hear the slight tremble in her voice
at the feelings he triggered inside her. She suddenly
had a compulsion to flee, but he was holding her fast.
Scared to make a scene, she lowered herself back onto
the bench. He loosened his grip, but instead of releasing her, he slipped his hand downwards, smoothing his
thumb over the delicate skin on the inside of her wrist.

She fought against closing her eyes to the sensuous
feeling. How could he make her feel such a mixed-up
jumble of emotions?

'We seem to have got off to a bad start this evening—
which is odd, as I thought you would be thanking me…'

Her eyes grew wider. 'Thanking you? What for?'

'For rescuing you from your wedding night.' He
grinned.

Instant outrage shot through her veins, despite the
fact she'd had the same thoughts earlier today. She
was starting to wonder if one brute had been replaced

with another. 'Rescuing me? Is that what you think you were doing?'

'Instead,' he said, ignoring her outburst, 'you shall be spending the night with me.'

Anne leapt out of her seat. 'I will not!'

The room was noisy, filled with the rise and fall of familiar voices, but all Brand could focus on was how absolutely perfect she was. And yet every pore of her gorgeous body screamed danger... Danger to himself and to his men. She was too much of a temptation and frustration rippled through him.

Right up until a moment before he hadn't been sure of his decision. But now that she was here, inside the walls of Kald, he felt responsible for the Princess's safety. If she made him this weak, how could he trust his own men to behave around her? He'd seen the way they'd looked at her as she had made her way through the crowd earlier and he didn't like it. He'd learned the hard way just how badly men could mistreat a woman.

A familiar wave of guilt washed over him from memories of not being able to protect his sister. No, he needed to keep Anne close, and there was nowhere closer than in his bed.

He'd made a promise to himself years ago: he might have failed when it came to Svea, but he'd be damned if he'd let anything bad happen to Anne.

Wasn't that the real reason he'd taken her from the castle? Yes, he'd called it a revenge plan to provoke Crowe, but he'd also wanted to get to know this girl who had once helped him—the girl who had consumed his thoughts since he was a boy. And he'd wanted to prevent her wedding to that monster from taking place.

But he'd acted selfishly. Bringing her here had put her in danger.

Brand was still holding her wrist, and as his fingers strayed over her skin he was sure she felt the same incredible spark he did. It was as if he could see every detail magnified: he noticed her breath hitch, her pulse quicken, her lush green eyes grow wider, darker.

He drained his cup and set it down next to hers on the table. 'Let's go.'

Gripping her hand, he led her in the direction of the door and out into the yard, despite her best attempts to tug herself free of his grasp and drag her heels every step of the way. But he wasn't holding her that tightly. He felt she could have swung free of him if she'd truly wanted to remain in the hall with everyone else.

The warm summer evening was dressed with the familiar salty scent of the sea and dark was closing in. There were only a few other people milling about outside, and Brand was pleased to see they were heading back indoors. He didn't want an audience for this.

As soon as they were out of view, Anne escaped from his hold and turned on him, her green eyes flaring. The neckline of the dress Svea had given her enhanced the pale swells of her breasts, which were rising and falling unsteadily, and the cotton dress, tied tightly around her waist, drew attention to her exquisite curves. Brand could see her pulse flickering erratically at the base of her throat, and as for the two tiny brooches fastening the front of the material...they were screaming to be ripped undone.

She pinched the bridge of her nose. 'I am tired and I wish to go to sleep now. If you could just direct me to where I will be sleeping, I can make my own way there.'

He stared at her. She was unbelievable! He couldn't have her walking about the place on her own! She was far too innocent and trusting. He didn't even trust his own men with her.

He took a step towards her, forcing her to take a step back so her shoulders grazed the wall of the barn behind her. 'Are you mad? Do you really value yourself so little?' If so, it made him wonder why. 'It would take a man less than a second to back you into a corner, just like this...'

'You told me I'd be safe here...'

'Yes, with me or Svea protecting you. Not wandering around the place all alone! You seem to forget, Highness, that right now I own you. You'll eat when I say, speak when I say, and sleep when I say...all for your own safety while you're under my roof.'

He could feel the anger vibrating off her. 'And I suppose I will have to bed you when you say, too?'

The rebellious heat and challenge in her eyes made all the blood in his body rush to his groin, making him hard, and for an insane moment he felt his body lean into hers. His face hovering over hers, he watched her tongue dart out of her mouth and tentatively trail over her parted lips.

So she was aware of such things, although he knew she had no experience.

He took a deep, steadying breath and took a step back. 'There you go, putting ideas into my head again,' he scolded. 'Now, come on.'

He pulled her across the square to Svea's farmstead, but he didn't make for her entrance. Instead, he began to lead her up a small staircase towards a door. It was an effort to get her to the top as she resisted him all the way, but she was no match for his strength.

He momentarily released her hands to grip her by her tiny waist and throw her over his shoulder, and she yelped. He took the stairs two by two and swung open the door at the top, before placing her down on her feet inside the room.

Brand had always been proud of the settlement he and his men had built here. It was the only place that had ever felt like home to him. He'd made his way out of the Saxon hellhole he'd been tossed into and he'd achieved his father's dream—well, most of it. But right now the cool caress of the sea breeze and the calming views of the bay through the smoke hole did nothing to ease the tension strumming through his body.

He drew a hand across his face. He was tired—the result of too many nights without sleep. And he'd gone too long without a woman. These days he could have his pick of Kald's most beautiful maidens, yet his interest never lasted beyond an evening or two. He had never allowed himself to care, nor even wanted to have a relationship with anyone. He'd learned that if he kept people at arm's length he wouldn't have to suffer any pain if anything should happen to them.

But Anne... Since last night, when he'd stolen her from her home, he hadn't been able to get her out of his mind and he hadn't even bedded her. He could never sleep with her—she was off-limits. He wasn't naive. He knew she would be worth more to her father if her virginity remained intact. Her father might not buy her back for a fortune if she was tarnished by the hands of a Dane.

When they'd finally arrived home this afternoon, and he'd handed the Princess over to Svea, he had missed the feel of her in his arms. He'd told himself he was being a fool, that it would soon pass, but this evening, when the door to the longhouse had swung open and she had walked into the room, his heart had literally stopped beating. It was insane!

Yet wasn't the sight of the Saxon Princess wearing a simple smock and a blue overdress that dipped subtly at the cleavage a vision to make any man question his sanity? Long, dark lashes framed her almond-shaped eyes, and her full, soft lips seemed pinker in the warm glow of his room. With a combination of small, pert breasts, a slim waist, and legs that seemed incredibly long in that dress, she was simply divine, and the desire he'd tried so hard to crush began to run riot inside him.

She had been so brave. And the stiffening in his groin made a mockery of any thoughts he'd had of being indifferent. Instead, that disconcerting, peculiar feeling of possession surged through his blood again.

Ulf, the youngest of his men, had lit the torches

on the wall and in the warm glow of the firelight he watched Anne's expressions as she took in her surroundings. The room was small, but comfortable, and a large bed dominated the space, which was lined with straw and covered with animal skins and fur. Still, the symmetrical dimples that had appeared as she'd smiled tentatively at his sister earlier this evening were nowhere to be seen.

His lips twisted. She had not yet extended that warmth to him. And as she looked up at him now, her green eyes clashing with his, his chest constricted. What had he been thinking? That her expression would slowly change from one of shock that he'd brought her to his room to one of pleasure? What a fool!

'These will be your new quarters,' he said, leaning in the doorway. 'Do they meet with your approval?'

'They do not.'

He grinned. He hadn't expected anything less. 'That's rather rude, given the room is mine. I do hope you will find it comfortable.'

'Do you live here with Svea?'

He nodded. 'She has the room below.'

'So you're not married?'

'No,' he answered, amused at the pink blush creeping up her cheeks.

'Why not?'

'Because I already have enough people to take care of.'

He had determined never to marry and have a family of his own. He couldn't be responsible for anyone else's life. And if you lived alone, you couldn't be broken by your enemy hurting someone you loved.

She nodded, seemingly satisfied with his response, and then her eyes came to rest upon the bed again. 'And where, might I ask, will you be sleeping?'

He offered her his best smile. 'I could sleep in here with you…' he teased, but instantly regretted it when Anne's exquisite emerald eyes widened in a flash of panic.

'You cannot. I will not. I'd rather you put me in a cage…'

He felt a muscle flicker in his jaw. 'That can be arranged,' he said darkly. 'And, believe me, that's where some of my men would like you.'

He came towards her, pushing his tunic sleeves up his arms. 'Look, you have nothing to fear. I am not in the habit of bedding Saxon women—especially ones who aren't willing… Where would be the fun in that?'

'But I thought—'

His blue eyes lanced her. 'You thought wrong, Highness. You shouldn't believe everything you hear. It seems to me you need an education in what Northmen are really like, based on fact, not rumour,' he said. 'Don't judge us on the actions of a few. And besides, you are not to my taste…'

'And neither are you to mine! You are the last man in the world I would ever want to be…intimate with.'

He felt as if she'd punched him in the gut as hard as a Saxon soldier might, and he sighed. 'If you stay in here you will not be harmed. You will not be touched. If you sleep out there in the hall I will not be able to vouch for your safety. Here, Svea will be just downstairs if you need anything, and I shall be watching the door.'

'Am I supposed to be grateful?' she spat.

'Mind who you're talking to, Highness,' he said, his voice like acid. 'Now, make yourself comfortable…get some rest. I'll have Ulf guard the door until I return.' He stalked over to the door and heaved it open.

'Where are you going?'

'To fetch my sister!'

Brand slammed the door and stormed down the stairs, heading back inside the longhouse and pushing his way through the throng of people. He wanted to head straight for the ale—he needed something to settle the rage and the lust coursing through his body. But he thought better of it. He needed to keep his wits about him.

All he wanted to do was go back to his room and coax her into allowing him to satisfy his need inside her beautiful body. But he was no barbarian, despite what she might think.

Anne's heart-shaped face had grown into that of a goddess over the years, and he wanted to take her long, billowing hair in his hand, twist it round his fist and pull her lips to his, silencing her far too talkative mouth.

But even as those feelings entered his mind, disgust also ripped through him. He should not be having these thoughts about her. She was a princess—spirited, brave and good—and he was exactly the type of person he should be protecting her from. Especially right now, when she was vulnerable. But their scorching kiss earlier today had caused a rush of heat to tear along his veins, making him wonder what one night would be like.

His primitive response to her was just as maddening now as it had been when he was a teenage boy, when they'd met for the first time. Back then, she'd stared at him—at his bruises and battered nose—as if he was something out of a nightmare. And perhaps she'd been right. Now he was covered in scars, both inside and out, so had he become the monster she'd once thought he was?

Yet everything he'd done had been for the good of his people, and in a way for Anne. Only she didn't realise it yet.

From a distance, he'd thought about her a lot. Too much, considering their first meeting had been fleeting. But now she was here, hadn't he made things a whole lot worse for himself? And for her?

He shouldn't have brought her here, and a wave of guilt crashed over him again. He knew only that he must keep her safe, and somehow he had manipulated the situation so she'd be sleeping in his room, in his bed. Yet he also knew all too well what would happen if he spent time with her alone—he wouldn't be able to resist her. And, disturbingly, it wasn't just her body he wanted to get to know. He found himself wanting to discover her hopes and dreams, what her life was really like. But she'd put up a barrier and avoided telling him. She was keeping her distance, and he had to do the same. He had to maintain control.

So much for getting some rest. He had the feeling he wouldn't be getting a lot of sleep tonight.

* * *

Anne lay awake in the darkness, listening to the sounds of the gathering going on in the longhouse. This bed was nothing like her grand one at home, but even so it had looked inviting and she'd curled up on it and shut her eyes, hoping slumber would come. But she was too warm, despite the balmy night breeze drifting through the smoke hole, and although she was exhausted, still sleep eluded her.

She had heard Svea enter the room downstairs and had listened to her moving around for a while before it all went quiet.

Anne hated to admit it, but she was waiting for the Barbarian to return. Enveloped in the furs on his bed, she breathed in the male scent of him, somehow needing to know and understand her captor better. He was certainly a mystery. Would he keep his word and guard the door? Or would ale reveal the rumours about his sexual appetites to be true? She had seen far too many of her father's advisors' real characters come out after they'd been at the mead halls in Termarth.

She imagined he'd retired to one of the back rooms in the hall with any one of those women who had been fawning over him…maybe he wouldn't even come back. And why did she even care?

But finally, as she lay there waiting, she heard deep voices in conversation, heavy footsteps on the stairs and a dull thud as if someone had slumped against the door. Her whole body tensed and she willed herself to lie as still as possible. She didn't dare breathe.

There was the sound of a sword being removed from

its hilt and being placed on the ground, a creak of the wood, and…nothing.

She waited again. She strained to hear his breathing. Was it the Barbarian? And was he asleep? What was he doing? Damn the darkness.

She couldn't bear this. She sat bolt upright and as quietly as she could tiptoed over to the door. She sat down, resting her back against it. 'Brand, is that you? What are you doing?'

'What?' His silken voice sounded in the pitch-black, through the wooden panel.

'I said, what are you doing?'

'Trying to get some rest—which is exactly what you should be doing after our long journey today.'

'Out there on the stairs? In the cold?' She felt hysteria rising.

'Someone has to make sure you're safe while you're here. What did you think I was going to do? I told you I won't touch you. I meant it.'

She couldn't believe it. He really did mean it. This wasn't the man she'd heard about, who didn't wait to be invited, who had a thirst for the conquest of Saxon villages and virgins.

She had been stoic throughout the journey here, trying to conserve whatever strength she had left to put up a fight should she need to. She would never have surrendered her body willingly to a man who would use her like an object. And yet he had surprised her by not even attempting to take her. He'd even confessed he didn't desire her.

'Why? Where would you like me to sleep, Highness?'

She tipped her head back against the door. Argh! He had to be the most infuriating man she had ever met. 'Out there, of course!' she ground out.

What was the matter with her? Of course she didn't want him to be in here, lying next to her—he was a ruthless killer who cared for nothing and no one.

And yet he did care about his sister. Images of him joking with Svea flashed through her mind, his wide smile and glinting eyes…and she'd seen the pained look in his face when he'd pushed his horse away earlier. He clearly cared for the animal. And he obviously wanted to keep his people safe. They certainly had that in common.

Was there more to Brand Ivarsson than she had originally thought?

'Fine, then we're both happy. Go to sleep.'

She reached out for a blanket from the bed and pulled it over her. He had somehow managed to awaken feelings in her she had never experienced before and couldn't even begin to understand. She didn't even think she wanted to—they were far too dangerous a response—and so she'd tried to push them down.

Perhaps it was just a heightened reaction to the terrifying situation. Maybe she'd feel better in the morning.

She played around with the animal furs, trying to get more comfortable.

'I do hope you're not going to be fidgeting around in there keeping me awake all night,' he said.

'You could always sleep elsewhere. Outside another room, perhaps?'

The wood creaked again and, straining to hear, she thought she heard him cross his arms over his chest.

'That's not going to happen.'

She sighed, and then decided she'd feel too guilty to sleep all night if she didn't at least offer him a blanket. So she stood and gently pulled open the door a little and peered around the edge.

'That staircase can't be very comfortable.'

'It's not. But I didn't think you cared.'

She could tell he was grinning in the darkness.

'I don't,' she said. 'But I don't want you to catch your death on my account. Here, take this,' she said, holding out the fleecy material.

His fingers brushed hers as he took it from her. 'Thank you,' he said. 'Now shut the door and go back to bed.'

She pulled the door closed and sank to the floor again.

'I said get some sleep!' he muttered through the door once more.

'I can't!' she fumed.

'Why not?'

'Why do you think? I'm miles from my home and I'm here—with you!'

'So you are homesick?'

'Not exactly,' she said.

'You do not like your home? Is that why you don't want to talk about it?'

'Of course I do! I would do anything for my kingdom, my people. It's just…'

'Go on,' he urged.

And something about the invisibility that came with being in the dark made her want to tell him. Perhaps he'd realised that she couldn't stop talking when she was nervous...

'It's just not as if my father will be sitting beside the fire, longing for my return. In truth, I fear you will not get the reaction you crave—he may not come at all. He might not think I am worth the fight.'

'He does not love you?' the Barbarian asked. 'I find that hard to believe. Among our people, family is everything.'

'He is not the man people say he once was. Not since he lost my mother when I was small. It is as if I am unimportant to him.'

She heard him release a long breath. 'I know what it is like to lose a parent. What happened to her?'

'She died in childbirth, having my brother. She never really warmed to my father, but he was obsessed with her. She was very beautiful. My brother was sickly and passed away when he was just a year old. I always felt my father wished it had been me who'd died instead.'

There was silence, and Anne bit her lip. She didn't know why she'd told him that. She was babbling again, but talking was helping to ease some of the tension of the past few days. In this absolutely absurd situation, it was helping her to relax. But she knew she mustn't reveal too much of herself—it would make her weak against her captor.

'That must have been hard on you. And your father,' he said. 'And yet I still think he'll send his men to fetch you. You *are* important, despite what you may feel.'

'As a bargaining tool, perhaps.'

And she wondered, not for the first time, how her life might have been different with a mother to love her and a little brother to play with. Would her father have behaved differently towards her and become a better king to his subjects?

She wondered if that was why she helped the people so much—to bridge the gap between them and her father. She had grown up understanding her position in the world, knowing she must heed her father's wishes and do her duty. Before the Barbarian had taken her from the ramparts all her dreams seemed to have been lost. And now... Now she wasn't sure about anything.

Did she really want to be rescued, to return to Termarth and marry Lord Crowe, now her world had been turned upside down?

'You are lucky to have a sister,' she said. 'To have the kind of welcome she gave you today. She would do anything for you.'

'And I her.'

'What happened to your parents?'

There was a long pause, and Anne wondered if she'd asked the wrong question, or if perhaps he'd fallen asleep. She stretched and curled her toes, waiting.

'My mother died on our voyage to England,' he said, his voice taking on a cooler edge. 'My father died not long after we arrived here.'

Her heart went out to him. 'I'm sorry for you too, then,' she said. And she meant it. 'No one should have to suffer burying a parent before their time.'

Her thoughts flew to how he must have had to grow

up quickly, to learn to take care of his sister and all these people.

He cleared his throat. 'All right—enough chit-chat,' he said. 'Now, please go to sleep. You must be exhausted.'

And at some point she must have drifted off, because the next time she woke the room was drenched in daylight. She opened the door, wondering if the Barbarian might still be there, but instead she'd found the young lad, Ulf, guarding her door. He told her he was under orders to keep her there, and she was still alone in the room by the time the sun was burning bright in the sky in the afternoon.

Anne paced the floorboards for what seemed like the hundredth time. She had watched through the smoke hole as the surprisingly beautiful kingdom of Kald had come alive. Children ran free, chasing chickens and a menagerie of other animals across the central square, and men and women emerged from their farmsteads and milled about chatting, milking goats and cattle, before heading off to the grain fields to farm.

Anne had been fascinated by the different clothing, their mannerisms and activities. It had been an education in Danelaw.

Svea had delivered her water for washing, breakfast, and lunch—but being cooped up was beginning to feel like torture. It wasn't the cage with bars she'd been expecting, but knowing she couldn't get out was making her start to panic.

She couldn't stay in this room all day, knowing she was trapped—she'd go mad. She needed to walk, to breathe in fresh air. But every time she tried the door handle it was locked, and the young Dane on guard on the other side of the door told her to stay inside, repeating that he was under the Barbarian's strict instructions not to let her out.

She was livid. He had lied to her again. He'd told her she wasn't a prisoner and yet here she was, locked up. She had seemingly swapped one prison at home, where she'd been caged by her father, for another. Well, she was sick of it!

She tried to focus on the view, on the sunlight dancing on the ocean in the distance, but that only made things worse. It was awful being this close to the sea and not being able to explore it. Her skin felt clammy and she was struggling to breathe. After pacing the room some more, she threw up her hands, exasperated, and made another try for the door.

Pulling and pushing at the handle, she felt it finally come free, and she fled past the young Dane and down the stairs.

'My lady, stop!' he said, struggling to keep up with her as she tried to calm her breathing, heading towards the longhouse full of purpose. 'You can't go in there!'

'Nonsense!' she said. 'I will not be locked up all day long.'

At home, she had begun to fight her father on the very same matter. But here she was surprised to find the hall empty, with just a few serving maids milling about. It had a different atmosphere in the daytime, with the fire slowly burning and animal skins strewn about, offering comfort and serenity.

She stepped back outside into the square, shielding her eyes from the sun with her hand. 'Where is he?' she asked, turning to the young lad.

'In the barn, my lady—but, please, you can't go in there. He told me you had to stay upstairs. You'll get me into trouble.'

He was really quite sweet, she thought. And she didn't want the Barbarian to punish him. But equally she would not stand being kept in a box. She would have to make the Barbarian see there was another way.

She headed in the direction of where she'd seen the men lead some horses and pushed open the door to the livery, which seemed to double up as a workshop. She found six men, some of whom she recognised from the barbican yesterday, huddled around what looked like a long, narrow boat, and her bravery wavered. She suddenly wondered how she'd had the gall to burst in here. But her irrational fear of being confined, of losing control, had propelled her forward without really thinking.

As she approached the group, they all turned to stare in her direction, some greedily looking her up and down, others bemused. Even the horses in pens on the other side of the barn started whickering at her flurried entrance. Undeterred, she concentrated on placing one foot after the other on the straw-covered floor as she drew nearer.

'My, my, what have we here?' Torsten sneered.

'I'm looking for Brand,' she said, finding her voice. She sensed these Northmen were in a rowdy mood—

perhaps they always were—and she tried to quell the uneasy feeling the redhead evoked in her.

'Is he here?' she asked, standing firm.

The group parted and stepped away from the vessel just as the very man she was looking for pushed himself out from beneath the craft, staring up at her from his position on the ground.

For a moment, looking into his steely blue eyes, she felt a bolt of unexpected heat strike low in her belly, and the sudden realisation that she actually found him attractive momentarily outweighed the anger he stirred in her.

She braced herself against it. 'I thought I'd find you here,' she said, taking a deep breath as she regained control of her racing heart.

He flicked his gaze over her, looking her up and down in that disapproving way she was growing used to, and she resisted rolling her eyes.

'Highness,' he said. 'This is a surprise. I thought I ordered you to stay upstairs and wait for my return.' An undercurrent of anger laced his voice, and he glared at Ulf. 'You have one moment to explain what you're doing here.'

She placed her hands on her hips. 'I came here to tell you that I will not stay locked up all day, waiting for you to grace me with your presence. I will not wait in a box until my father or Lord Crowe come to claim me. I will die of boredom!' she spat.

Annoyance lanced her as her outburst raised a laugh from the men.

'I'd be happy to keep you entertained, my lady, if Brand would only allow it!' Torsten grinned.

The Barbarian scowled and slowly stood in front of her, blocking the path between her and Torsten. He loomed over her, dominating the space between them. His sculpted frame, probably honed from fighting or from hard work on the land, seemed even more imposing than she remembered from the day before, and her heart began to pick up its pace again.

'So to what do I owe the pleasure of this little visit? Boredom?' he mocked, making her feel as if it was an inconvenience.

Not for the first time, she wondered why he disliked her so much. He didn't even try to make a secret of it. Was that why he'd been avoiding her—why he wanted her out of his sight? Well, the feeling was reciprocal. And it had grown ten-fold since he'd put her under lock and key. If Ulf hadn't let it slip that the Barbarian was working in the barn, she might never have been able to get near him. And she refused to be ignored! But she knew she needed to get him alone, to appeal to his better nature without these brutes being around.

'I was hoping we could talk. In private.' The words felt like blades in her throat, as she remembered what she'd spat at him last night—that he was the last man she would ever want to be close to.

He raised a dark eyebrow and Anne thought in that moment how he was rather like the stallions in the stables—no doubt a wild ride, but way too dangerous to take a chance on.

She anticipated that he wouldn't make this easy for

her. Why should he? He was wiping his hands on a rag while studying her face. Was he contemplating telling Ulf to take her away and lock her up again? She refused to give him the opportunity.

'It's important,' she pressed.

The crease between his brows deepened and he turned to his men, who were watching them with amusement. All except Torsten, who seemed to be looking at her in a hungry way that made her prickle with discomfort.

'Men, can you leave us?'

Anne released a long, steady breath. She was relieved, but also surprised. It was unusual for a man to honour a woman's wishes so publicly, wasn't it? Especially a prisoner. She didn't think her father had ever let her opinions be voiced. And yet didn't that make the Barbarian seem even more powerful—stronger somehow—because he wasn't afraid to let a woman be heard? She'd half expected him to throw her over his shoulder, take her back up to the room and chain her down. But everything about this place and her captor had caught her off-guard.

Then, as if for her benefit, he added the warning, 'This won't take long.'

The Barbarian busied himself with scrubbing a patch of dirt from the side of the wooden boat, and continued doing so even when they were alone, so Anne came round the craft to stand in front of him, crossing her hands over her body, feigning a confidence she did not feel.

He sighed. 'What is it that you want, Highness?'

It irritated her that he never used her name, Anne, yet at the same time, she liked the way Highness or Princess sounded like an endearment on his deep, velvety tongue. She wondered what else that tongue—that perfect mouth—could do, before stopping herself short.

Where had that thought come from? What was the matter with her? She'd had a taster of his kisses yesterday and she did not want more—did she?

She tossed her hair over her shoulders, and with it her appalling thoughts. She was a clever, strong, and capable woman, who just needed to keep herself sane until she was returned safely to Termarth.

'You can call me Anne,' she said. 'It might help me to fit in a little more while I'm here if you don't use my title.'

The Barbarian threw the rag onto the floor and finally turned to face her, bracing his hands behind him on the stable rail. 'I don't think you'll ever blend in here,' he said. 'But what is it that you want? I'm pretty busy here, *Anne*.'

She felt a tug in her chest—that same irresistible pull as when their eyes had met across the battlement at Termarth—and her mouth dried.

'Have you sent word to my father, to let him know I am here?'

He studied her carefully. 'That is no concern of yours.'

'I was just thinking… If it is a ransom you are after, you will need to let him know of my whereabouts.'

'I'm sure your father's dogs will sniff us out. We were careful to leave enough tracks. Is that all?'

She wrung her hands together. 'Last night you said that I didn't have shackles and chains because I wasn't a prisoner. That I was free to do as I pleased…' When he didn't speak, she rushed on. 'Well, you and I both know that I can't exactly walk out of here and find my way home, so I shall wait for my father's men to fetch me. Which will be soon, no doubt. But I cannot stay in that room, day and night, cooped up like one of your animals. I will go mad. Please…'

He must have noticed her pale skin, or perhaps even recognised the consternation in her eyes. 'What's the matter, Princess? Are you lonely up there? Needing someone to talk to?'

She tilted her chin up. 'If you must know, I'm scared of small spaces.' *Of having no way out.*

His eyes narrowed on her. 'Are you?'

He thought she was playing him.

'I mean it,' she said. 'I've hated it ever since I was young. I panic.'

He took a step towards her, concern clouding his blue gaze. 'Why? What happened?'

She sighed. She didn't want to tell him, but she knew he wouldn't believe her otherwise, and might send her back to that room in bonds.

She twisted her hands some more. 'After my mother died, my father would lock me away for long periods. He said he was worried that something would happen to me, and the only way to keep me safe was for me to stay in my room. I'd spend days and days up there, with no one to talk to and nothing to do. Then he'd soften and let me out for a while—until he had another

one of his episodes and he'd do it again. Each time it happened I'd be up there for longer and longer, and I began to worry he'd forgotten about me. I started to pace and scream, begging to be let out, but it was as if no one could hear me.'

She thought she saw a flash of anger light up the Barbarian's eyes, but he didn't say anything.

'With you locking me in that room, I think it brings it all back,' she finished.

He took a step towards her. 'So what do you suggest? I can't have you roaming about the place—it's not safe,' he said, his eyebrows pulling together.

'Safe for whom? What do you think I'm going to do?'

'For *you*!' he said, exasperated.

Again, not what she was expecting.

'Some of my men have taken a shine to you, Highness. You may have no regard for your safety, but I do.'

'Anne,' she said.

'And some of them don't feel the need to be gentle with Saxon women, *Anne*,' he added.

Her skin chilled. 'I understand. Which is why I suggest you put me to work with your sister.'

For a moment he looked bemused. 'I do not put my sister to work—she does as she pleases.'

'Then I envy her,' she said. 'No man has ever let *me* do as I please.' He drew in a breath, but she carried on anyway. 'I can sew...or wash pans.'

He stared at her, incredulous. 'You can't be serious. You are a princess. I can't imagine you have ever done a day's work in your life!'

'Then you don't know me at all. Perhaps you need an education in Saxon women,' she said, twisting his words from the night before.

His amusement dried up. 'I am sorry if I've misjudged you, Highness, but I thought princesses drifted around in their palaces, being waited on hand and foot. They don't work.'

He picked up a tool, as if at the mention of work he needed to get back to whatever he was doing to the boat.

'This one does—even if my father forbids it. I can sew, or even cook. I need to do something. I know we don't exactly see eye to eye, you and I...' She waited for him to deny it. He didn't. 'But I'm serious. I need to keep busy.'

'Look,' he said, tossing the tool aside with a loud clatter. 'You're of no use to me dead, but if you promise to be careful, and not to leave Svea's side...'

She smiled at him then—perhaps for the first time. 'I don't especially want to end up dead myself...'

His lips twisted.

'Thank you,' she said. Then she turned her gaze to look at the boat. 'Did you build this?'

'I did.'

'It's beautiful. You're good at it.'

'Was that a compliment? From Princess Anne of Termarth?'

Her smile widened as she considered him. 'Brand the Boat Builder...' she said. 'It has a nice ring to it. What is it for? Are you planning to go somewhere?'

His brow furrowed. 'Ulf!' he called, and the lad came running in.

He obviously didn't want to tell her, and he was cutting their conversation short.

'Take the Princess to my sister and ask her to give her a job to do—or at least to keep her occupied until I am finished here.'

'Yes, Brand.'

'And don't let me down again.'

'No, Brand.'

'Thank you,' Anne said again, and began to walk away. Then she stopped and turned slightly. 'And for keeping your word last night.'

He inclined his head, narrowing his watchful eyes on her.

'I am starting to think you are not the barbarian people believe you to be.'

In fact, she was starting to wonder if any of it was true. Who *was* the man behind the fearsome name?

'Well, we can't have that...' He smiled. 'Perhaps I need to start living up to my reputation.'

Chapter Four

Brand knew he was letting Anne affect him more than she should. They were waiting for an enemy to arrive at his gates, getting ready for the battle he'd longed to fight for years, to take his revenge—and yet his mind was consumed with thoughts for this woman. His rival's woman.

But didn't they say you should keep your enemies close? Perhaps he should get to know everything about her, inch by silky inch. He found himself wanting to know more about the woman beneath the beautiful exterior too—the one who had handed him a blanket last night so he wouldn't get cold.

And yet he could not allow himself to care for her. He had a whole fortress of people to look after, and a sister he had vowed to spend his life making amends to. It was why he had determined never to have children of his own—he didn't need anyone else depending on him.

It had been hours since he had spoken with Anne in

the barn, and he'd kept himself and his men busy with reinforcing the castle walls, making more longbows and stockpiling food, preparing for Crowe and his men to arrive. But his thoughts were tormented. When she had smiled at him for the first time she had taken his breath away. She was more mesmerising than his beloved ocean. And more dangerous.

He needed to get some self-control.

He understood Anne's need to keep busy—he often sought solace in his workshop. His father had spent most of his time there too, tinkering away on whatever his latest project was. And it helped Brand to feel close to him.

His father had a lot to answer for... Ivar Bjarnesson was the reason their Danish shield brothers had joined them on their quest to England. They'd followed his vision, his search for fertile land and a good trading route. A better life. And it was why Brand was determined not to give up on what they'd built here.

Only he didn't know if his father would approve of his latest move of practically stealing a princess from her wedding bed...

The well-worn old longboat that had carried them to England was still here, and Brand smiled, running his hand over the bodywork. To anyone else, the bare shell of the vessel would have looked like scrap, but to him it was still beautiful, amazingly free from any major damage, just a slightly dented keel. A fierce dragon head was carved into the prow. One day he would strip it down to its core, discover its weaknesses—rather like Anne had begun to do with him last night...

Why did she keep interrupting his thoughts? Why was he letting her get to him? He needed to focus.

He knew he was purposely trying to keep his distance from her. Having just a piece of wood between them all night had been bad enough, but spending the day with her too? Hell, no. He'd been prepared to lock her up for the remainder of the time she was here, so he wouldn't have to be around her, until she'd stormed in here, refusing to behave the way he'd expected her to and breaking down his resolve. Again.

Everything she'd told him about her upbringing so far had shocked him, made him angry. How could her father have locked her away like that? Although wasn't he guilty of wanting to do exactly the same? Couldn't he understand why? When something was so precious, it was tempting to keep it tucked away, to keep it safe. And yet Anne had felt her father wasn't interested in her. The King had neglected her. And still, in spite of his harsh treatment of her, she had grown up to be kind-hearted. He'd seen it in the way she'd helped him as a boy and the way she'd cared for his horse when it was hurt.

He sighed, knowing he should seek her out, check that everything was all right and that his men weren't tormenting her. But when he headed into the square and inside the longhouse, there was no sign of her or Svea. They weren't in the cookhouse either. When he couldn't find them in Svea's room, his skin began to chill with alarm. His strides became longer and faster as he searched for her back in the barn, in the smokehouse and all the other houses. Nothing.

She wouldn't have made a run for it, would she? Yes, she was impulsive, strong-willed and tenacious— he wouldn't put it past her to try—but the gates were locked and his men were on guard. Someone would surely have raised the alarm. And Svea was nifty with a blade should an enemy have come close.

Then a thought occurred to him. The beach. He could tell she'd felt drawn to the sea—she hadn't been able to take her eyes off it on their journey to Kald. She'd been practically mesmerised. And although she had wanted to hide her fascination from him, she'd failed miserably. Would Svea have taken her there?

Fear thundered through him. Yes, the sea looked beautiful, and to a strong swimmer like himself or Svea it was glorious, but to someone unprepared for the currents—someone like his mother or Anne—it could be lethal.

He signalled for his men to open the fortress gates and then took off on the path that led downhill to the cove, picking up his pace.

Reaching the bay, sheltered on one side by the fortress, the rest a vast expanse of golden sand, he noted the tide was in and the waves were thrusting forward, rolling at full speed onto the shore. The sun was getting lower in the sky as he looked up and down the beach, but he couldn't see them.

Memories washed over him, of the boat rising over each crest then crashing back down, and watching his mother fall. He'd cried out to warn his father, but it had been too late—her head had slammed into the vessel, and he'd watched as her body had slipped beneath the surface. The last thing he remembered—would always remember—was the sound of his mother's last breath and the shattering of his own heart breaking.

In these past few years he'd been stronger than he'd known he could be—he'd had to be for Svea. He'd had to grow up quickly, and give over his time to making sure she was all right, that she had everything she needed. But he was certainly no replacement for their parents. And it had put him off ever being a father himself. The burden was too great. And should anything untoward ever happen to his own children, it would be more than he could bear. He often took comfort in the fact that his father had died without having to witness what had happened to him and Svea.

A movement near the rock pools caught his eye as a solitary figure began to walk towards him. He made his way in that direction, and through the fading sun he saw that it was Svea.

He cursed under his breath. 'Where have you been? I've been looking everywhere for you. Is Anne with you?'

'We've been here. I thought I'd allow our guest to wash while the men were otherwise occupied.'

'Good idea,' he said, relief flowing through him. 'Where is she?'

Svea pointed to the tidal pools, and as Brand registered the lone silhouette in the water he released his bunched-up fists, running his fingers over his hair and down his beard.

'Don't worry, she's safe,' Svea said, tapping her sword as if to reassure her brother.

These days his sister was one of Kald's fiercest warriors, and he was incredibly proud of the woman she'd become. Crowe had changed her, of course, as he'd changed them all. That man had torn apart the beautiful web his family had built, hardened their hearts, and he knew Svea longed for revenge, as did he.

If he could cause that man pain, it would assuage the guilt he felt for not being able to protect Svea and his father. And they'd had infinite patience, like a colony of spiders, constructing a new, beautiful but fragile home in which to take shelter, and it wouldn't be long now until Crowe fell into their trap.

'You know, if I didn't know better I'd think you had a soft spot for our prisoner,' said Svea.

His eyes narrowed on her. 'That's ridiculous.'

She grinned. 'Just remember she's a Saxon—you're a Dane. We stick to the plan.'

'How could I forget?' he said. 'You know I won't let you down.'

'Be sure you don't.' She squeezed his arm. 'Well, she's all yours. I need to go and see how tonight's food is coming along. See you up there.'

He paced over to the pools, needing to see with his own eyes that the Princess was all right.

'Anne?'

The water parted and she stood suddenly, in shock, water sluicing off her glorious body—and he froze. Never before had he experienced a shot of lust so strong, so powerful. He couldn't move.

They could use her as a weapon in battle, he thought, to paralyse men—she was that beautiful. He blinked his eyes, trying to block out the image of her loose dark hair cascading over her wet undergarments, the flare of panic in her green eyes.

He saw Anne glance down and gasp. The white material of her undergarments had turned see-through in the water and was clinging to her body in all the wrong places, highlighting the shadows under her small, pert breasts, the peaks of her rosy nipples. A little squeal slipped out of her mouth, and just as quickly as she'd stood her divine body disappeared beneath the water again.

'There's no need to stare!' she shouted.

He would have to disagree. But she was a little too perfect—especially for the likes of him. And knowing that helped him to keep his hands to himself.

He forced himself to be courteous and turn around.

'What are you doing here?' she screeched.

'I didn't know where you were. I came to find you to check everything was all right.' His back to her, he closed his eyes and tried to swallow down his lust, but it was futile. 'It's getting late. We should go back up before it gets dark. Svea's gone on ahead.' His throat felt incredibly dry. 'But you might want to get changed first,' he said.

Snatching up her cloak, he wondered how he had missed the neat pile of clothes on the rocks. He threw it to her and she stood again, holding the wool across her body, and with extremely unsteady fingers she reached for her dress too.

He was glad to have another moment with his back turned to pull himself together. He heard her hoist herself out of the water and begin to dress. There was the unmistakable sound of wet clothes dropping to the sand, and he heard her tussle with the wool as she dried her smooth skin. He could imagine every action and his blatant desire wasn't going away.

An agonising moment later, he heard her soft footsteps on the sand behind him.

'Are you decent?' he asked.

'I am now.'

Turning round, he knew he would never be able to erase the image of her perfect round breasts and the flare of her hips from his mind, as she rose out of the water like the Norse sea goddess Rán. And she'd definitely snared him in her net.

'I thought you weren't keen on bathing in public,' he said.

'I didn't have much of a choice, did I? And your sister assured me no one was here.'

'So how was it?'

'What?'

'The water?' He grinned, keeping up with her as she began to make her way across the beach.

He saw the faint flicker of a smile at the corner of her mouth. 'You were right. It was good—if a little cold.'

He knew how enticing the water could be. If it hadn't been for her teeth chattering and his stomach beginning to rumble he might even have tried to convince her to go back in with him. And not just into the rockpools, but the shallow surf.

An image of her body in his arms, slippery from the

water, made him hot and hard. He breathed in a lungful of sea air, hoping it would steady his racing heart, as they began their ascent up the steep, winding cliff path.

The dark fortress always took on a different character at night time. The light was rapidly beginning to fade and the tall wooden walls stood in a mighty silhouette against the setting sun. He wanted to know what she thought of the home he had built. He didn't understand why he cared, but he wanted to know if she liked it. It wasn't exactly like the castle she had grown up in, but it was still pretty impressive, and enough to put off even the fiercest of opponents from attacking.

Still, he knew Crowe would come. That man had a thirst for power and bloodshed. Brand had seen it first-hand. What was taking him so long? If Anne had been taken from *him*, he would have gone after her in a heartbeat. But he wasn't her rescuer, was he? He was her captor. And right now he wasn't sure he liked himself very much. He only hoped she knew by now that he wasn't going to hurt her. If anything, he wanted to protect her.

It was the gulls circling in the sky above them that first caught Brand's attention—and then he saw the field, well churned up by horses' hooves. Every muscle in his body tensed and his blood chilled. Out of the corner of his eye, not twenty feet ahead of them, he saw a wall of Saxon soldiers gathering on the heath.

He covered Anne's mouth with his hand, mirroring his movements in the forest the day before, enveloping her body in his arms as she tensed. If they'd carried on just a few steps more they would have been seen.

He nodded towards the field and she followed his line of sight. 'It seems your lover has come for you at last.'

He glanced over to the fortress gates. There was no sign of Svea. He reckoned she must have made it back just in time, thank goodness. If she had seen the Saxons, there was no telling how she might have reacted...

He backed Anne into the hollow of an old English oak where he'd played hide and seek with his sister as a boy. He manoeuvred her round to face him in the tight space, blocking her exit. She was enclosed, and he knew she wouldn't like it.

'Are you not going to scream, Princess?'

Her chin tilted up. 'I wouldn't dare. I know what my punishment would be if I tried.'

He grinned. He'd spent his childhood growing up in the marsh and heathland, so he knew this terrain inside out. The soldiers ahead of them looked like hired mercenaries, rather than free peasants fighting for their King. It would make them harder to fight, if it came to that, but Brand knew he had the upper hand having the fortress.

Only he saw instantly that those fifty or so men were blocking their way to the entrance of Kald.

Heading up the group was Crowe, and Brand felt a cold curl of wrath seep through his veins.

He reached for his sword.

'Don't!' Anne said, gripping his arm.

He glanced down at her hand, then back at her. 'What's the matter? Worried that your lover will get hurt?'

She shook her head. 'He is not my lover. If it was up to me, I would not be marrying him at all.'

He inclined his head. 'Worried about me, then?'

'I don't want anyone to get hurt. And you'd be a fool to fight all those men on your own. See reason!'

He would happily die trying... But, although he hated to admit it, he knew she was right. Now was not the time to fight. There were too many of them for him to take on by himself—even by his standards. No, he had to bide his time and first get back within the walls of Kald without being seen.

He released his grip on the hilt of his weapon.

'Do you have a death wish?' she added.

'I do not fear death, if that's what you mean. Every Dane wishes to fight with honour and to die bravely in battle.'

'But surely not yet? Not now?'

He nodded, taking her chin between his thumb and forefinger, gently tipping her face up to his. He was so close to her he felt her breath hitch. 'You're right. I should be patient.'

In all things, he thought, as he stared down into her eyes. He could get lost in their green stormy depths.

So what should he do? They could wait it out—see if the soldiers moved away, so he could signal to his men in Kald to open the gate for him and Anne to slip inside. Or they could return to the beach and make the hard climb over the rocks to the other entrance at the back of the fortress. But it was only accessible by water. Could Anne make it?

He peered around the oak and took another glance

at the men. They looked as if they were set to stay, so he made his decision.

Anne gasped. 'Brand, they're wearing black and yellow—the markings that man in the village spoke of.'

'I wondered if you'd noticed.'

She shook her head. She couldn't believe Crowe and his men would do such a thing. Why? Had Brand been right all along?

'I'm sorry I doubted you. What do we do now?'

He liked the sound of 'we', and he trailed his hand down her cheek, over her arm, and down to hold her hand in his. And when he thought she might resist, to pull back and protest, or cry out to Crowe, she didn't.

'They're blocking our route back. We'll have to go this way. Come on.'

Chapter Five

Anne supposed she should struggle against his touch, but she felt dazed and disorientated. She was sure that Brand had nearly kissed her for a second time. Would she have pushed him away? The way her body was reacting to him disturbed her. It seemed to have a mind of its own, burning for his touch, and she didn't understand it.

Was this what desire felt like? And why was she feeling it with this man?

Keeping low and quiet, so as not to draw any unwanted attention, Brand led her back down the narrow cliffside path and she let him, her tiny hand in his large, strong one. She wondered why she wasn't trying to escape. Why was she following this Northman down a dark, dangerous path when her fiancé's men had finally come to get her?

But if she'd made a run for it, or cried out, it would have led to certain bloodshed. Brand would have put up a fight and been killed, and she told herself she didn't want him or anyone else to get hurt. And wasn't there a tiny part of her that wasn't yet ready to go back to her old life? Back to Termarth to be married off to Crowe or the next highest bidder?

Her fiancé was practically within shouting distance, but she was no longer sure who was the enemy. Was Crowe a friend or a foe? Could it really be true that he and his men were responsible for the devastation of that settlement the other day? She felt sick. If he had killed all those people in that village, she needed to let her father know. Surely the King wouldn't want such an ally?

She wondered if Brand was right—were the Danes being blamed for Saxon atrocities?

'Where are we going?' she whispered.

'Back down to the beach. We can't stay here on the cliff all night, and at least there's shelter in the caves. We can get into Kald if we go the back way, but we might have to wait until first light. The rocks are lethal, even when you can see where you're going.'

Anne stopped dead, tugging her hand out of his grasp. 'You want us to spend the night on the beach? But there's no one else around.'

Maybe she was making a mistake. But she had her reputation to think of! She could not be alone with this man—especially when she was having such strong reactions to him. She thought she was even starting to like him. The yearning to have him kiss her again was becoming a concern, and as for the throbbing heat between her legs—it was terrifying her.

'What's wrong? Don't you trust yourself alone with me?'

He offered her a dangerous half-smile. Damn him,

how did he do that? How did he know what she was thinking?

'Come on, we don't have a choice,' he said over his shoulder. But he stopped again when he realised she wasn't following.

'We do,' she said, shaking her head. 'You could stop this madness and hand me back to my people.'

His face suddenly turned mutinous. 'What is it, Princess? You've caught a glimpse of your lover and are desperate to go back to him? Is that it?'

'I told you—he is not my lover. I barely know Lord Crowe and I do not care for him,' she bit back. 'All I know is that I can't be alone with you!'

Somehow her words and her anger seemed to appease him. He exhaled, slowly raking his hand over his hair. 'Look, I promised I wouldn't kiss you again, if that's what you're worried about, and I meant it. I'm not going to hurt you, Anne. I will hand you back to your father soon enough—I promise. But for now just keep walking. We don't want to be on this crumbling path in the dark.'

And, like a deer being led off into the unknown—either to freedom in the forest or to be made a sacrifice—she allowed him to take her hand again and she followed him.

When they made it onto the sand it had lost all the warmth of the sun and felt like a cool embrace around her feet, and yet Brand was right—it was much more sheltered from the elements down here. It was also out of sight of Crowe and his soldiers. Out of sight of anyone...

'Won't your men be wondering where we are? Won't they come looking for us?' she asked. 'Won't they attack Lord Crowe?'

'Svea knows we were at the beach. She'll realise we're stuck. And, no, they won't do anything without my command.'

Brand tugged her along the undulating sand to the opening of a little cave.

'Take a seat,' he said, motioning for her to sit on a smooth rock.

The sun was setting on the horizon and it was an incredible show of rich purple and glorious gold, casting a brilliant amber glow over the beach and illuminating the rippling water. When she was younger there had been so many times when she had longed for escape and had dreamed of seeing the ocean, of experiencing places and scenes like this one. But never had she thought she'd experience it with a Northman.

She had heard stories of men like Brand Ivarsson crossing the seas. 'Giant sea wolves', her father had called them. Unafraid of anything or anyone. Pagans to be feared and fought. And yet the man who stood before her now, trying to pull some green leaves from the rocks, was nothing like the men her father had described. Yes, he looked fierce and dangerous, but he was also extremely attractive—and she had not once seen him act like a barbarian. He had actually treated her rather well for a prisoner.

And, although she was deep in Daneland, Anne realised the barren beauty of the place was getting under her skin—just like her captor.

'What are you doing?'

'I'd normally spear some fish and cook it over a fire, but the smoke would give away our location, so we're going to have to make do with this sea spinach for our meal tonight. I hope you're not too hungry?'

Brand passed her a handful of green leaves with fleshy stems and she took a tentative bite. It wasn't too bad—she'd had worse. He ate a few stalks himself but he was quiet…brooding.

Was it because he had an army at his gates and knew battle was now imminent? But men such as Brand Ivarsson yearned for battles and glory, didn't they? They lived to fight—he'd told her so himself. Perhaps he was just desperate to get back up there and get on with it.

'We don't get sunsets quite like this in Termarth,' she said, trying to think of something to talk about. 'What an incredible view. I could get lost in it, couldn't you?'

'I could,' he said, but when she turned to look at him she saw he wasn't admiring the horizon. He was looking at her. And the more he looked, the more she babbled.

'I can see why you decided to settle here. What was it like where you originally came from?'

'Cold,' he said.

'Just cold?'

'Desolate. There were no crops, no harvest…' He shrugged. 'Nothing like this,' he said, waving a few of the green leaves around. 'I was just a boy; I don't remember too much. But I do recall we had no land. No land that wasn't waterlogged, anyway. And we were always hungry. There wasn't enough food. We came in search of a better way of life…better things.'

Anne thought how bad things must have been for his parents to make the decision to put two small children in a boat and travel across perilous seas—to risk their lives and start a new one. She tried to picture Brand as a boy, but struggled. She didn't like the thought of him being starving and cold, but then she wouldn't wish that on anyone.

'And is it?' she asked. 'Better here?'

'Some things.'

He was staring at her again, with heat in his eyes.

'I always longed to escape too…to get far away from home.'

'Is life as a princess really so bad?'

'I know I should not complain. I certainly cannot moan of ever being cold or hungry. But it's not all feasts and festivities either. There are so many rules and restrictions. It's lonely. I envy the way you and your people live so freely—the way Svea can do as she pleases. I spend most of my days lost in books, wanting to explore the places I read about, longing for an adventure of my own.'

'Are you not having one right now?' His lips curved up into a smile.

'Battles and bloodshed aren't really my type of thing…' she said, glancing away, trying to remind herself that she was *not* on an adventure, she had been abducted. Snatched from her home. And now her father had sent Crowe and his army to steal her back.

It was as if she was like some kind of toy the men wanted to play with, to throw around for a bit and see what bargain they could strike with her. If only they would leave her be to make her own life, to rule her own people. If only her father would see her as capable of doing that one day... But it seemed a husband had to be thrown into the deal.

Her thoughts flew back to her fiancé. 'What if we're not there and Lord Crowe attacks? I mean, Svea may not start it, but the Saxons might.'

'Worried you're missing the fight, Highness?' he mocked.

'No, I'd just hate him to storm the fortress for nothing. I can't bear the thought of innocent women and children getting hurt.'

'You are a good person, Anne.'

He placed a hand on her shoulder, trying to comfort her. And it did. She wanted him to keep it there, and yet she hated herself for feeling reassured by him when he was responsible for all this, so she shrugged him off.

'I told you—I doubt they'll attack tonight. Not after their long journey, nor in the dark—and definitely not if they think you're inside,' he said. 'They wouldn't risk it. They'll want to negotiate first. Anyway, no one needs to get hurt if your fiancé complies with my demands.'

She held his gaze. 'And what are they?'

'I told you. Crowe's life in my hands.'

As he began to rake the sand with his sword, she realised there was much more to this than kidnap and a possible ransom. She could tell that a burden lay heavy on his set shoulders and she wanted to know what it was. She had a right to know, didn't she? He was using her to get back at the man, after all.

'What is it driven by, your obsessive need for revenge? What did Crowe do to you? What scars did he cause you?'

He looked at her then, ice-cold. 'You're staring right at one.'

Her skin prickled. She studied the silver track carved into his face between his forehead and his high, defined cheekbone, interrupting his dark brow. It wasn't unattractive. If anything, it added a certain allure to his impressive face. But it must have been a deep wound originally.

'He gave you that? How?'

'I'm surprised you don't remember, Princess. After all, you were there.'

'What?'

He was practically glowering at her, his face taut, and she could feel the tension rolling off him. She felt as if they were each pulling one end of a tug of war rope, like those she'd seen the Danish children playing with in the square, and it was ready to snap.

'You don't remember me, do you?'

She stared back at him, felt a tremble starting in her knees. Whatever was coming, she knew it wasn't good…

'We met before, a long time ago…' he continued. 'You helped me when I was hurt.'

He stabbed at the sand with his blade again, as if

to give his hands something to do, his eyes something to focus on.

An image of a boy, battered and bruised, entered her mind. It was so vivid it took her aback. A boy with winter-blue eyes...

It had been a balmy summer's day and she a young teenager. She'd been walking outside the castle gates, where she hadn't been allowed to go. But she'd been desperate to explore, to see new things. It had been just after one of her father's episodes, and she'd been locked up inside for weeks. She'd thought even one afternoon of freedom would be worth getting caught for.

She'd heard barking dogs and male voices and had panicked, taking cover behind a little wooden shack in a meadow. She hadn't wanted her father's guards to find her, knowing she'd be punished, but then she'd seen they were soldiers from Calhourn, not Termarth, and that they were chasing a boy who was about the same age as herself.

She'd lingered to watch, to find out what all the commotion was about, and she'd seen them pummel his face and kick him, over and over again, until he'd stopped moving. She'd been horrified, clasping her hand over her mouth so she wouldn't cry out.

When the soldiers had finally retreated she'd crept closer, to check if the boy was still breathing. He'd been left for dead, his face covered in blood. Yet it hadn't been his terrible injuries that had shocked her; it had been his dark skin and long blond hair, and when he'd opened his pale blue eyes something about them had made an instant impression.

He was, without doubt, the most beautiful boy she'd ever seen—even with his appalling injuries. She'd sensed he was trouble. He didn't look like the usual boys who hung around the courtyard of the castle, and he was clearly a danger if the Saxon soldiers had been after him. And yet surely no child deserved that treatment?

Anne had felt a shift in her blood that day—a desire to piece him back together, to help him. But when she'd heard the sound of the Royal Guard approaching, sent to retrieve her, she'd realised how foolish that idea was.

Her hand flew to her mouth. 'That was you? And Lord Crowe?' She shook her head, allowing the information to sink in. 'I always wondered what had happened to you after they took me away.'

Before this moment she had never been able to imagine the warrior before her as a young boy. But now she knew with crystal-clear clarity that it had been him. And her heart went out to him for what he had suffered and the shadows that now haunted him.

'Well, now you know,' he said, frosting over, standing up as if to say their conversation was over.

But she hadn't finished. She shook her head, rising to join him. 'But why did he hurt you? For being a Dane?'

'You'll have to ask him that when you next see him, Highness. But, yes, I believe that was my only crime.'

She understood his rage now. Lord Crowe had nearly beaten him to death. And yet he'd lived to tell the tale. Yes, Crowe deserved to be punished, but she still couldn't see how taking the man's life would make things better. It would just make everything worse. Had the Barbarian told her everything?

'Thank you for explaining it to me,' she said.

He nodded. 'I have always wanted to thank you for helping me that day. I have never forgotten it. Never forgotten *you*. When I heard your father was marrying you off to such a man, I felt I needed to repay the favour... You have said you don't want to marry him. Hopefully you won't have to. Is it just him you're averse to, or the institution of marriage altogether?'

The question took her aback. No one had ever asked her opinion on the matter before. It was just a given that she would do her duty and marry whoever her father told her to, whether she wanted to or not.

'I had always hoped to marry for love, but as that cannot be I am prepared to marry for the good of my people, to help keep them safe. But now I see this marriage would not be good for anyone.'

'You know, we are not so different, you and I...' He smiled. 'You will marry whoever your father thinks will give your kingdom more protection. I will not marry for exactly the same reason—to protect my people.'

'Our people depend on us,' she acknowledged.

He nodded. 'Now you should try to get some sleep,' he said, drawing a line under their conversation. 'Whatever happens, it's going to be an interesting day tomorrow.'

She reclined against the wall of the cave, trying to get comfortable. Above them the magnificent sky glittered with faraway stars and the dramatic waves crashing onto the shore helped to calm the storm inside her. But every time she closed her eyes she was haunted by a pale blue gaze and a boy's bloodied face. He was hurt, and no matter how hard she tried, she couldn't reach him.

She shivered.

'Are you cold?'

'A little.'

'Here,' he said, passing her his cloak. 'Take it.'

Her brow furrowed. What was this—kindness now? He continued to surprise her.

As she took it, her fingers brushed against his. 'Don't you ever sleep?' she asked.

He muttered something under his breath, and she could have sworn he said, 'I did before you came along.'

Anne's head kept rolling forward in her sleep, and when she shivered for the hundredth time Brand made his decision. He sat down next to her on the sand and wrapped an arm around her, pulling her head into the curve of his shoulder. He drew her close, hoping his body heat would help to warm her up. He tucked the cloak around them and allowed himself to shut his eyes.

At least this way maybe he would get some rest too, without worrying that she might try to make a run for it or that she would freeze to death. She wouldn't thank him for touching her again, though, and the instant his body curved around hers, his hip resting against the side of her bottom, he didn't thank himself either. His erection was immediate.

What was it about this woman that made him want

her so much? Seeing her launch her half-naked body out of the water earlier had taken that desire up a notch.

And what was it about her that made him open up and tell her things? Things about his childhood that he'd buried deep, trying to forget them—like how his family had been starving and why they'd come here. All things that had made him the man he was today. Wasn't that why he'd vowed he would always keep the people under his protection fed and warm, whatever it took? And hadn't those memories of going hungry, and never wishing it upon another soul, led to him being here now, with Anne in his arms?

She could help him to help his people... She was valuable to her kingdom and her father would no doubt be willing to pay for her safe return. And yet he was starting to realise she was right. She really was priceless...

She muttered a few words in her sleep and turned into him. He could take her so easily. He knew that was what the Saxons expected of the Danes. Her tiny frame would be no match for his strength. But fundamentally he didn't agree with it—especially after what had happened to Svea. And he'd never had to use force to get what he wanted from women. Usually seduction came easily to him. But this was much more complicated.

If only Anne *wanted* to be with him... But that would never happen. She was far too good for the likes of him.

He must be insane... Here he was, stranded outside his fortress, with fifty or so Saxon soldiers at his gates, and he couldn't keep his feelings for this woman in check. Right under her fiancé's nose.

But wasn't there something deeply satisfying about that? Wasn't that part of her allure? He wondered if he would still want her if she wasn't engaged to Crowe, but as he stared down at her beautiful face, softened by slumber, he had his answer. *Helvelte*, yes. He wanted her. And now that she'd told him she didn't even know or particularly like Crowe, and didn't want to marry him, he desired her all the more.

In any other circumstance this would be an ideal setting to court a woman, with the backdrop of the ocean and the canvas of stars lighting up the night sky, the silk-smooth sand beneath their bodies... But he had to think of her and her reputation. He needed to stop being so foolish and he needed to rest, so that tomorrow he could focus on his vendetta.

He closed his eyes again and tried to put all thoughts of his captive out of his mind.

When Anne woke she felt warm, safe...and then she realised she was nestled into the side of a man's chest. A heavy arm was draped around her shoulder, a big hand curved around her waist, and she froze in alarm. Brand had promised not to touch her again and yet here he was, holding her in his arms. Arms that were solid and strong and seemed almost protective—or was their purpose purely restraint?

But as she listened to the steady beat of his heart, and felt the rise and fall of his breathing, she realised he was asleep. Heat was radiating off him, and he wasn't trying to harm her or imprison her. He was just holding her, perhaps to keep them both warm.

In the upstairs room he had told her he didn't find her attractive and she should have been relieved. Instead, it had hurt—more than it should. Was she unlovable? Her father had always been so cold, and he had made her feel that way. She had never had a close friendship with anyone except one or two of her maids, who were paid to look after her and be kind to her.

And yet this man, huddled next to her on the sand, had revealed that he had thought about her all these years—since they'd met as children... He had revealed he had stolen her away to protect her from Crowe. And now he was holding her, keeping her warm, and she had never felt so cherished.

She was lying here in the darkness, actually willing him to pull her closer into his chest and hold her even tighter, to run his fingers through her hair again, as he had done the other day. And her thoughts scared her, because she had only read about these feelings and been educated in how things were between a man and a woman through reading books—she had never experienced it first-hand.

Who was this woman she was becoming? She didn't even recognise her.

And as she lay there, trying to steady her erratic breathing, taking in the musky male scent of him, she couldn't help but nuzzle closer, enjoying the feeling of his solid chest muscles beneath her cheek, the heat of his thighs against hers.

But when she felt his breathing change and his arms tighten around her, her whole body tensed. She didn't dare move. *What had she done?* She knew she should act quickly and feign disgust at his closeness, but her body wasn't listening to her mind and she couldn't bring herself to pull away. And then, almost unbelievably, impossibly lightly, he began circling her shoulder with the tips of his fingers, sending goosebumps down her arms, making her shiver.

'Still cold?' he asked.

'No... You promised you wouldn't touch me again,' she whispered, turning her face to stare up at him. But her voice didn't sound as if she minded. Damn. Why couldn't she stir up some of that anger? 'You said it was a mistake...'

Sleepy hooded blue eyes gazed down at her. 'I didn't say I wasn't willing to make the same mistake again.' His husky voice was just a breath away from her lips. 'And if you don't stop looking at me like that I'm going to have to do something about it...unless you tell me to stop.'

But she didn't. She couldn't.

And this time Brand was gentle. His fingers brushed her cheeks as his firm mouth lightly grazed hers and her eyelids fluttered shut. Her thoughts were incoherent as her lips slowly yielded, giving in to the delicious sensations he was creating as he took possession of her mouth with persuasive, tender strokes of his tongue.

It was a kiss that seemed to start as a question, a soft enquiry, but soon deepened into a thorough examination of her mouth, demanding some kind of answer. And instead of pulling away Anne responded by pressing herself closer, bravely letting him know that she wanted this just as much as him. Her hands moved up to rest against his strong jaw, holding him in place as her tongue experimentally stole into his mouth too, over and over again, gliding against his in a deep, passionate caress.

Heat bloomed inside her—or was it hope?—and her hand slid down over his chest, brushing aside the material at the neck of his tunic so she could explore the feel of his skin, as hard as the rocks on the beach but as smooth as the sand. Brand moaned and dragged her down to the ground, so they were lying side by side, and then he tugged her body against him as he continued to educate her in the art of the perfect kiss.

As heat coiled down low in her belly she tried a little wriggle against him and he growled, his careful control seemingly about to snap. Drifting his hands down to her hips and cupping her bottom, he hauled her soft curves against the hardness of his length, binding her to him, and an insane need lanced her. She didn't want him to stop. She wanted him to put his hands on her. All over her.

Rolling her onto her back and hovering over her, he skated his fingers up her ribcage to curve over one pert breast. She knew she should pull away, stop this madness, and yet still her body arched into him, and a flutter of excitement blossomed between her legs as he kneaded her breast through the material of her dress, making her quiver.

She wanted more.

Her head rolled back against the sand as he left a trail of delicate little kisses along her throat, and then his thumb moved over her nipple, tweaking it into a hard peak. He pushed one knee between her thighs, his thick erection nudging against her stomach, leaving her in no doubt of his desire, or of where this was heading.

It must have been her little gasp of shock that made him pull back slightly. Anne's fingers were suddenly unmoving at the back of his neck as they stared at each other, their foreheads touching. And then, with an almost violent, urgent curse, he was up, leaving her lying on the sand, her arms outstretched, wondering what the hell had just happened.

'*Det var som faen!* We shouldn't be doing this. Not here. Not now,' he bit out, stalking away.

Anne's cheeks burned as she struggled to sit up, straightening her clothes. *What had she done?* She didn't know what had come over her, to act so brazenly. And yet still a part of her wanted to beg him to come back and finish what he'd started. But she had no experience when it came to things like this, and she'd certainly never expected to feel like that! Especially with Brand Ivarsson the Barbarian.

But she had welcomed his touch...willingly opened her mouth so his tongue could explore her. Her hands flew up to her hot cheeks. She had writhed against him, silently encouraging him to put his hands on her. What was the matter with her? After all, he was only doing all this to cause injury to Lord Crowe, wasn't he? Had their kiss been just a part of his revenge?

It hadn't seemed as if he'd been kissing her for anything other than his own pleasure. And surely if he wanted to wound Crowe he would have taken her already?

His touch had been potent, bringing her to budding

life, and as he'd held her against his chest her nipples had peaked as they'd grazed against him. She'd found herself holding on to him as if he was a lifeline, and then, just as quickly as he'd started, he'd pushed her away. He'd stopped. Whereas she would have continued.

She felt a little sob rise up in her throat. Oh, God. How would she ever find the strength to stand and face him?

He had his back to her, tying up his boots. And now she felt just as she had as a child, when her father had closed that door on her in the tower. Shut out and alone. She knew she should say something, but her lips were quivering and she felt tongue-tied. This whole situation was new and terrifying to her.

She stood on trembling legs and tried to focus on her footing, squaring her shoulders, trying to tear her thoughts away from him and the taste of his mouth on hers, the feel of his warm skin under her fingertips, his bearded jaw grazing against her chin.

Stop!

'Brand—?'

'We should go,' he said, cutting her off, his curt voice piercing her heart. 'The sun's rising and we've wasted far too much time here.'

Chapter Six

Brand hadn't been wrong about the hard climb over the rocks. It was a slippery scramble over ridges and little rock pools, and Anne reluctantly had to keep taking his outstretched arm to hold her balance.

He was used to the terrain and surefooted, easily making large strides from one boulder to another and then waiting for her, gripping her tight with his firm fingers as she jumped the distance to meet him. Her boots weren't appropriate, and as she landed on each uneven slab of stone she plunged into his solid chest and thigh muscles. Each time, she wasn't ready for the impact, and each time his big hands came up to circle her arms, grounding her.

'Steady.'

It certainly wasn't helping her to regain her usually cool poise. But if she was honest, she hadn't been in control of her own destiny since she'd met him. Yet she would like to salvage her self-esteem.

She scraped a hand over her face, as if to rub her

thoughts away. Was he regretting kissing her? she wondered. After all, he had described it as a waste of time. Was that why he was being so short with her?

The blistering hot sun beat down on her skin, making her overly warm, and still all she could think about was his lips on hers. She glanced out over the ocean and wished she could cool off in the water, like the little fish in the shallows, float away with the waves and be engulfed by something far bigger than her fear and shame.

When her body collided with his for the hundredth time her composure finally snapped. 'Don't you have any regard for keeping your distance?' she bit out.

'I didn't hear you complaining about that this morning.'

Her eyes narrowed on him. 'Oh, so you're acknowledging it now?'

'What?' His long legs straddled two seaweed-covered rocks.

'Nothing.' She sighed, suddenly thinking better of broaching the subject as he tugged her to join him. 'I just want to forget it.'

He moved on to the next boulder. She took a big stride and met him, meshing with his body again. 'You need to stop talking nonsense. I'd say it was pretty unforgettable, wouldn't you?'

Heat flooded her cheeks. He reached out to tuck a strand of hair behind her ear and she couldn't help but lean in a little closer.

He inclined his head. 'But that doesn't mean it was a good idea. It definitely was not.' He moved on again.

'I behaved badly. I'm sorry. I'm just not in the habit of abducting beautiful, clever, and spirited Saxon princesses and finding myself wanting to kiss them.'

Her breath caught in her throat. He thought she was clever! No one had ever considered her intelligent before. In fact, her father hated it when her nose was stuck in a book. He didn't believe she needed to be educated because she would have a husband who would make decisions for her. It had made her want to read all the more—even if it had to be done in secret, late at night by candlelight.

They continued on the rocky path in silence. Perhaps they both thought it safer, but from that point on he held her hand in his and didn't let it go.

The route seemed endless as they scaled huge boulders and clambered around smaller, sharper ones, being careful not to tread on the little creatures that lived among the rocks.

It must have been mid-morning when Anne began to tire, and Brand finally pointed to something up ahead of them.

'Look,' he said. 'We're almost there. Come on.'

She put up her hand to shade her eyes from the glare and see what he was looking at. She spotted a little jetty and a boat. But there was no path, no passageway into the fortress.

'Where do we go from here?'

'I forgot to mention…' Brand grinned sheepishly '…we have to sail around the headland the rest of the way, to take the mouth of the river into Kald.'

'Sail?' she said, her heart picking up pace. Her eyes

darted all around them, searching for an alternative route, a way to get out of this. 'I can't get into a boat! You know I don't like tight spaces. Brand—'

He continued to hold her hand in one of his, and tilted her chin up with the other, so she was looking up into his eyes. 'You're going to have to trust me, Anne.'

She swallowed. Easier said than done.

As they neared the crystal-clear water lapping at the jetty, she realised the long, narrow boat was just like the one she'd seen him working on in the barn. She felt redundant standing there, watching Brand jump knee-deep into the water to untie the vessel, while her mind made a mental tally of all the things that could go wrong if she got on board.

She reached up to feel that the back of her neck was damp with perspiration under her loose locks. She hadn't had a chance to braid her hair since she'd bathed at the beach last night. She must look a complete state.

Brand waded back towards her and held out his hand to help her onto the boat. 'Anne, it's perfectly safe,' he said, coaxing her towards him.

Chewing on her bottom lip, but accepting his help, she descended into the longship and as soon as she was in sat down on one of the benches to avoid making it rock. Brand pushed them away from the jetty before hoisting himself in.

'Welcome aboard the *Freyja*,' he said, and smiled.

'Named after one of your gods?' she asked, grimacing at the motion as Brand walked to the middle of the hull and sat down, taking up a pair of oars.

'Actually, my mother.'

Anne glanced at him in surprise. For such a supposedly unfeeling man, he had a tendency to say and do some rather sentimental things. 'She's beautiful. Did you build her?'

'I did.'

'Is she seaworthy?' she teased.

When he grinned in response, her stomach did a little somersault.

'Of course.'

'And you're sure you can row this thing on your own?' she asked, looking around at the oar holes which, if she'd counted correctly, were meant for thirteen rowers on each side—not one man. Even though the man in question was larger than life itself.

'I think I can manage.'

He began to rotate the oars to manoeuvre the vessel. She started at the sudden movement and gripped the side of the boat. There was no turning back now. Fortunately, there was no cabin, and although she was seemingly trapped in this prison on the water for a while, she was relieved that she didn't feel confined.

She pointed to the intricate carving of a sea serpent on the prow. 'You like these monsters. They're on all your ships. Are they meant to frighten people?'

'That's the *Midgard* Serpent—the world serpent.'

Her eyes widened. 'Surely such things don't exist?'

'Let's hope we don't find out!'

He laughed, and she began to relax as they glided through the shallow waves, the force of his powerful strokes meaning they were soon quite a distance from land.

'You asked me yesterday why I was building boats,' he said, and she wondered what it was about the sea that was making him more open. 'It was my father's dream, and is now mine, to build ships and use them to trade—to carry cargo in land or across the sea.'

She hadn't expected him to be a man of quiet ambition. 'I thought... I thought they might be for sailing to and raiding other places,' she said. 'I have overheard my father talking about Northmen landing on beaches and attacking monasteries and villages and then sailing away again.'

'You should know by now that's not what I do. Nor my people in Kald.'

She nodded. What other dreams did Brand Ivarsson have? she wondered. And why did he not want a wife...a family?

Images of gorgeous children with wild blue eyes and dark blond braided hair stormed her, catching her off guard. What was she doing? She was dreaming of the impossible, a Saxon and a Dane, when he had merely been telling her about boats. In fact, hadn't he implied he might even be leaving this island?

A vision of him sailing away from her caused a sharp pain in her chest.

'So, what do you think?' he asked, lightening the mood. 'Keep going and sail to distant shores, or go around the headland and face your fiancé?'

His joking, despite the subject, amazingly made her smile. It was actually a tempting offer... She realised this was what total and utter freedom felt like. They were out at sea and no one knew where they were. The scene around her was serene, the sound of the restless waves were gently rippling against the side of the boat, and it was hard to deny their newfound camaraderie.

She caught his gaze and heat snaked between her legs. Perhaps there *was* a sea serpent after all...

Brand seemed so at ease and carefree out on the water, as if this was where he belonged. His hard features had softened, and the only tension in his body was in the muscles pulling the oars, propelling the boat forward.

'Rowing suits you,' she said.

'I love being out here. Like you, I don't do very well stuck in a box.'

'Where's the furthest you've ever gone?'

'Apart from Daneland to England? Only so far as the little islands to the north and south of here.'

'What were they like? Will you tell me about them?'

She realised she might never get the chance to do this again, so she decided to drink in the moment. Leaning back, she tipped her head, turning her face up towards the sun and briefly closing her eyes, and felt her worries melting away under the heat as she listened to Brand talk.

He spoke of magical islands formed of forests and beaches, where no people lived, just animals. And he told her of grand monasteries and castles he'd seen while sailing along the coastline here. And as he rowed he pointed out shoals of fish swimming alongside the boat, or moonlike jellyfish with delicate dancing tentacles.

She delighted in his witty commentary and his observations, and she voiced her wonder at all the new sights and sounds. When he spotted a seal bobbing in and out of the waves she was overcome with a desire to get closer, and threw herself half over the side of the boat in awe, forgetting all about her earlier fear of its motion.

Brand stopped rowing, not wanting Anne to miss the seal swimming in the surf. Her rapture at seeing all the creatures of the ocean had him spellbound. He'd seen seals before, many times, but seeing one through her eyes made it much more appealing. Her face had lit up at everything he showed her and her pretty smile was genuine.

He wished they could stay out here forever. He didn't think he'd ever tire of her company, her sense of humour, and hearing her views on the world. When she'd stretched out catlike in the sun, his body had responded with force. He knew he should wipe the morning's kiss from his memory, but still his thoughts kept straying to the way her lips had sealed against his, to the taste of desire on her tongue and the feeling of her small, exquisite breasts pressed up against his chest, cupped in his hands.

He had instigated it, of course. He'd been the one to pull her into his arms and to press his mouth against hers. Then, staring down at her, seeing her cheeks flushed, he had come to his senses and pushed her away. And she'd looked confused—startled, even.

He had done some reckless things in his past, especially when he was just a lad, chasing fun and danger.

But he wasn't sure he'd ever done anything as hare-brained as this. He'd taken advantage of Anne's wedding to kidnap her and bring her to Kald. He was using her to get revenge on Crowe and now he was trying to seduce her.

Yet, clutching her so close, he hadn't had the strength to resist. One minute he'd been kissing her, going out of his mind with desire, and the next he'd been holding her at arm's length, unable to forgive himself. He'd never been so confused.

He was so irresponsible. He'd promised he wouldn't touch her again, but he'd broken his word and ruined her trust—what little he'd had of it. She must despise him for all he'd done to her so far, and she wouldn't thank him for what was to come, either.

And yet as she leaned over the side of the boat and skimmed her hand through the water she seemed content in his company, and he wanted to keep her to himself a while longer. Even though he knew everyone at Kald was waiting, he wasn't ready to take her back. He wanted this one moment, free of responsibility.

The instant they rounded the headland they'd be turning into the river and reality would come back to bite them. Anne would have to watch him fight her fiancé, and she would no longer look at him as she was looking at him now.

He didn't think Svea or Kar would engage in any kind of communication with Crowe and his men while he wasn't there. And he didn't think Crowe would attack or negotiate until he had some kind of confirmation that Anne was inside the fortress.

He hoped his gut instinct was right, because he was scorching in the burning sun, rowing a heavy ship, and the water looked too inviting. It was calling to him, and he made his decision. As they passed the secluded cove where he often came to be alone, he dropped the oars and put down the anchor.

Anne glanced questioningly up at him. And when he tore off his tunic, throwing it down by her feet, her eyes widened.

For a moment she just stared in astonishment at his body—in awe or in horror? He wasn't sure. His chest was adorned with dark blue ink, which also covered his entire torso and back, and he knew it was intimidating. It often struck fear into the heart of his enemies. He'd had it done when he'd become leader at Kald. He needed to know what she thought of the markings—whether she found them unattractive.

'What are you doing?' she choked.

'What does it look like? I'm going for a swim. Want to join me?'

He tugged off his boots. Next, his belt dropped to the floor. For a moment he reached for the tie on his trousers, and considered stripping them off and going in naked, but when he saw the consternation on her face he thought better of it. He'd probably shocked her enough for one day.

He dived over the side and the cool salt water instantly soothed his hot skin. He'd hoped the water might wash away his desire, but when he resurfaced Anne was dangling over the side of the boat again, watching in wonder, or concern—he wasn't sure which—and he knew that it hadn't.

'Well? Are you coming in?' he grinned.

'In this dress?' She shook her head vehemently.

'You're wearing undergarments, aren't you?' He smirked.

'I can't even swim!'

'I could teach you.'

For a moment she looked almost tempted. But then she shook her head again, biting her lip.

'Coward.'

He wanted to drag her in after him, to hold her in his arms, free and weightless in the water. But as his hands sliced through the water, while he swam to the shallows and back, he realised they'd reached something of an accord and was reluctant to do anything to damage it. He'd enjoyed her company this morning, probably more than he should. In fact, he was enjoying everything about her.

He wanted her, pure and simple, and that could only be resolved in one way. But taking her and satiating their desire was something he just couldn't do if he wanted a ransom for her safe return.

He made his body work hard, his muscled arms streaming through the water, cooling himself from the sun and his heated thoughts of his companion. By the time he finally heaved himself back into the boat he felt slightly more in control of his tormented mind and body.

Anne squealed as the ship lurched from side to side, then righted itself, and he noticed she did everything possible to avoid looking at his bare chest, suddenly finding the seam of her dress incredibly fascinating. Was she holding her breath? He grinned.

'Here,' he said. 'I got this for you.' He held out a large pink seashell with a smooth spiral core.

Now she had to look at him, and he enjoyed seeing a delicate flush appear in her cheeks. He crouched down in front of her and held the smooth open surface of the shell up to her ear.

'Listen,' he said.

At first, she looked confused, and then her eyes widened in amazement. 'I can hear the ocean!' She gasped, and he grinned again. 'It's the waves rolling onto the shore. How is that possible?'

He shrugged. 'I'm not sure, but it's yours. So you can hear the waves no matter how far from the sea you are.'

No matter how far away from me you are...

Anne nimbly took it from his hands. 'Thank you.'

She met his eyes and a moment passed between them. The tension in the air around them almost glittered, and it took every ounce of his strength to keep himself from leaning in and kissing her again. She was so close...

No! He stood and pulled his tunic back on, and she practically wilted with relief, making him grin even more widely.

'Ready to go?' he asked. He hoped she'd say no—that she wanted to stay out here with him for a while longer. But she just nodded and glanced away.

'Those clouds over there look a bit ominous,' he said. 'We'd better move on.'

She seemed to be analysing him as he rowed, running her fingers through her rumpled hair. He liked it. It reminded him of winding his own hands through it, drawing her lips towards his.

'What are you thinking about, Princess?'

She started fiddling with that seam on her dress again. 'Why do you cover your body in ink like that?' she asked.

So it was his markings that were playing on her mind. Did she find them off-putting?

As he pulled hard on the oars again, and they began to venture round the peninsula, the breeze began to pick up and the sea became choppier. But Brand was in full control. He knew it was rougher out here, where it was less sheltered. He hoisted the square sail to harness the power of the wind and help them pick up pace.

'We use ink to say something about our personalities and to honour the gods. Or, in my case, to cover up some pretty bad scars. I know it takes a bit of getting used to. Do you not like it?'

'I hadn't given it any thought,' she shrugged.

He smiled at the lie.

'What does your ink mean?' she asked.

'I will tell you about it some time, but right now the weather is turning faster than I'd predicted. I'm sorry. I shouldn't have stopped for that swim.' He stalked around the ship, holding on to the side, tying things down.

When a large splatter of rain landed on Anne's hair,

and then began pelting down into the boat, for the first time he felt real concern.

He didn't mind towering walls of water, the wind and the rain—in fact, there had been times in his life when he'd come out in search of a storm, wanting to test himself, war against the waves, even get lost in them. He'd buried a lot of his anger in this ocean. But he'd never have chosen to subject Anne to this. He was a fool, putting her in harm's way. They could have been home by now if he'd just stuck to his plan.

It wasn't long before the skies had turned grey and churning water was curving over the boat. He wondered if the gods were angry with him. It was the first time he regretted the open deck, where a woollen cover was their only protection from the elements.

He made a few more strokes with the oars, but it was becoming impossible to fight the waves. He couldn't believe it when he saw Anne bailing water with a bucket.

'What are you doing?' he asked.

'Trying to be useful!'

She never ceased to amaze him. She certainly wasn't the delicate flower he had originally thought. She always wanted to help.

'I'm going to have to take down the sail and lower the anchor again,' he shouted over the raging noise of the sea. 'We'll have to ride it out. Sit by the mast and hold on,' he instructed. 'I'll grab the cover.'

'Will the boat take it?' she asked, raising her voice so he could hear her. 'The waves are pretty big.'

'I built it to withstand storms like this. We should be fine.'

'Should?' she said, smiling.

It was her smile, even in these dangerous conditions, that made him feel a connection with her, and he stopped securing the oars and came to sit down next to her in the cramped hull. They huddled together and he brought his arms around her and the mast, holding them both tight as the boat rode the waves for what felt like an endless amount of time.

Swells of water rose and fell, taking them up to great heights, and then they'd crash back down with a bump. He saw Anne's face was turning greener by the second, and he felt like the world's worst person. He was worried she'd bump her head, or fall overboard, so he tightened his grip and she clung on to him. They were a tangle of limbs, but she didn't moan or blame him once.

He thought he would have preferred it if she had. He was finding her silence disturbing. And the way her body kept bumping into his was agonising. Although how he could even think of sex in these conditions was beyond him.

Suddenly she lurched forward and vomited over the side. He moved with her and held her waist as she did it again.

'Are you all right?'

A violent spray of water hit them, and she coughed and spluttered.

'I've been better,' she said, sagging down onto the floor, her eyes fluttering shut.

'But will you be all right?'

She looked up at him through the battering rain. 'The next time you feel like going for a swim, just don't—is that clear?'

He grinned. 'Clear,' he said, tugging her into his side and smoothing her hair. 'That's a promise.'

'You'd better swear it instead—you're not very good at keeping promises.' She smiled weakly.

He couldn't believe she was trying to make him laugh at a time like this. Who *was* this incredible woman he'd stolen and brought into his life? And how was he ever going to be able to give her up? She truly was a priceless gem. No amount of treasure would be enough for a woman like her.

After what seemed like the longest storm Brand had ever battled, the heavy rain began to slow and the dark clouds started to disperse. His heart lifted when a sliver of gold lit up their path towards Kald again. Anne might just forgive him yet. That was once she'd warmed up.

She was now sitting under the woollen cover completely wet and shivering again. He knew he had to get those clothes off her, but he didn't think she'd agree to that if he suggested it.

With a newfound burst of energy, he lifted the anchor and rowed the boat again, hard and fast, feeling the need to get back to the fortress as soon as possible now. And when the archway over the river into Kald came into view he breathed a huge sigh of relief.

He launched himself out of the ship and dragged it up the slipway to the boathouse before helping Anne out. She walked a few steps before sinking onto the grass, collapsing on her back, and he lay down beside her.

'I never thought I'd be so glad to see Kald again,' she said, her hand over her forehead.

Another flicker of admiration for the way she'd handled herself flashed through him. He rolled towards her and propped himself up on his elbow, staring down at her. He lifted a few wet strands of hair from her face, and was glad that she let him. She was either too cold to protest, or no longer so opposed to his touch… He hoped it was the latter.

But the moment was short-lived. The unmistakable sound of an arrow whistled overhead, and Brand was on his feet as fast as the storm had hit, his fight instinct kicking in.

'*Skit!*' he swore. 'Did you hear that? Something's happening. We need to get back. Do you think you can walk? It's just up the hill.'

She nodded, curling herself up to stand, and followed him as he took her hand again and began to ascend the grassy slope where remote farmsteads were dotted about, although the owners were nowhere to be seen.

'Is that Crowe attacking?' she asked. 'I thought you said he wouldn't.'

Brand couldn't believe it to be true. He wouldn't be so foolish to send arrows into Kald with the Princess inside, would he? Did Crowe not care for the safety of his bride?

Anger lashed through him. And yet even as these thoughts rushed at him he wondered if he was any better. Wasn't his imminent betrayal of her far worse? Would she understand if he said he was doing it for the good of his people? He doubted it.

A pain burned in his chest when he wondered what would happen when Anne discovered he was about to put a price on her head. That he was planning to sell her back to her family for gold.

They raced up the hillside, passing working horses and sheep grazing in the fields. It was tricky to run in her saturated clothes, and Anne felt her heart burn from the sudden exercise—or was it from the way Brand had taken care of her when she'd felt unwell, and how a moment ago he'd been staring down at her as if he wanted to ravage her mouth again?

But soon they reached a ridge and she realised they were back in the square, amid a flurry of chaos, the air tinged with a mixture of excitement and fear. Men were grabbing their shields and swords and taking up defence positions on the ramparts.

Anne knew their time alone was well and truly over.

They glimpsed Svea's retreating frame, and Brand dropped her hand as he raced to catch up with his sister. 'What's going on?'

'Where the hell have you been? I was starting to get worried,' Svea scolded him. 'They shot an arrow. It hit Ulf.'

'No...' Anne whispered, concern clouding her spirits.

'Come quick—he's in here.'

They raced towards the longhouse, where Ulf was

writhing in pain on a bench, an arrow sticking out of his upper arm and blood seeping into the animal skin he was lying on.

Anne's hands flew to her face in worry. 'This is your fault!' she said, turning accusingly on Brand, suddenly filled with anger. 'If you hadn't brought me here this would never have happened.'

'They shot just one arrow?' he asked his men, ignoring her and leaning over Ulf to inspect the wound and the weapon.

'This was attached to it,' Torsten said, handing him a piece of parchment.

Brand glanced at it before placing it in his tunic.

'They obviously want to get our attention, and they prefer to send notes rather than a messenger,' said Torsten. 'We need to cut off this arm. If we don't, the boy's not going to make it.'

Anne stepped forward. 'If you cut off the arm he will certainly die,' she said, speaking up bravely against the red-haired brute. 'He'll lose too much blood. I've seen it before.'

Brand looked between her and his friend. Unbelievably, his eyes settled on her. 'What do you suggest, Anne?'

Did he actually want her opinion? 'If we pull it out, the wood may come loose from the arrowhead and it could get stuck in his body. But I can try to cut it out…' Anne said.

'You?' Torsten mocked, his face darkening. He turned on Brand. 'You're not going to listen to the

Saxon witch? What's she even doing here? She probably wants the boy dead!'

Anger flared. 'That's not true!' Anne gasped.

Brand must know she wasn't lying. He'd seen her interact with Ulf. She liked the boy. Would he believe her?

He stroked his beard, taking a moment to think before giving her a steady look. 'Do what you have to do.'

'You've lost your mind! She's playing you—turning your head!' Torsten raged, and he kicked a barrel of mead as he stormed out of the longhouse.

'Anne, what do you need?' Svea asked, resting a hand on her shoulder to bring the focus back to the boy.

'A knife, a needle and thread, sage and garlic, if you have them—and some kind of liquor to numb the pain.'

Brand nodded to Svea. 'Go. And bring a blanket for Anne.'

'What are you going to do?' he asked, coming down to kneel beside her.

'Extract the arrow, then treat the wound. It's his best chance. But there's a lot of blood.'

'How on earth do you know how to do this, Anne?'

'I've helped my father's soldiers before...when they've been shot.'

'Unbeknown to him, I bet.'

She met his gaze. She liked it that he understood her. It was as if he knew her better than anyone. How was that possible?

'And did they make it?' he asked.

'Some... I'll do my best. Should we fetch his parents? Tell them he's hurt?'

Brand gave her an odd look. 'His parents are dead, Anne. He's a Saxon.'

Anne inhaled sharply. 'Ulf is a slave?'

Disappointment crashed over her like the giant waves had done earlier on. She'd thought Brand didn't buy people.

Svea came rushing back, holding the things Anne had requested. 'Here,' she said, and Anne took the items she needed first, while Brand reached for the blanket and placed it around her shoulders.

Ulf was murmuring now, squirming in agony, and Anne knew she'd have to wait for answers about the boy's family and his role here. She indicated to Svea to pour some alcohol down Ulf's throat, and then Anne doused his shoulder in the liquid.

'You'll have to secure him,' she said to Brand.

She wished she could tell him to leave, because he was a huge distraction. But she needed his strength to hold the boy down. If Ulf moved, she'd cut him and make his injury worse.

Had Brand really taken Ulf from his home and enslaved him? Ulf wasn't much older than Brand had been when Anne had helped him that day when he was in Termarth. She had somehow thought he was better than that—that he didn't trade people. It made her doubt him and his reasons for taking her.

But she couldn't think about that now—she needed to focus on helping Ulf.

It was hard, working in such subdued light, but she managed to cut the arrowhead out. The wound wasn't as deep as it had looked, but the loss of blood was proving tricky. She cleaned the wound and, using a needle and thread, carefully stitched it up, then sat back on her ankles to study her work. She hoped the herbal ointment would be enough to bind the flesh and stop any infection. Thankfully, Ulf was now asleep, and the wound looked clean at least.

'Thank you,' Brand said, resting a hand on her shoulder and giving her a squeeze. 'You have done well.'

His touch spread an unwanted warmth through her body. She turned to look at him and the rush of his all too familiar scent brought back the feeling of his lips moving against hers, his tongue filling her mouth, his hands on her breasts. Images of his half-naked body diving into the water flooded her mind.

When she'd seen that his muscular chest and back were completely covered in ink, at first she'd been shocked, and then she had been curious—transfixed. She'd wanted to let her eyes roam over every line, to explore the patterns with her fingers. And she'd wanted to know what they said about the man beneath. She'd been disturbed and enthralled all at once. Her pulse had been erratic as she'd watched his powerful torso channel through the water.

She had hoped this task—stitching Ulf back together—would help her to forget all about it. Incredibly, the storm hadn't, and she was sure he'd been about to kiss her again before they'd heard the humming sound of the arrow. She had wanted him to, and yet if he bought and sold slaves she would not be able to abide it…

She removed his hand and busied herself with clearing away the mess she'd made on the bench.

Brand reached for the note in his tunic and unrolled the bloodstained parchment. 'You can read?' he asked Anne. 'Will you read this to me?'

She nodded, astonished that once again he wasn't too proud to ask for her help.

'It seems you have no end of talents, Anne. You clearly like healing people, and are good at it.'

He was analysing her with those perceptive eyes. 'Is that so wrong?' she asked.

'It is not a criticism.'

She laid a hand on Ulf's forehead and was glad to feel that he didn't have a fever.

'After that day I helped you in Termarth, when we were much younger, I found myself wanting to study the art of healing. I read books on anatomy and herbs—anything I could find in my father's library,' she said, washing the blood off her hands. 'Not that he approves.'

'Surely he sees your knowledge as an asset?'

'Apparently not.'

'Then he's a fool.'

Anne's heart leapt. This man—this Barbarian—valued her education. How was it possible that he managed to bolster her confidence, her self-worth, more than any other person ever had?

'You didn't answer my question. How did Ulf come to be here? Did you snatch him from his home too?' Her chin tilted up in provocation, her eyes simmering with displeasure.

Brand held her gaze. 'No—I told you. I don't make

a habit of kidnapping Saxons. Is that what you think of me?'

'What should I think? You have a Saxon boy in your midst, helping you to do your dirty work.'

He came towards her, crowding her with his big body. 'His father attacked Kald—not the other way round. He brought him to the battlefield. A nine-year-old boy! He was left an orphan, so we took him in... treated him like one of our own. He doesn't know anything different now.'

Once again, he'd shocked her. 'Why would you do that?' she asked, her throat feeling tight.

He reached up to wipe a smear of blood from her cheek. She flinched. 'Because, like you said, perhaps I'm not the barbarian people believe me to be. I think children should be nurtured, not beaten or manipulated.' He inclined his head. 'Nor neglected and shut away and deprived of learning and adventures.'

Anne floundered at this hint to her own upbringing, suddenly feeling awkward that she'd doubted him. She nodded to the parchment to distract him—and herself—from the fresh curl of intimacy enveloping them.

'What does it say?' Brand asked.

'It seems my fiancé wants me back and he's prepared to fight.'

Chapter Seven

The longhouse was far from the jovial scene it had been the night Anne had arrived in Kald. She was washing her hands at the back of the room, and noticed that after dinner most of the women and children returned to their farmsteads, while the men were out on the ramparts, guarding the walls.

Brand's trusted few were gathered round the long wooden table in the centre of the room, deciding on their course of action.

'Crowe demands an answer and I say we spear the bastards!'

'They struck the first blow. Now we should darken the sky with arrows.'

'They should pay us in gold not to kill them while they sleep.'

So this was their great plan, Anne thought. And all this because Brand had taken a beating when he was a boy? Yes, the Saxons had left him for dead, but as he'd survived this all seemed too much, somehow.

Had he given her the full story? Was it really about Crowe attacking villages and blaming the Danes for it? He certainly deserved to be punished for that.

'They say we are to hand over the Princess or they'll send smoke and fire.'

'Then we take the fight to them!' Kar said.

'No.'

Brand's deep, authoritative voice cut through all the others. He had been sitting at the head of the table quietly observing until now, his long fingers steepled in front of him, and everyone turned to listen.

'I have said no one is to fight but me. I will make a square with Crowe. This is my battle.'

Anne felt a strange flutter of fear in her chest. She didn't want him to fight.

'It's as much mine as it is yours,' Svea said fiercely, stepping forward.

'It is a fight for all of us,' Kar said.

So they all loathed her fiancé. How could her father intend to marry her to a man who inspired such hatred?

Anne rubbed her temples. She was getting a headache...

'I know,' Brand said, placing a hand on his sister's shoulder. 'But this is how it's going to be. Kar, tell Crowe we will speak with him at dawn. If I go out there now there'll be no holding me back.'

'You should take the bed.'

'No, you take it.'

'I can sleep downstairs with Svea...'

'*Faen I helvete*, Anne!'

Brand and Anne were standing in the doorway of the upstairs room and he was losing the will to live. It had been a long day and he didn't want to argue with her any more—especially not in this small space and not about sleeping arrangements. His anger was causing a lick of arousal in his groin and that was the last thing he needed to feel all night, sitting outside her door. It would certainly hijack his ability to sleep.

He pulled off his boots on the staircase.

'If you're planning on fighting tomorrow, you'll need to sleep.'

Anne was talking a lot. He'd noticed she did that when she was nervous. And she was wringing her lovely hands.

'Are you always this stubborn?' he asked.

'Yes.'

'Well, stop it. With an army at the door I've got to keep an eye on the men through the night anyway, to check nothing is amiss, so you may as well take it. Now, stop talking and get out of those damp clothes. Put on the fresh ones Svea gave you.'

He closed the door and braced his hands on the wooden rail, releasing a long sigh. For the third time in as many days Anne was undressing just an arm's reach away from him and the constant ache in his groin was becoming excruciating, making him downright irritated.

A few moments later the door swung open again and he turned to find her standing there, in a fresh, plain white smock, minus the pinafore. She looked every bit the pure, innocent virgin. His mouth dried and he sighed. As much as he wanted her, he really did need to get some rest tonight. He had a date with destiny tomorrow. And tomorrow night he'd either be celebrating his revenge on Crowe, bathing in his enemy's blood, or dining in the Great Hall of Valhalla with the gods.

'I was thinking we could share the room,' Anne said, waving her hands about, looking flustered. 'I know you won't let me sleep elsewhere, but I can't let you sit outside all night either. And this...' she motioned to the animal skins and furs thrown over a chair in the corner of the room '...looks comfortable enough to sleep on.'

His eyes narrowed on her. 'What about your reputation?'

'Everyone is either on the ramparts or in bed! I doubt anyone will see or even care. They're not *my* people, after all. No one need ever know.'

'Stop babbling, Anne. But if you're sure, then I accept. With the Saxons surrounding us I don't really want to let you out of my sight, and that chair looks a lot more appealing than the floor out here.'

He took a last glance around the quiet village square, before striding into the room and shutting the door.

'I could do with getting out of these wet clothes, so if you don't want to watch me strip you might want to look the other way.'

He was half hoping she'd say she wanted to watch, but he knew she wouldn't. That was just a fantasy. Instead, she quickly turned around, facing the smoke hole, and he put on fresh trousers, leaving his torso bare. She'd just have to deal with it.

He poured them both some water from a jug and offered her a cup. She must have been thirsty as she drank it all in one go. He took the empty jar out of her hand and placed it down on the table. He caught her looking at his ink again, but he cut her visual tour short by putting out the torch flame.

He stumbled around in the darkness and cursed quietly as he crashed into the wooden chest before reaching the chair. He heard the bed shift under her weight as she got in, and he waited for what seemed like a moon's whole cycle, listening for the sound of her gentle breathing, waiting for her to go to sleep so he could finally relax.

He couldn't believe it, but he'd actually never shared this room with a woman before. The women he had were brief distractions, and they usually happened on mutual ground—either at the back of the hall or in one of the farmsteads. And, as leader of the clan, he always left before morning. No one needed to see him coming home after dawn.

But up here was his space—the only place where he could be alone, apart from out on the water, and having Anne here with him was both infuriating and...*nice*.

'Are you awake?'

He sighed. 'Yes. What is it, Princess? Do you need a bedtime story?'

'Will you tell me about the markings on your body? What do they mean?'

He knew she was fascinated by them. And he knew why. They were dark and intricate, and the sword on his chest and the ravens on his back were all combined together with trees and knotwork in a labyrinth of complex tangled lines.

He turned to face her in the darkness, his eyes adjusting to the blackness. With just the pale moonlight filtering through the hole in the wall he could see the outline of her beautiful face, just a stride away from him.

'The sword represents power, protection, and strength. And the ravens—they symbolise the death of my parents. But they're also a nod to our god Odin and his wisdom and intelligence, the good and the bad...'

'They're amazing. Who did them for you?'

'Svea. She's very talented.'

'What about the symbol on your neck?'

'That's *Ægishjálmr*—the Helm of Awe. To frighten off our enemies. Do they scare you, Princess?'

'No.' He heard her shake her head. 'Did they hurt?'

'We use wood ash—and, no, they didn't hurt. But then I have a high threshold for pain. Why? Are you thinking of having some ink too?'

She giggled at the absurd suggestion. 'No, somehow I don't think it would suit me.'

He smiled into the darkness. 'What design would you have?'

'What would you suggest?'

'None. Your body is too perfect to be covered with any kind of ink...'

He heard her swallow and saw her turn her face towards him.

'But if you had to choose one for me?' she pressed.

'Then I'd have to go for *vegvisir*, the symbol used

for protection…or a little primrose. It's our goddess Freyja's sacred flower. It also reminds me of our first kiss…'

The silence stretched between them. He wondered what she was thinking.

'You know, you really aren't anything like the person people describe you to be,' she said.

He ran his tongue over his lips. He was *everything* people thought him to be. He didn't know why he'd been trying to convince her otherwise. He was a brute and he was out for revenge; he would use her to gain wealth. Yes, he had taken her to protect her from Crowe, but in doing so he'd put her in harm's way. And right now he didn't like himself very much.

'Why do they call you that? The Barbarian?'

'Let's not talk about it now,' he said. 'You must be tired after our long day today. But you're safe to sleep now, Anne.'

'I won't wake up and find myself in your arms?' she questioned lightly.

He groaned. Now he had all kinds of images flicking through his mind—and he was hard. 'For pity's sake, don't put ideas in my head, Anne!' he said. 'Now, please, go to sleep.'

But if he wasn't mistaken, she'd sat up in the bed. 'I can't… I'm worried about tomorrow.'

He sighed, sitting forward, resting his elbows on his knees. 'How so?'

'I don't want you to fight.'

He reached out to catch her chin between his fingers in the darkness. 'Why?'

There was a long silence before she said, 'I don't want you getting hurt. It's all madness, Brand. If Crowe kills you, then it was all for nothing. And if you kill him, then what? Will you feel satisfied? Will it be over? No! You'll start another battle between Danes and Saxons.'

'It's a little late for that, Anne.'

She didn't need to tell him the stakes were high— he already knew. If he lost, Anne would belong to that man forever and Svea would never have peace... But if he triumphed, Anne would soon learn of his betrayal and he'd end up without her anyway.

'I don't see why it has to be like that. Why can't everyone just be friends?'

'Like us, you mean?' He grimaced.

He heard the bed shift again, and his whole body tensed when her hands came down to rest on his shoulders and she lowered herself into his lap.

His eyes narrowed on her in the darkness. Was she playing some kind of trick on him? He had the sudden notion that perhaps she was trying to deprive him of all reason now that rescue seemed imminent. Was this some idea she had to scramble his brain so he wouldn't be able to fight?

But he pulled her gently into his body and she rested her head against his bare chest. She placed a hand on his cheek. He should remove it. Hell, he should lift her body from his and put her back in the bed. But instead he turned his face into her palm and pressed a soft kiss to her skin.

'At least I can say it wasn't my fault when you wake in my arms in the morning. Now, please, stop babbling and go to sleep.'

Chapter Eight

The startling sound of a horn echoed around the fortress of Kald and travelled out across the land. Anne thought it was the most terrifying sound she had ever heard. It signalled a warning, a battle, death.

She was standing on the bridge, leaning over the parapet of the guard tower, above Kald's sturdy wooden gates. From there, she could see across the marsh and heathland to the vast expanse of golden sand and ocean. She longed to be back out there on the water again—not here, watching this harrowing scene unfold.

On any other day, she imagined the view would be breathtaking, but the sight before her now filled her with ice-cold dread. Her father had sent an army! Beneath them, it wasn't just the fifty men she and Brand had seen the other night—there were another seventy or so Saxon soldiers, all sent to fight for her release. But instead of feeling relief at her imminent rescue, she just felt numb.

'And you said your father didn't care about you,' Brand said, one eyebrow raised.

'Brand,' she said breathlessly. 'You must hand me back before anyone gets hurt. I'm not worth all this.'

'Actually, you are,' he said. 'Now, keep quiet. Stay out of sight.'

Brand was naked from the waist up, legs planted wide, a bearskin thrown around his shoulders. He held a wooden shield in one hand and a sword in the other. He looked like a ferocious warlord, all hard muscle and dark skin. His ink-covered body, although deeply fascinating, was enough to strike fear into his enemies, and his heavy brow didn't give away one ounce of feeling.

He looked like a different man from the one she'd shared a room with last night. Worlds apart from the man who had held her so tenderly, who had spoken of primroses and protection and stroked her hair as she drifted off to sleep.

Her throat felt thick. 'Why aren't you wearing any armour?' she asked, appalled.

'I have all the protection I need.'

'Don't you have any fear?'

'The only thing I fear is not being able to protect the people I love. I do not fear death.'

She wanted to throw herself down at his feet and beg him to stop this. She'd happily marry Crowe and be miserable for the rest of her life if it meant he'd spare Brand's life. But she knew he wouldn't retreat now—no matter what she said. This fight would go ahead. She was as certain of that as she was that the sun would still rise tomorrow, but by then her whole world would be changed.

Two figures emerged from the wall of Saxon men

and trotted forward on their horses. Anne recognised one of them to be Lord Crowe. He was the epitome of arrogance, playing with the gloves on his hands, cracking his knuckles. She had often thought he looked like a hefty dog, with a thickset body and a pushed-in nose. Taking in the black and yellow markings of his armour, she still couldn't believe that he and his mercenaries were responsible for the desolation of that village. It sickened her to the stomach.

She thought the other man, wearing a navy tunic over chainmail, was the Ealdorman Lord Stanton of Braewood. She had seen him before at the King's witans and knew her father thought highly of him.

Brand stared down at them from the bridge. 'My lords, welcome to Kald.'

'You must be the heathen they call Brand Ivarsson. I am Lord Crowe of Calhourn, and I believe you have something that belongs to me.'

Anne realised she had forgotten to breathe. Her heart was in her mouth.

'To you? No, I don't think so.' Brand shrugged. 'Though we have been enjoying the company of Princess Anne of Termarth.'

Crowe's lips thinned into a sneer. 'And how have you been getting on with my bride?'

'Very, very well,' Brand said, offering up a hard smile.

Crowe moved his neck from side to side. 'Well, fortunately she is not my wife...yet. If she has been touched, that will be most disappointing. I was so looking forward to breaking her in.'

Anne's stomach rolled. She saw Brand's fist tighten

around the hilt of his sword, so hard his knuckles began to turn white.

'But I doubt you have been so foolish as to touch her. You will know the King and I have no use for damaged goods. And you must be expecting some kind of reward for her safe return. No, if you'd harmed her, the fate of you and your people would have been sealed. I have no qualms about burning you all to the ground—the Princess as well, if she's been whored. But let it not come to that. Why don't you make it known what you want, Pagan? Why would you take such great pains to steal away my bride? Is it gold you are after? Or more of our land? Although I must admit she means little to me, so your price must be reasonable. I am prepared to make you a deal, but I wish to see my bride first.'

'There will be no deal,' Brand said. 'Tell your men to stand down and my men will do the same. Then get off your horse and fight me, man to man.'

Anne could tell Crowe hadn't been expecting that as his head snapped up. 'You wish to face me in combat, boy?' He smirked.

'You needn't have brought an army to fight your battle. It is only *your* blood on my hands that I desire.'

Crowe chuckled, spittle forming in the corners of his mouth. 'Very well—we fight. And to the death. But if, on the off-chance, I lose, you still won't win the Princess. My men have orders to attack if I am harmed. I must insist on seeing her first, though.'

Brand gently took Anne's arm, almost reluctantly bringing her into view on the bridge at the top of the gate. She stared down into Crowe's cold, flinty eyes and felt a flicker of disdain. She could smell Brand's musky skin and feel his heat, and she wanted to turn into him, bury her face in his shoulder and pretend none of this was happening.

'Highness,' Lord Stanton said, coming forward. 'I trust you have been well looked after?'

'I have, my lord. Thank you.'

'And is the honour and virtue of Termarth still intact?' Crowe barked.

She swallowed, feeling the heat of Brand's fingers burning into her arm. Thoughts of his lips against her mouth flooded her mind, his hand to her breast. For a moment she wished she could say no, then maybe Crowe wouldn't fight for her. But she thought of her father and knew she couldn't.

'It is, my lord.'

He nodded, and his gaze snapped back to Brand's. 'Very well, Heathen. We fight.'

Anne let out a little sob and her knees sagged.

'Take her,' Brand said to Kar, and she felt herself being pulled back, watching, helpless, as Brand made his way down the wooden steps.

She struggled against Kar's muscled restraint. 'They'll kill him,' she whispered, horror on her lips.

Kar shook his head, looking at Brand with admiration in his eyes. 'Brand is the best warrior I've ever known. Have faith, my lady…'

She watched, as if a pit were emptying in her stomach, as the huge wooden gates opened and Brand walked out into the fray. Something in the set of his shoulders suggested that he was bent on one purpose.

His hands clenched and unclenched on his sword and shield, and his nostrils were slightly flared.

Crowe had lowered himself from his horse and his eyes were narrowed on his opponent.

She strained to hear what was being said between the men. They looked like a bear and a wolf about to do battle, circling each other.

'Do I know you, boy?'

'I'm surprised you don't remember.'

And with a quick flick of his sword, which glinted in the sunlight, Brand sliced the Saxon's forehead open, through his eyebrow. It was an injury that matched his own. There was a rumble through the Saxon troops, the horses braying.

'I am the Danish boy you said you wanted to teach a lesson to a few years back…'

Crowe gave an animalistic growl as he touched a hand to his injury. Recognition lit up the deep-set eyes in his ruddy face. 'Ah, yes,' he sneered. 'A girl who screamed and a boy who watched. You, I presume? A good day. Just like today is going to be. Although I rather thought I had finished you off back then. I meant to.'

Anne's head swam. There was more to this than Brand had told her! What was it? Why hadn't he given her the whole story?

The men squared up to each other and began to cross swords, as all pairs of eyes looked on. Crowe's sword crunched against Brand's shield. Brand slammed Crowe against the wall, and metal clashed against metal. There was cheering from both sides, and Anne couldn't understand why the Saxons and Danes were enjoying it as if it was sport. Crowe rounded on Brand and he ducked, just missing his opponent's blade as it sliced through the air. Then Brand brought his weapon down on Crowe's shield so hard the yellow dragon splintered.

It was the most brutal, savage fight Anne had ever seen, and yet she couldn't bring herself to turn away. She needed to know what was happening. There was blood already, and she suffered every blow, wincing and gasping at every stab of their weapons. Brand was agile on his feet, dodging Crowe's sword, and his own iron kept striking his opponent's shield.

When Crowe was flung to the floor she could tell he was flagging—he was clearly no match for Brand's strength—and then Brand was on top of him. Crowe was pinned beneath his weight, his weapon discarded and his bare fists flying. Brand was wild and unrelenting, pounding and pummelling, almost overcome with rage, seemingly lost in revenge. And now she knew that this man, right here, was the Barbarian she had heard of.

Her hand flew to her mouth as they thrashed around on the ground and Crowe tried to crawl away. But he was pinned beneath Brand's weight again, writhing and convulsing in pain, and when Brand finally wrenched him up onto his knees the Saxon whimpered, begging for his life to be spared. Both sides looked on in hushed silence, waiting for the Barbarian to finish the job. He had earned his victory.

'Brand—no!' Anne said, launching herself towards him, her voice wobbling.

Lord Stanton cantered forward at the same time. 'Show mercy. Let us come to an arrangement.'

Brand glanced up at her, his eyes cold, devoid of emotion, his face splattered with blood. 'Get her out of here!' he yelled at Kar.

It was all too much. Anne heard wailing, and before she realised the sound was coming from herself she was being dragged across the courtyard and back to the upstairs room.

'Anne?'

Brand pushed open the door.

'Go away.'

She couldn't bear to look at him. The brutal scene kept replaying over and over in her head. Brand and Crowe's bloodied bodies and Brand seemingly going berserk.

She squeezed her eyes shut. She wanted to rid her mind of it. She wished she could return to this morning, when none of it had happened. How could she ever erase those images from her memory? No doubt he had finished the job and killed Crowe.

She was sitting on the floor in the corner of the room, hugging her knees to her chest, her face streaked with tears. She had never seen anyone fight like that before. Barbaric was the only word to describe it. So now she knew where his name had come from. If it was Brand's wish to stand out and be noticed by his gods, then he had achieved it with this bloodthirsty vendetta.

She had seen it too, and she wasn't sure she could forget it. But there was also a part of her that wanted to understand it better…to understand *him*. What had made him behave like that?

'Anne,' Brand said again, his hands on his hips. 'I've never pretended to be a good man, you know that.'

She bristled. He had seemed so devoid of feeling it had shocked her.

'It was a fair fight, Anne…'

'So now I know where you get your name from. You have fought like that, behaved like that before. How else would you have garnered your reputation?' She shook her head. 'Did you kill him? Oh, God, you don't know what you've done.'

He'd surely started a war. She was terrified of what this meant for Kald and for Termarth. What would happen next? The Saxons must be trying to break through the gates even now.

'No, I didn't kill him, but I should have.'

A cool trickle of relief flowed through her.

'You don't know what he did, Anne!'

'That's because you haven't told me!'

The silence stretched like the string of an archer's bow, until Brand came down on his haunches in front of her.

'You really want to know? I was trying to protect you from him. From the monster you were going to marry. The truth isn't pretty, Anne.'

'Tell me. I need to know.'

He stood and went over to the smoke hole, raking a hand through his hair. He was still caked in Crowe's blood and his wounds hadn't been seen to. How badly was he hurt? She wanted to reach out to him, but she couldn't. She needed to hear this first.

He took a deep, steadying breath before he began. 'When Svea and I were younger, our father took us to Termarth. He had a dream, as I told you, to build boats, to sell them, so we went there looking to trade. We managed to find a potential buyer and my father was in great spirits. His dream was coming true. Before we left for home we went to a mead house to celebrate, but just after we left the castle walls Saxon soldiers came out of nowhere, surrounding us. One of them had taken a shine to Svea and he made it clear what he wanted.'

Brand had started pacing as he spoke, the tension rippling off him like a raven shedding its dark feathers.

'My father didn't stand for it, of course,' he continued. 'He would have done anything to protect us. He drew his sword, but that gave them the excuse they were looking for to strike. They beat him, ten to one. They waited till he was broken and on his knees, and then they…'

He drew his hands over his face, and it was as if he had the weight of the world on his shoulders. She wanted to tell him to sit down, to rest.

'Sorry,' he said, his voice cracking. 'I don't ever talk about the events of that day. It makes me feel a mixture of hatred and shame… Because they killed my father, Anne. They severed his head from his body. And then they grabbed Svea and made me watch as they took turns with her. She had just turned twelve.'

Anne felt as if an archer had released his arrow and

it had hit her in the heart. She couldn't believe what she was hearing. It was tragic. Horrific. Her heart lurched for poor Svea, for having to go through such an ordeal. And it ached for Brand.

'That was Crowe? Crowe did that?' She wanted to reach for Brand, to comfort him, but he was so deep in thought, dark and brooding, she wasn't sure he'd want her to.

'Yes. Afterwards, they beat me, but somehow I managed to get away and run.' He stared down at a spot on the floor, his neck bent forward. 'They came after me—as you saw. But I thought I deserved it because I hadn't saved my father, or Svea. I deserved to die for not protecting her.'

Anne shook her head furiously. 'Brand, it's not your fault. There was no way you could have fought all those men on your own. Unarmed. They would have killed you. They tried to kill you!'

'After they left—after *you* left—I spent the next few days looking for Svea. I was so ashamed that I'd run out on her. When I eventually found her she'd been cast out onto the streets and she was in a really bad way. I stole a horse—the only crime I'd ever committed up until that point—' he laughed bitterly '—and got her home. It took a long time for her to recover. They'd hurt her. Badly. And I vowed that when I was strong enough I'd make that man pay for what he did.'

Anne didn't trust her voice to speak. Her throat was aching. How could Lord Crowe have done that?

'Brand, I had no idea,' she said, fresh tears pooling in her eyes.

Deep down, she wondered if a part of Brand held her responsible—after all, they were talking about her father's ally, her fiancé! *Ex*-fiancé. How could her father have wanted to marry her off to such a man? Did the King know what Crowe was capable of?

She shuddered.

'After that day, I vowed never to let another Saxon hurt my family or my people. I learned how to fight like a warrior, so the next time the Saxons attacked I could protect the people I loved. And I did. Those first few years after my father passed away I lived for the fight. I was filled with hate and desperate to punish any Saxon for what Crowe had done. I took my anger out on them. When the Saxons repeatedly tried to get us to leave Kald by laying siege, part of me was glad. I wanted to fight them with fury, to kill them. And so my reputation grew. And if that's what's needed to keep my people safe, then so be it. If my name instils fear into Saxons and keeps them away from our lands—good. But I never provoked the battles, Anne. I was just defending my people from your people. And as the grief eventually passed, and the years wore on, I realised there was only one man I truly wanted to destroy...'

So this was why Brand had taken her...why he had provoked this fight. And she was glad he'd won.

'Why didn't you kill him?' she asked.

He ran a hand over his beard. 'Because to kill a monster sometimes you have to become one,' he said quietly. 'And I didn't want you to see me like that. You have always soothed my rage, Anne. And I held Crowe's life in my hands and I made my decision. But there are always consequences, aren't there? I had just thrown down my weapon when I heard a guttural roar come from behind me. It was a sound like no other I've ever heard before. One that held grief and pain and torment. I turned and saw Svea running towards me… She must have sensed me pull back, decide to spare his life. It all happened so quickly, but I kicked Crowe to the floor and grasped hold of Svea and she broke down in my arms.'

'Is she all right?' Anne asked, concerned.

'I've just been with her, holding her as she wept, trying to calm her down. At first she was furious with me, but now I think she's just relieved that he's finally been seized and is no longer a threat. That he can no longer hurt anyone else. Deep down, she's tough.'

'Where is Lord Crowe now?'

'He's in chains in a room at the back of the hall. I've been waiting years for this moment, and today I've settled my promise to my sister and avenged my father's death. I shall send Crowe back with you to your father, and I ask that you tell him of all the atrocities he has committed—against my people and yours. I hope your father will punish him accordingly.'

Anne's head shot up and she stared at him. Brand was standing on the other side of the room from her, his hands braced across his chest. She'd been wondering what he would do with her, now he had got what he wanted. Now she knew.

'You're sending me home?'

Wasn't that what she'd wanted? Or had she hoped he would ask her to stay? But that was surely impossible. He was a Dane and she was a Saxon. And yet, did she not mean anything to him?

As she stared at him, there seemed to be a giant void between them, a great chasm opening up.

'That is what you want, isn't it?' he asked.

'Of course,' she said, tears welling in her eyes. 'It's time.'

He gave a curt nod and stalked to the door and pulled it open. 'It's been a long day. I'll leave you in peace now, Anne, while I work out the arrangements.'

Chapter Nine

Brand knew the exact moment Anne entered the longhouse—and the exact moment she discovered that he had always meant to sell her for a price.

She had come into the hall with Svea, but while his sister had joined the men at the large table, Anne had made a beeline for Ulf, at the side of the room, who was now sitting up and looking a lot brighter.

Her wispy floral scent alerted Brand to the fact she was close, and the hairs on his arms bristled in anticipation. But jealousy smarted when she smiled at the boy and tended to his wounds. Had *he* not suffered far greater injuries today?

Brand had washed the blood from his skin and inspected his multiple cuts and bruises. The worst was a deep gash to his arm, which Svea had tried to patch up as best she could. And he thought he might have broken a bone in his foot. He was having difficulty bearing any weight on it, which was making it increasingly hard to walk, but he would tolerate the pain.

It was Anne caring for someone else and saying that she wanted to leave that he couldn't handle. His blood had been up ever since.

He knew everything had changed. The intimacy that had blossomed between them had been crushed by his brutal behaviour. She had thought the worst of him, thinking he had killed Crowe, and she'd even shed tears over it. She'd said she wanted to leave and, frankly, he was as angry as hell with her.

But even so, when she'd stepped into the hall and he'd seen that she no longer had a red, puffy face, that she was composed and in control of herself, she had detonated his desire all over again. How did she do that?

Mainly, he was furious with himself. He knew she was safe from Crowe, but that meant he now had to give her up—and he wasn't sure how to go about it in a way that would keep both her and his people happy. He had promised them a reward. He couldn't let them down. But he didn't want to let Anne down either.

'I say we stick to the original plan and demand five hundred pieces of gold for the witch!' Torsten was saying, trying to work the other men into a fury. 'That was always the plan—what's changed? We tell the Saxons we won't murder them all while they sleep, and that in exchange for our leniency they can have her back once they give us the gold.'

Brand saw Anne's back stiffen, saw the realisation of what Torsten was saying dawn in her eyes—that Brand had intended to fetch a ransom for her all along.

Her chin thrust upwards sharply, in that proud, dignified way it always did.

A wave of fists began banging on the table by all
those who were in agreement with Torsten, and now
Brand felt the swell of rage against his men as well. He
understood that they wanted gold, to provide for their
families, but it was his decision to make—not theirs.
And he'd grown weary of fighting. He longed for peace
and stability—didn't they?

'Enough!'

The air in the room was so thick that it seemed almost
tangible, but Brand placed his hands flat on the table
and the pounding stilled. It was strange… He'd got his
vengeance—they should have been celebrating—but he
felt dissatisfied. He still hadn't got what he wanted. But
what exactly was that?

He glared at Torsten and felt the tension between
them simmering. 'What's the matter with you? Your
thirst for blood is even worse than usual! Do you have
something you want to say?'

'Aye, I damn well do.' The older red-haired man
stood up. 'You've been getting your cock wet with
that Saxon whore this whole time,' he said, his hands
on his hips. 'And you've become fixated on her. Cast
your mind back a few years. We followed your father
to richer lands and we were promised an equal share
of any spoils. Land, treasure, slaves… Is she not a
treasure? I demand that you share her before we give
her up and then share the ransom you get for her. You
owe us that.'

Brand saw Svea blanch, and he put a hand on her

shoulder to reassure her he would deal with this. He studied his old ally, his cool eyes full of disdain, and felt the anger vibrating off his body.

It had been one hell of a day. He'd beaten his enemy in the most brutal of fights, he'd had words with Anne and watched his sister cry, and if he didn't negotiate with the Saxon soldiers soon, they would no doubt attempt to breach the fortress walls. But he wouldn't stand for Torsten giving him orders, or speaking to him as if he wasn't the leader of Kald. It was *his* leadership that had kept them all safe these past years, and he expected loyalty now.

Quiet rage had him rising to his feet, squaring up to his father's old friend. He realised theirs was an acquaintance that had run its course. 'Like I said right from the start—she's mine to do with as I please. If I want to bed her, I will, and if I want to sell her, I will. *I* will decide what happens to her, not you. You're far too hot-headed, Torsten. You always think with your cock, and therefore you make bad choices.'

His adversary glowered at him, his face turning puce.

But Brand continued. 'You'd like to sleep with her? You'd like a bit of fun? Well, you're a fool. You'd be selling us short. The minute any one of us touches her, she loses her worth. She's nothing.' His eyes lanced her across the room. 'We'll make much more gold for her if we return her to her father, the King, her virginity intact. And that's the prize here, yes? Gold—not her body. So go and take a mistress tonight, but keep your hands to yourself when it comes to the Princess. Now, are you with me or against me? What's it going to be?'

As he glanced around, his men's fists began pounding and pummelling the table in agreement...

Anne rose to her feet and met Brand's steely gaze. His final insult had taken her breath away. She had felt his anger from across the room as soon as she'd entered the longhouse, but she hadn't been able to understand why it was directed at her. There had been a hard edge to his voice and words, and she'd felt the blow of each and every one. When Torsten had mentioned the ransom treasure they were all expecting, her heart had frozen over.

She felt rooted to the spot. Now she knew Brand's desired outcome in this dark game he was playing. This was the truth.

She took in his set jaw and unreadable eyes and felt her temper spike. He had deceived her. He had told her he'd taken her to provoke Lord Crowe, in revenge for the wrongs that man had done, and to protect her from marrying a monster. But all along he had been planning to sell her back to her father for gold, which he'd said he wouldn't do.

She felt winded by the betrayal and by his cutting words. He'd called her nothing. *Nothing!*

She had stupidly convinced herself he felt something for her, and had begun to believe she cared about him too. But it was all lies. It had always been about the treasure. He was no different from her father—or any other man. He was treating her as an object for his own gain and she felt like such a fool. She'd let him kiss her, touch her... She'd even thought about going further... Yet he had held back, and now she knew he would never have taken her anyway, because then he wouldn't have earned his gold.

Oh, God! She felt tears sting her eyes and furiously blinked them away.

He'd promised he wouldn't hurt her, but right now she felt more wounded than she ever had before in her life—as if he'd pierced her heart with his iron sword.

But Anne had never been one to keep her mouth shut when she felt she'd been wronged.

'You bastard!' she said, as she placed her cup down on the table and rushed from the room.

The men all around him cheered, back in good spirits, but for an awful moment Brand was at a loss, as if he had made an enormous mistake. He rolled his shoulders. He was so wound up. The thought of Torsten laying a hand on Anne had spiked his rage. He'd said what he'd needed to say to ward off his once-friend from following through on his dark desires. But had he gone too far?

He rubbed his chest. He'd lashed out at his friend and then at Anne, wanting to hurt her as he was hurting because she'd agreed to leave. But then she had looked at him, her emerald-green eyes two wide pools of vulnerability...

He really was a bastard.

He pushed himself away from the table. 'I'll go and make our demands known to the Saxons,' he said, and stalked out of the hall after her, leaving the men to their revelry.

He followed Anne, a mixture of rage and lust propelling him forward as she fled across the square, and finally caught up with her in the stables, just as she threw herself against one of the horse's sides, her fingers curling over its mane.

'Anne—wait.'

'For what, Brand? For you to enlighten me as to why you're such a brute?' Her stare was full of judgement, her cheeks wet as she wiped away a tear. 'This was all about gold the whole time... But not everything has a price. You're no better than my father.'

His brows knitted together. 'Anne, we need to talk... What I said to the men, I didn't mean it. It was just to keep Torsten's wandering mind and hands in check.'

'So you're not going to ask for a ransom?'

He paused before answering, and she laughed bitterly.

'Oh, but of course you are.'

She dug her heels into the horse's sides and mounted the animal. It reared up. He was forced to step back as he realised she meant to ride it—without reins or a saddle—and she sped off in a cloud of dust across the square.

For a minute, he felt off-balance, stunned. There was a connection between them that made her so familiar to him this whole situation felt absurd. Part of him wanted to rant and rage, tell her off for daring to run away from him, and another part of him wanted to pull her to him and thank the gods she was still here. Safe.

And yet without a saddle she could fall off that horse and—*Skit!* When was she going to start taking care of herself?

The spike of irritation in his groin spurred him into action. He mounted one of the stallions and tore off after her, across the yard and over the grain fields, down to the track they'd come up earlier that afternoon from the boat.

He was livid, his boots digging into the sides of his horse, and he was gaining on her, travelling at speed over the long grass, down the hill, the horse jolting and jerking over the uneven terrain. His arm burned, his foot was agony—but he didn't care. Where the hell did she think she was going?

The stallion's nose was finally aligned with Anne's mare and he swerved to the right, recklessly making contact with her. Steering into her, he forced her to turn abruptly, backing her against the boathouse.

When her surprised horse came to a halt, she flung herself off the animal and he jumped down too, meeting her anger with his.

'Are you out of your mind?' she yelled.

'Quite possibly.'

And as he stared down into her blazing eyes he knew she wanted him as much as he wanted her, and he hauled her to him, crushing her mouth with his.

He thought for a second that this was what insanity felt like—wanting someone so badly that you didn't have a choice. Her stifled gasp sent a warning signal to his brain that he shouldn't be doing this, but he'd already made his decision. And, by the way she was pressing her body against his, she had too.

He'd half expected her to shove him away, had even hoped she would, to put a stop to this madness. But she was responding with fire. He grabbed her round bottom and almost welded their bodies together, his length pressing into her flat stomach, and she groaned—a delicious, needy sound that made him want to cause more of a reaction.

He carried her a few strides to the boathouse and, placing her on her feet, pinned her up against the wall. Her hands were around his neck, and as he ravaged her mouth with his tongue he put his hands possessively over her breasts. She whimpered, and his need for her was like an excessive thirst that he had to quench.

He tore his lips from hers, and as he ripped open the brooches that fastened the straps of her pinafore together, letting the material cascade to her waist, he said, 'I didn't mean any of what I said to my men, Anne. I was just telling them what they wanted to hear. Believe it or not, I'm still trying to protect you.'

Her under-gown was still in the way of his destination, and he urgently tugged the collar down over her shoulders, peeling away the material. Small, pert swells of creamy skin spilled into his hands. At last. She was so beautiful...so pale and perfect under his tanned palms. He kneaded and stroked her sensitive flesh, and loved it when she groaned, her head rolling back.

Staring down at her thrusting pink nipples, he realised they were too much of a temptation, and he lowered his head to take one hard bud into his mouth and suckle. She let out a gasp at the indecent torment he was creating, and his hot tongue and teeth tugged at her sweet and salty skin, his beard brushing against her.

She held his head to her chest, her hands roaming through his hair. 'And what about the gold, Brand?'

'To hell with the ransom, Anne. It's you I want.'

Her hands slid over the taut muscles in his shoulders and down his broad back, securing his body tighter to hers, and then they began to roam up and under the material of his tunic, exploring and caressing the ridges of his solid but smooth skin. Her tantalising soft caresses were torture. They weren't enough. He wanted and needed more.

Pushing up her dress, seeking out her other intimate places now, he wrapped one of her legs around his thigh so that he was right there, his hard shaft pressing against the already damp heat of her undergarments. And the last shreds of his self-control were gone.

'I've been fighting this with all the strength I've got, but it's not working. This is the only way…'

And as she wildly, desperately grasped for him, her hands under his arms, pulling his chest closer to hers, the ache in his groin grew hot and heavy. He had to have her. Now.

'Then take me, Brand, and put us both out of our misery so we can move past this.'

He longed to spread her legs wide, his weight holding her down, to thrust deep inside her, to rid himself of this rage and longing. But her words had sliced through his fierce need. He didn't want to just take her and move on, and the thought brought him up short. That was a first.

What he really wanted was to savour every moment of her sweet submission. And, realising this would be her first time, he wanted it to be special—not a frantic moment up the side of the boathouse.

Anne's hands slid over the taut muscles of Brand's stomach and around his broad back, securing his body tighter to hers as the soft material of his trousers brushed against the bare skin of her inner thighs, making her hotter by the second. And when she felt his thick erection nudge against her most intimate places, waves of heat spread like a raging inferno through her body.

Brand lifted his head to meet her lips again, his tongue filling her mouth, entwining with hers—but something had changed. His caresses against her skin became less urgent and his touch was suddenly excruciatingly tender, gentle, as he stroked her neck, her breasts, teasing her nipples between his fingers.

It was driving her mad. She wanted more. It wasn't enough. She never wanted him to stop. He was stealing her away to places she had never even known existed. And maybe this was what she needed—to forget everything, just to feel total, utter pleasure.

She believed that he had said those things to warn off his men. And now she knew that if he continued to lay his hands on her, if they carried on down this dizzying path, she wouldn't be worth a ransom...

She flattened one of his hands against her breast

before pushing it down over her stomach, and lower, guiding him over the bunched-up material of her skirts to reach between her legs. Her eyes opened and met his blue heated gaze. His lips curved up into a dangerous predatory half-smile as she encouraged his fingers to carry on their descent, leaving him in no doubt as to where she wanted him to touch her.

She grazed her mound against his hand, impatient. She had no idea what she was doing—she just knew she needed him to touch her right there. Now. The ache that had been throbbing between her legs the past few days was becoming impossible to ignore.

'I wanted to touch you here that night on the beach.'

Her hand still covered his as he skilfully drew the material of her underwear to one side, and her breath caught in anticipation of his intimate touch. 'Then why didn't you?' A breathless whisper.

Momentarily, she felt fresh air drift over her exposed sensitive skin, before it was replaced with his warm, strong fingers. Parting her with one slick slide of his thumb, making her legs buckle, his thighs held her up and in place as he gently pushed one long finger inside her.

Languid heat bloomed. Need lanced her. 'Oh, God...' Her head fell forward, her forehead against his. So this was what it felt like. She had never imagined it to feel so good.

As he drew his finger out, bringing with it a rush of wetness, he masterfully, mercilessly, circled her sensitive nub, slowly, incredibly gently, making her head spin.

'Because I was waiting for you to want me as much as I want you…' he said.

She would have responded, only he'd ruthlessly pushed two fingers back inside her again, causing her to cry out in shocked pleasure.

'Quiet,' he said, before he caught her mouth with his to stifle her moans. 'We don't want to wake the villagers.'

His fingers weren't acting as if he wanted her to be quiet. They were unrelenting, seeking, pulsing in and out of her, demanding more of a reaction, and her leg curled higher and tighter around his, holding him to her, never wanting this to end and yet at the same time urgently wishing for the release only he could give her.

Her head fell forward on a sob of swelling emotion and pure white-hot blinding bliss, her teeth sinking into his shoulder to stop herself from crying out. His fresh, musky male scent enveloped her and the boat-house wall bit into her bottom, grazing her as she rode his masterful fingers, which were bringing her to the mind-blowing brink, and she cried out into the curve of his neck.

She didn't know how long they stood entwined like that, neither of them moving. He must have been giving her time to get her breath back, but it was a while before he spoke. He smoothed her damp hair either side of her face.

'I'm sorry for all that I said in there, Anne,' he said quietly, cutting through the haze of lust and the torrent of pleasure strumming through her body. 'I was angry

with Torsten for the way he was speaking about you. I wanted him to back off.'

He sighed and took a step away from her, the last of his anger seeming to ebb away. He helped her to straighten her clothes while she still clung to him. She didn't think she could stand without his support. Her legs were still trembling. She gripped his upper arms to steady herself, and he blanched beneath her grasp, grimacing.

'You're hurt!' she gasped.

'It's just a little cut.' He grimaced again.

'I don't believe you. How bad is it?'

'Don't worry about me, Anne.'

'But that's the problem. I do…' She brought her hands up to his jaw and drew his mouth down to hers, and their tongues found each other again in a long, lingering kiss.

His hands stroked down her arms to find her hands, and he tugged her around the side of the boathouse, leading her to the jetty so they could take in the view of the moonlight shimmering on the water. He pulled her back into his chest and kissed the top of her head.

'What are you going to do about my father's army, Brand—and the ransom you've promised Kald? Your men are talking about the price you want for me, but where does it end? What about the cost of all this conflict between our people?'

He sighed. 'The men expect me to earn a ransom for your safe return—but I promised them the gold before I got to know you, Anne. I wish I could take it all back… Now, if I send you home and they come out of

it empty-handed…' He shook his head. 'Try to remember they don't come from a life of privilege, like you.'

She inhaled sharply. 'That's no excuse.'

'You're right,' he soothed, his arms tightening around her. 'And I don't intend to go through with it. I shall have to provide for Kald in some other way. I will come up with something. I promise that I'll make all this right, Anne.'

He tipped her head back so he could access her neck, placing soft little kisses along her jawline, and she moaned softly. She could feel his hard length pressing into her back and knew she had to be brave and touch him too. And she wanted to—she just didn't know what to do. What if she didn't please him?

So she turned in his arms and forced her trembling hands to stray downwards, tracing the thin line of dark hair that descended from his stomach, and then she plucked up the courage to flatten her palm over the ridge in his trousers.

He groaned, resting his forehead against hers as he began to run his hands down her body.

'Anne, you are so exquisite… I want to cover your body in kisses,' he whispered into her ear, and he pushed open the door to the boathouse and pulled her inside.

She had no idea what she was doing. She just knew she wanted to accelerate the intimacy between them. She wanted to drive him as wild as he was making her. So she tugged open the tie fastening his trousers and moved her other hand beneath the material to take

hold of him, wrapping her hand around the intimidating, huge, hard length of him.

He growled. 'Anne, you're driving me insane. Can you feel how much I want you?'

She pushed him back against the wall she gave him a few quick strokes before he moaned into her mouth, but he stilled her roaming fingers.

'Anne,' he whispered. 'Not here. Not yet.'

How did he have such control when she was losing her mind?

Brand lowered her to the wooden floor on her back as he kissed her, stroking her arms as their tongues continued to tangle. He pulled away slightly to look at her in the mellow moonlight, sprawled beneath him, her hair cascading across her shoulders, and when she smiled up at him, trying to pull him back towards her, he'd never seen anyone or anything as beautiful in his whole life.

He gazed down at her as his fingers traced the edge of her dress, over her cleavage. He lowered his head to follow the path with his tongue. If he wanted to kiss her everywhere he needed her naked, so he found the hem of both her garments and rolled them up her legs, tugging her up so he could gently peel them away from her chest and over her head.

And when he lay her back down on the straw he allowed his eyes a moment to linger over her body, soaking it in in the moonlight, before he dipped his head to her naked breasts. She was perfect, so pink and pert and soft, and he showered her sensitive skin with endless kisses, making her nipples wet, swirling his tongue around them, causing her to writhe beneath him and arch her back, wanting more.

She moaned softly and his cock soared. He stretched out beside her, his hands trailing over her flat stomach, his fingers moulding to the gentle curve of her hips and moving round to squeeze her smooth bottom. But his exploration didn't stop there. His fingers dipped further below, to her soft, silky entrance, once more.

'Brand...' she spluttered.

This was exactly where he wanted her. Compliant, wet and willing. His for the taking. He knew that if he wanted peace between Termarth and Kald, as she did, he must take her back pure and chaste. But he could still make love to her with his mouth, couldn't he?

Leaning over her, he let his eyes glance down to take in the intimate dark curls at the apex of her thighs, and his mouth watered to kiss her right there.

His mouth had left her lips and begun to kiss an indecent burning trail down her body, not leaving any part of her skin uncovered. His beard tickled the soft, sensitised skin of her stomach, while his fingers skated up and down her parted thighs. And then, before she knew what was happening, he'd hooked her legs over his shoulders.

Too late, Anne realised his intention, where he was planning to kiss her next, and despite her gasps of shock and her half-hearted protests he held her fast. She threw her arms over her eyes and gave in to the burning intimacy and the incredible sensations his tongue was causing as it swirled over her silky thighs, keeping their course upwards.

Finally, he bent his head and placed his lips where she wanted him the most. He ran his tongue over her most sensitive nub. She bucked, but he ruthlessly pushed her thighs further apart to give him better access. And when he flicked his tongue down her crease, opening her up to him, she cried out, letting him know he was driving her wild.

She reached down to clasp his head, never wanting this to end, and as his tongue inched inside her fingers bunched in his hair in disbelief and her bottom arched off the floor, rising up to meet him, demanding more. She had never known such things were done, or even possible.

Her muscles began to clench and her thighs quivered. He must know she was on the brink. But still he didn't stop. His clever tongue continued to lick, tease and torment her, tipping her over the edge, and he brutally gripped her hips to hold her in place as she cried out in her intense swirling climax.

He dragged his head up her body until he was hovering over her, his hands braced either side of her shoulders, and he was so hard. But he just pulled her into his arms and kissed her gently, until the tremors stopped coursing through her body.

A while later, she allowed him to deftly pull her under-gown and pinafore back into place, sorting out the straps. She watched as he fumbled with the pins. Were his hands shaking?

She bit her lip, suddenly shy. 'What of your needs?'

He smiled. 'I want you, Anne, but not now—not here,' he said, tucking her hair behind her ears. 'Not when your father's men are still banging on my door. And not until I've made amends. But before this is over, Anne, I will make you mine.'

Not long after that Brand left Anne talking with Svea in his sister's room. Svea seemed in much better spirits, and he was glad. His heart warmed as he watched her and Anne busy themselves with making hot drinks and a fire. It took all his strength to leave the cosy scene, but he knew he must come to an agreement with the Saxons before it was too late and things took an ugly turn.

He exited the fortress gates and began to pace over to the soldiers. They were readying themselves to fight, and as he approached the men bristled like the hairs on a huge hog. He couldn't blame them—they'd all seen what had happened between him and Crowe, and as far as they were concerned he had two Saxon hostages.

He asked to speak to the man in charge, and as he waited, with an army of men staring him down, all he could think about was what had happened between him and Anne. The realisation that she wanted him as much as he wanted her made him restless, and even had his fingers shaking.

Just remembering the way she'd felt in his arms, the way his fingers had moved deep inside her, made his blood heat. She'd practically demanded that he touch her, then shown his hands the way to the secret parts of her body. And he'd needed no further encouragement. He'd had his tongue down her throat, her bottom backed up against the wall, her dress gathered up around her waist and his long fingers buried inside her within seconds.

Did he have no shame? To seduce a virgin Saxon princess against the boathouse wall? And yet he couldn't bring himself to regret it. His fingers had fitted her tight body so perfectly, and she had been so responsive to his touch.

He had wanted to claim her from the moment he'd first laid eyes on her. She had been his dream girl as a boy, and she was still his fantasy as a man. He'd thought that when he brought her to Kald those feelings would soon pass, as they had always done with other women. He took them to bed, he grew bored, he moved on. But his need for Anne was becoming greater, not less, and he hadn't even made love to her. All he wanted to do was shove down his trousers and lose himself inside her. He wanted to make her his forever. But a little voice inside his head made him hold back.

She stirred feelings inside him that he'd never felt before, and he knew that was dangerous. Especially when she would be leaving him soon. Now Crowe was in chains Anne was free to marry someone else…and he knew he had to return her to her father to have any hope of making things right. He just wasn't sure how he was going to let her go.

She had made him remember the love his parents had shared. She'd stirred up his memories of the happy times they'd spent together as a family when he was a boy. Did he really not want what they had had—did he not want a wife and children? Was he going to deny himself all that love and joy just because he was fearful of losing all that he would cherish and hold dear?

He raked a hand over his head. He wasn't getting any younger. What was he doing with his life? When this was all over, he needed to get his priorities straight.

Chapter Ten

'Fire! Fire!'

Anne had been sitting at Svea's table, sipping a hot drink and listening to her talk about her and Brand's childhood, enjoying the stories of Brand as a boy, when they'd heard shouting coming from outside. They'd dropped their cups and rushed out of the hut to find hordes of villagers gathered in the square, some scurrying about, looking up in horror at the wild blaze atop a section of the fortress ramparts.

Spitting and smoking, the flames were now blindingly bright and fierce, illuminating the dark night sky. Leaping from the battlements to the turf and timber rooftops of some of the farmsteads, the fire seemed furiously out of control, its thick smoke making people choke.

'Are we under attack?' someone cried. 'What's happening?'

The villagers were running around in chaos, gathering up children, animals, and their belongings, trying to get them to safety.

Anne was momentarily stunned. Where was Brand? Was he safe?

But when she saw Svea filling buckets with water she rushed to do the same, wanting to do something to help. But she didn't make it to the well. A large figure grabbed her from behind and clamped huge clammy hands over her mouth. As she was picked up off the ground and carried through the air, everything moved too quickly for her to process.

This was not Brand's firm but gentle touch, and fear lurched through her. Was this her father's attempt at a rescue? Had the Saxons set the fire as a distraction? And if they had breached the walls, what had they done to Brand?

Despite her kicking and screaming, her captor didn't throw her down to the ground until they were inside a building. He closed the door behind him—and locked it.

Dread pounded through her veins. 'What are you doing?' she asked, trembling. 'Who are you? Let me go!'

Eyes darting around, she tried to work out where they were, but she couldn't see anything in the blackness. Then the pungent metallic odour of hanging meat and fish hit her and she retched. They were in the smokehouse and she was trapped.

'What am I doing?'

The rough voice sneered, making her shrink back from it. It was Torsten. She knew it without a doubt, even before her eyes adjusted to the dark and his outline came into view.

'I'm going to show Brand that he doesn't always rule

the roost around here. Not any more. And I'm going to show *you* that you're nothing but a piece of meat.'

She felt sick, her skin crawling with fear. She had to stall him. Stop him doing whatever it was he was about to do.

'Did you set the fire to distract everyone?' she asked, playing to his ego, trying to keep him talking.

Her breath was coming in short, sharp bursts, and she was sweating. She was having difficulty focusing—the panic of being confined as well as being attacked by this man was overwhelming her.

He laughed. 'It should keep them occupied while I have my fun. And they'll think your Saxon fools did it,' he jeered, reaching out for her.

She dodged him, grappling around on the floor, searching for something—anything—to defend herself with. 'But when they realise Brand will come looking for me. He'll come storming in here at any moment,' she said, her survival instinct kicking in.

'Then I'd better be quick,' he spat.

He launched himself at her, grabbing her arms, and she struggled against him, lashing out and screaming. But he smacked her across the face, sending her into a crumpled heap on her back on the floor.

'I don't believe he has any intention of fighting your army. Or of sending you back and claiming our gold... You've turned his head, witch. Well, I've had enough of waiting.'

Shuffling backwards, and still fumbling for something to use as a weapon, Anne grabbed anything she could lay her hands on—pots, pans, cooking instruments, even a fistful of salt… But she was no match for his weight. He grabbed her hands and pinned her down, his vile breath hissing over her face. He smelled of stale sweat and ale, making her stomach churn, and she turned her head, struggling to gasp some air. He was rough as he tried to manoeuvre his big body in between her kicking legs, but she made it as difficult as possible for him.

'Get off me! Stop it!' she cried.

She could hear the tremors in her voice. She couldn't remember a time when she'd been more afraid. Brand had never made her feel like this.

But her resistance was making Torsten even more angry, and he hit her again, this time blackening her eye, knocking the wind out of her. He took the opportunity to grab her by her wrists and bind her with rope, then dragged her across the room and bent her over a table.

And then she realised she'd rather be dead than have this man take her.

'I've never known a Saxon woman to have such influence over a man. Let's find out what all the fuss is about, shall we?'

When she heard Torsten unfasten his trousers she gagged. *This is it*, she thought, bracing herself.

And then he was gone, pulled back by a force she couldn't see.

'What the hell do you think you're doing?'

Brand.

Her body almost sagged in relief.

'Taking a piece of what's rightfully mine! What I'm owed.'

She heard the crack of bone hitting bone. *'Dra til helvete!* She'll never be yours.'

'You've broken my jaw. Over a Saxon whore?'

She heard another blow and saw Torsten stagger backwards.

'Pick up your things and clear out your house. You'll leave Kald tonight. And if I ever see your face again it will be too soon.'

Anne could hear the anger vibrating in Brand's voice. She whimpered, the rope beginning to slice into her wrists. She could tell a crowd had gathered just beyond the door. She needed to get out, to get away.

'You're choosing her over me? I gave my life to your father. I've given years to you.'

'No, you have followed your own path of rape and pillaging. That was never mine or my father's. We are not the same, you and I. Now, get out!'

Anne realised with relief that the fire must have been extinguished if everyone had gathered round the smokehouse to see what was going on. She hoped no one had been hurt. She could just make out Svea, Ulf and Kar. She couldn't believe Torsten had set the buildings of his own village alight as a distraction, so he could attack her. He could have burned them all down to the ground.

'Get out!' Brand roared again.

She watched Torsten begin to stalk away, but as he did so she saw him slide Ulf's sword out of its hilt.

'Brand, watch out!' she cried.

And in a flash Brand, Kar and Svea all turned their weapons on him. The red-haired brute slumped down to his knees, dropping Ulf's blade in defeat.

'Take him away,' said Brand.

Anne felt a hand on her waist and she jerked.

'It's just me.'

Brand.

And that was when she felt an uncontrollable trembling start in her legs and the tears began to roll. And as Brand untied her and pulled her to her feet she collapsed against him, throwing her arms around his neck and clinging to him, never wanting to let go.

Chapter Eleven

'You're bleeding.'

'It's nothing. I'm fine.'

Brand had carried Anne up to his room and they were sitting cross-legged on the bed, face to face. Her skin had turned almost colourless, and she was bruised and dishevelled, her hair all over the place. But she was still so proud and dignified, still so beautiful, and it hurt to look at her.

When he'd seen her bent over that table in the smoke-house, looking so tiny and fragile, he'd felt an uncontrollable blinding rage shift through him. The thought of Torsten or any other man taking her against her will, hurting her, had filled him with nauseating horror. The warrior in him had thought only of helping her and he'd wanted Torsten's blood.

As he'd enveloped her in his arms her whole body had trembled, and she had clung to him, burying her face in his shoulder. He'd wrapped his arms around her and stroked her hair, soothing her for a long while.

Svea and Kar had dealt with Torsten, and the crowd had begun to disperse and make their way to their homes.

Brand had told them he'd come to an agreement with the Saxons and they wouldn't be attacking to-night. They were all safe. And then he'd scooped up Anne and brought her back here.

He pressed a damp cloth to Anne's split lip and she winced. He felt as sick as a dog. He'd broken his promise. He said he'd keep her safe. But it was his own selfish actions that had brought her here and put her in harm's way. By taking her from her home and bringing her to Kald he'd let a brute prey on her. This was all his fault. He'd failed to protect his sister, and now Anne too.

'Did he really set the fire to distract everyone, just so he could lure me away?' she asked, shaking her head.

'Looks like it.'

'Is there much damage? Was anyone hurt?'

'Anne, you've just suffered probably the worst attack of your life and yet you're worried about other people?' he asked, offering her a half-smile before it collapsed again. 'Danes?'

'I don't see your people as any different to ours. In fact, I've grown fond of a few of them,' she said quietly.

His heart lurched. Did she include him in that count? he wondered—and then stopped himself short. *No! Enough.* He must not wish for something that could never be. He had to let her go. He had to return her to her people, where she would be safe. His worst night-mare had come true—he had had a taste of what it would be like if something happened to her and it was more than he could bear.

'When I saw the fire and felt someone grab me I thought it was my father's men, making a rescue attempt.'

He nodded, moving the cloth to the cut near her eye. She flinched again. He wished that had been the case. He wished they had rescued her instead of her having to go through that ordeal. He should have been there with her, guarding her at all times. But now he'd lost her trust.

'Then I realised it was Torsten and I knew it was going to be bad...'

'I'm so sorry, Anne.' He hushed her, his mouth dry. 'You know we're not all like that,' he said, staring steadily into her eyes, his brows drawn together.

But even though he knew he wasn't like that—that he would never act the way Torsten had—he also knew with absolute clarity that he wasn't good enough for her.

Her fingers came up to take the cloth, brushing against his.

'Torsten gives us Northmen a bad name.'

'I know.'

And as if to prove it she leaned in and kissed him. It was the sweetest kiss to the lips, and one he definitely didn't deserve.

He cupped her face in his hands as he pressed his mouth against the tiny cut next to her eye, kissing it better, and then his lips moved back to her mouth, gently touching the cut there too. It was meant to be a goodbye kiss, and it took every ounce of willpower to pull away from her.

'I should leave you to get some rest,' he said, rising off the bed.

'Leave? Don't be absurd—this is your room,' she said, gripping his arm. He winced again. 'You are badly hurt, Brand! Let me see.'

'I have told you I'm fine. It's you I'm worried about.'

She pouted just a little. 'I've let you tend my wounds—you could at least let me do the same for you.'

The fact that his arm actually hurt like hell, and knowing she probably wouldn't let it go, made him relent, and he sat back down on the bed. Plus, he wasn't ready to leave her just yet. Would he ever be?

'Take off your top,' she said. 'Let me look.'

He rolled his eyes, but did as he was told and turned his bandaged arm towards her. Slowly, ever so gently, she peeled away the wool and he heard her breath catch.

'That is not just a little cut,' she scolded him. 'It's deep. Who stitched it for you?'

'Svea. But I fear she doesn't have your skills.' He smiled.

'I would have done it for you. Why didn't you let me?'

'I was being stubborn.' He shrugged.

'You? Stubborn?' She smiled too.

She cleaned the wound with water, and then reached for the ointment on the wooden chest—the one she'd made for Ulf. She applied it with the delicate tips of her fingers before wrapping the bandage around his muscular arms again.

'Svea has done quite a good job, actually. I'm impressed. There—how's that?' she asked.

'Better. Thank you,' he said, and as their eyes met the tension in the room was so thick he thought he could slash it with his sword. Or smash it to smithereens with a kiss.

But he didn't dare kiss her again. He must never kiss her again.

'You should get some rest now, Anne. Actually, we could both do with some rest.' He tried to stand again.

'Will you stay with me, Brand?'

He knew he shouldn't. He should walk out through the door and never look back.

'Please?'

It was the 'please' that was his undoing. He couldn't resist. Because what she was asking for was all that he wanted. He wanted to hold her and stroke her and make everything all right. He wanted to show her that Northmen could be gentle. And he knew that if this was going to be the last night they spent together, he wanted to hold her in his arms.

He gave a short nod and she moved over to one side of the bed and slipped beneath the furs. He did the same and pulled her to his side.

He could stay like this forever, he thought. This was what he wanted for his future, he realised. Anne at his side, always.

And this was what could never be now that he'd let both her and himself down. He could never forgive himself for that.

* * *

Anne woke with a start to see Brand fully dressed and leaning over her, his forefinger to her bruised lips.

'Don't talk, just come. Get dressed,' he whispered. 'Quietly.'

'What's going on?'

'No questions,' he said. 'Just do as I ask. Don't make a sound.'

It was barely light and she glanced at him, wary. She'd had just about enough drama to last a lifetime. Why was he dressed and wearing his leather and chain-mail vest over his tunic—the one he'd worn the night they'd met on the ramparts? And the shadows under his eyes told her he hadn't slept well. That was strange—she'd had the best night's sleep, wrapped in his arms...

She clearly wasn't awake yet—she couldn't think straight. Her limbs felt heavy and she wanted to stay in the warm cosy bed with him. Why was he pulling her to her feet and helping her pull on her pinafore over her smock? Why was he slipping her feet into her ankle boots?

And then she reached up to pat her hair, to see how much of a state it was in, and realised it was braided.

'Did you plait my hair?' she asked, incredulous.

'Not very well.'

'While I was asleep?'

'I used to do my sister's hair...after my parents died.'

A giggle escaped her lips. The Barbarian had plaited her hair. He would never cease to amaze her, she thought.

And then he was leading her down the steps and

across the square to the gates. The pink and golden early-morning light was hazy, just like her mind, as she watched Brand signal to Svea and the fortress guards, who were up on the bridge. They raised the wooden bolt, and then slowly the huge wooden gates began to open.

'Take care, Princess,' Svea said. 'We'll miss you. Come and see us some time, won't you?'

And Anne suddenly realised what was happening.

This was it. Brand was sending her home.

Her heart exploded in pain. She didn't know what she'd been expecting—but not this. She had thought he cared for her, so why was he sending her away? She was now wide awake, and she spun round to Brand, ready to say—what?

'Not now, Anne,' he said, purposely avoiding her eyes, and with his hands on her shoulders he propelled her forward, towards the awaiting convoy of Saxon soldiers.

She was completely taken aback, struggling to come to terms with what was happening. She felt like a caged bird, flapping its wings, desperately trying to escape—and yet it looked as if she was no longer a prisoner. She was being released, set free from his hold.

What was Brand thinking? Why was he sending her back after all the incredible things that had happened between them the day before?

Tears threatened, so she bit the inside of her cheek. She could not make a scene—not with the Saxon soldiers approaching—and he knew it. What she wanted to do was to grab him and shake him and yell at him, but mainly she just wanted to throw her arms around him and beg him not to do this.

Didn't she deserve an explanation? Shouldn't they have talked about this?

And then the ice-cold clench of betrayal gripped her. Had he made a deal after all? Had her father paid him a ransom? And, despite the explicit things he'd done to her yesterday, how he'd made her feel so special, she realised he still hadn't made love to her. Was that because, as he'd said before, she was worth more if her innocence was still intact? She felt sick.

Lord Stanton, who now seemed to be in charge of the Saxon army, cantered towards them on his horse. He nodded at Brand in recognition, then turned his attention to Anne.

'Your Royal Highness, I'm not sure if you remember me. I am Lord Stanton. I'm very pleased to see you.' A look of consternation crossed his face when he saw her swollen lip and blackened eye, but he refrained from commenting on them. 'Your father has missed you. It's time to take you home.'

Her eyes narrowed on them both, and a rage burning like the fire on the rooftops last night swept through her. How dare they make decisions for her? And yet it was as if she had an invisible gag on her mouth. She couldn't protest. What could she say? That she didn't want to go home? That she wanted to stay?

She couldn't. It wasn't appropriate, was it? And she didn't even know what Brand's thoughts were on the matter. For all she knew, he couldn't wait to be rid of her. Had their shared intimacy over the past few days not meant anything to him? It had meant everything to her. She had thought she was falling in love with him.

Instead of saying what was in her mind and in her heart, she took a deep breath, schooling her features. 'Thank you, my lord,' she said. 'I appreciate you and your men coming to fetch me. But might I ask what deal you have struck for my release?'

'Your father was willing to do anything to ensure your safe return, Your Highness.'

Anger seeped through her blood. She was livid now. If she had been sold like one of Brand's animals at a farmers' market, didn't she at least deserve to know what price her father had paid for her and how rich he'd made the Barbarian?

She swung a look at Brand and, damn him, he was acting so cool, so remote. This whole situation felt unreal. Especially as just yesterday she'd let him do unspeakable things to her naked body. He'd made love to her with his mouth—and now he was selling her like an object. Whatever the amount, Brand had made her feel dirty and cheap—like a slave.

And then she almost laughed. He didn't even have slaves. Most Northmen bought and sold slaves, yet this man didn't—it was beneath him. No, he only sold princesses.

Anne wrestled with her emotions, trying to keep them in check. She was on the edge of hysteria. Of course she wanted to go home—didn't she? She couldn't expect to stay in Kald forever, living as Brand's mistress. She was a fool to have entertained the idea, even for a second. It would destroy her reputation. And yet the things he'd done to her yesterday…

She had stupidly thought that he cared for her. That he wouldn't want to let her go. She'd thought he might even marry her. But all this time he must have been scheming behind her back. She didn't want to believe it, and yet the truth was there, right before her eyes, as the Saxon soldiers began to move off the heathland.

Her throat felt thick with the tears she refused to shed—she could not let him see her cry. She wrapped her arms around her midriff and determined not to look at him again.

Her father's messenger, Girladus, who they'd encountered on the way to Kald, came towards Brand, leading Rebel.

'I believe this steed belongs to you?'

'Thank you,' Brand said, taking the reins.

The horse was pleased to see her, and Anne could have wept. She nuzzled the animal's neck, needing the comfort, while Brand busied himself readying Rebel for her to ride. He moved to help her mount the animal, but she put her hands up in a warding-off gesture.

'I can do it,' she said curtly, backing away from him, increasing the distance between them.

'We'd like you to ride in the middle of us, Your Highness. It's the safest place,' Lord Stanton said.

He had treated her with respect so far, and she wondered if, after Crowe, he was next in line on her father's list for her hand in marriage. She imagined most women would find him ruggedly handsome—he had an attractive face—but for some reason he left her feeling cold. There was only one man who had ever stirred her heart and her desire.

Unwanted tears welled in her eyes and she suddenly lost the strength and the will to argue. She didn't even have the energy to talk. She spurred the horse into a trot and took her place behind the new leader of the army. She was pleased to note he was still wearing the navy uniform of her father's men, not the black and yellow that Crowe's close comrades wore.

When she saw Brand turn back towards the gates of Kald, for an awful moment she thought he was heading inside, walking out of her life without even so much as a goodbye, and the pain took her breath away. But then she saw Svea leading out two black stallions, one with a forlorn-looking Lord Crowe positioned on top, his hands bound.

She noticed Brand was hobbling. Did he have another injury she didn't know about? Why did she even care? Brand and his sister seemed to be having a heated conversation, and then Svea threw her arms around him, holding him tight. Why did Svea look so distraught? And then Brand mounted the second horse and fell in behind Anne in the convoy.

She couldn't understand it. None of this was making any sense. She rubbed her temple, where a dull pain was starting to throb.

'What are you doing?' she demanded, turning round in the saddle to speak to him, already breaking her own rule of not looking at him.

'I wanted to see you safely home. And Crowe locked up.'

She sat up straight. 'I was safe at home until you came along! My father's men can look after me from here.' And then a thought struck her. 'By escorting me home, you'll be putting yourself in danger. You might be arrested by my father's men the moment you set foot in Termarth.'

He shrugged. 'I've decided to come anyway.'

And as the snake-like trail of soldiers in navy uniforms began to leave the kingdom of Kald she knew she must withdraw from him. She could never forgive him for this. Any of it. And yet she still couldn't help but worry about what would become of him once they arrived at the castle.

They rode all morning in silence, along the coast she'd grown to love, and she wished he'd never come into her life and taken her away, opening her eyes to everything the world around her had to offer. Even the storm hadn't dampened her fascination with the sea, and she didn't think she'd ever tire of its wild beauty. Not seeing it every day would cause her great pain. Not seeing Brand every day would be...

No! She must not do that. She must not think of him.

Her mind kept running over the past few days for any signs she'd missed of his betrayal. He'd completely fooled her, and she resolved not to let it happen again. She knew she had to get away from him to process what had happened, but he was riding right behind her, keeping her in his sights, so escape was impossible.

It was unnerving—like having a constant dark shadow looming over her. She could feel his blue gaze burning a hole into her back and it was making her ridiculously agitated, her fingers trembling on the reins. She felt exposed, vulnerable, and sat rigid, trying to block him out. Everything about his nearness reminded her of how she'd felt in his arms last night, and in the afternoon, how she'd flourished beneath his touch. How he'd brought her to aching, throbbing life like a flower blooming in the sun, opening her up to a world of beauty and possibility.

And now he was tearing her down and she was literally shrivelling and closing up, making herself impenetrable.

But what surprised her and disturbed her the most was that she still wanted him. How could she still feel that way after all he'd done? She loathed herself and shuddered at her own weakness.

Suddenly Brand was right there, riding beside her. 'Are you warm enough, Highness?' he asked. 'You're shivering.'

She bristled at the formality of him using her title. 'Why are you still here?' she bit out, rounding on him.

She saw the Saxon soldiers raise their eyebrows at her furious tone, but right now she didn't care. She'd had enough of men and all their schemes, their thirst for power with no regard for anyone else's thoughts or feelings.

'Now that you have what you want, why don't you just leave?'

She thought she saw him recoil slightly from her words, but his eyes remained cool and steady. 'I told you—I promised to see you safely home.'

It was like looking into the unwavering gaze of one

of the carved heads of those monsters mounted on his ships. How could he be so cold, so unfeeling? She had the sudden desire to lash out at him, to try to hurt him as he was hurting her, to provoke a reaction.

Her chin tilted up. 'Lord Stanton, after the fall from grace of Lord Crowe, and therefore the cancellation of my wedding, are you aware of my father's plans? Does he have any other potential suitors lined up for me?'

Brand's eyes narrowed on her and she saw him tighten his grip on his horse's reins.

'I'm afraid I don't know. You'll have to ask your father that, Your Highness, when we arrive back at Termarth.'

'I'll be sure to do that, Lord Stanton,' she said, smiling sweetly, cutting Brand a look. 'As soon as I get home.'

She knew she was being childish, but she couldn't help herself.

The time seemed to drag, and when they finally stopped for a rest, and Lord Stanton tied up Rebel and helped Anne down from the horse, she made sure she stayed away from Brand. He tried to approach her and offer her some bread, telling her she should eat something as she had missed breakfast, but she shunned him.

'You're so wilful—do you know that?' he said, raking his hand over his hair.

'I pride myself on it.'

He grimaced, stuffing his hands into his leather vest and stalking away. It was then that she realised, in dismay, that they were surrounded by a swathe of pretty yellow primroses. They'd stopped in the forest where they'd shared their first kiss. And, no matter how much she wanted to hate him, her heart still ached for her Barbarian.

Every sight or sound on this journey stirred a memory, and Brand was finding it increasingly difficult to keep up a front.

He shifted in his seat. Anne had been travelling further and further ahead of him for the past few hours, ever since they'd stopped for a rest in the forest where he'd first kissed her. He'd been a brute since that first night, proving she could definitely do better than the likes of him. But when she'd mentioned her father finding another suitor for her it had felt as if she'd taken his axe and swung it into his chest, ripping it open.

He knew this journey would be different. For a start, Anne was no longer his prisoner, and she was surrounded by the King's men and their protection, not nestled in his arms, between his thighs. And she was heading back to Termarth. He was not whisking her off to Kald, bringing her home.

This time, the journey would be slow and steady, and she'd have people to look after her every need. He knew this was how it should be, and yet he longed for it to be as it had been before—just the two of them. He wanted her as much now as he had when he'd pulled her into his chest that first night. Actually, he wanted her more.

By the time they stopped to pitch their tents that evening, in a sheltered redwood grove, his mood was black. Listening to her talk to Lord Stanton and some of the other men, rather than speaking to him, was infuriating. He was glad she didn't have to sleep out in the elements, surrounded by monsters like Torsten, and yet watching the Saxon men fall over themselves in their attempts to help her off Rebel, or to show her to her tent, was maddening.

He nestled down to rest against a tangled tree trunk, far enough away from the soldiers cooking meat over a fire and close enough to Anne's tent to keep an eye on it, to check she was safe.

Yesterday at the boathouse it had been incredible, and he wanted to relive it over and over again. That was where he'd choose to spend his life—in her arms, with her looking at him as if he was her whole world. But last night, as he'd held her and soothed her to sleep, he'd told himself it was for the last time. He'd proved he couldn't protect her…that he wasn't good enough for her.

He'd hardly slept, watching her sleep, playing with her hair and wondering if he was doing the right thing.

He had made no deal with the Saxon soldiers. He realised he had never really wanted a ransom for Anne—he'd just used that as an excuse to get to know her. But if she wanted to believe he had accepted a reward for her return, then so be it. It was his way of gently pushing her away, of letting her go.

He had been honest and told Lord Stanton that Crowe had killed his father, and when he'd insisted on escorting Anne home the man had been decent, agreeing to him joining them on the journey. Brand knew he was risking capture and punishment when he reached Termarth, but he was prepared to take that risk—he would do anything to ensure Anne's safety.

And if he did make it out of this alive, he would just have to find another way to appease his people and provide for them.

He should have told Anne about his talk with Stanton and about her leaving Kald before he'd slept beside her all night, but he'd put it off. There had been a large part of him that had wanted to break the agreement and sail off with her into the sunset this morning, but he'd known that was impossible.

She didn't belong to him. She could never be his. He had to hand her back.

But he wouldn't be without her until he'd deposited her into the hands of the King. Yet being this close to her and not being able to talk to her, or touch her, was torture.

He knew she was furious with him for making a deal behind her back. He could tell she was trying to distance herself from him by the way her body stiffened every time he came near her, by the way her chin tipped up, the way she stumbled away to avoid touching him. And that was the way it had to be—what needed to happen. But knowing that didn't help. It still hurt. It wasn't what he wanted.

They'd barely spoken since they'd left Kald, and now Brand wanted to storm into her tent, take her in his arms and kiss her. To cut through the tension. To forget everything else and just seek pleasure in each other's bodies. But he knew the guards wouldn't let him anywhere near her. Hell, she might not either. And saying goodbye to her tomorrow would be easier if she was still furious with him.

He was just settling down for another uncomfortable night, watching the entrance to her tent, when the canvas was cast aside and she stepped out. Their eyes collided with the force of two shields clashing, bringing him to attention, before she turned and headed in the direction of Lord Stanton and the smell of roasting meat. He saw the ealdorman offer her a plate of food and she accepted it with a smile. Jealousy burned.

He took his knife out of his belt and began to sharpen it against a stone…just for something to do. He knew the Saxon men were wary of him, and he didn't blame them. They'd all seen his fight with Crowe. It seemed Crowe's men had returned to Calhourn, though, and Stanton was responsible for his own *fyrd*, who would do the King's bidding.

Would Stanton be King Eallesborough's second choice of suitor for Anne? he wondered. He would probably be considered much more attractive to a woman than Crowe, with his easy smile and his full head of dark hair. Had Anne had these thoughts earlier—was that why she'd mentioned it?

The thought of her with any man except him made Brand incensed and he ran the blade harder across the stone, foolishly slicing his finger open. *'Skit!'*

'Are you all right?'

He glanced up to see Anne coming towards him.

'It's just a scratch,' he said, popping his finger in his mouth to draw off the blood.

'You should be more careful. Here, I've brought you some food.'

He looked up at her, suspicious of her kindness.

'I'm fine, thanks. I can fend for myself.'

'And you have the nerve to call me stubborn?' she said, shaking her head. 'Well, just for once, why don't you swallow your pride and eat what my father's men have cooked and be grateful?'

She bent over and set the plate down on the grass next to him.

'Is this where you're planning to sleep?' she asked.

'Why not? It'll be the third or fourth time I've slept out under the stars this week. I'm getting used to it.'

'Lord Stanton says he can find room for you in one of the tents if you like.'

He narrowed his eyes on her. 'How kind of him. Will you be finding room for him in yours?'

'What?'

'He seems to like you, and you him. What's stopping you?'

He knew he'd gone too far. He saw it in the wounded flare of her eyes, the stricken set of her mouth. But he was hurt. And he was angry—but with himself mainly.

'How dare you?' she spat, her quiet anger unfurling. 'After all you've done. How can you sit there and criticise me? I hate you. I—I think I shall go to my bed early. And I shall ask if I can ride at the front tomorrow, so we don't have to see or speak to each other again.'

She turned on her heel, started to walk away.

'Then they'll really know how I affect you, Princess.

Bringing me food, then complaining about being in my company… They'll think you're afflicted.'

She stopped and glanced back, her lips pursed together. 'I don't care what they think. All I know is that I was wrong about you. And if I ever have to speak with you again it will be too soon.'

She stalked back to her tent and threw the canvas flap shut.

Well, at least she hadn't gone to Stanton, Brand thought wryly. He ran a hand over his face. What the hell was he doing? He didn't even know why he'd said those things. He didn't mean any of it. But if he was trying to keep her feeling furious with him, he was certainly going about it the right way.

When the walls of Termarth finally came into view the next day, Anne was surprised at how much the sight of the castle comforted her. The dramatic silver stone walls around the tower had always made her feel trapped before, but when the drawbridge was lowered and the gargantuan wooden doors opened up, she felt as if the walls were giant arms, reaching out to capture her in a welcoming embrace. Despite her lonely upbringing, it was still her home, and after everything that had happened, she felt so weary and out of sorts.

She had stuck to her word and ridden at the front with Lord Stanton today, rather than in the middle of the convoy, so she didn't have to talk to the Barbarian. And she'd forced herself not to look at him at all—even though she'd found it excruciatingly hard. Just as water was vital to her survival, she'd found herself needing to drink him in, to check he was still there. But the cruel words he'd spoken to her last night had struck deep, and she knew she couldn't forgive him for all this.

She took in the familiar landmarks of the pulsing kingdom, trying to lift her spirits. People lined the streets to celebrate the safe return of their Princess, cheering and waving, and she plastered on a smile, moved her hand to and fro in the air. But her mind was in complete and utter chaos.

She had been gone for less than a week, but she had changed so much in that time. Everything was different. She would have to face her father and pretend everything was fine when it was far from it, and she didn't know how she would be able to move on with her life. She couldn't picture her future without Brand in it.

Most of the army dispersed when they were inside the city walls, and just a small group of Lord Stanton's trusted soldiers, as well as Brand, escorted her to the steps of the castle keep. She was shocked when she saw her father was waiting for her, his eyes shining with tears.

As Lord Stanton helped her down from Rebel the King extended his hand and his thanks to the man, before enveloping Anne in a warm hug. She couldn't remember the last time her father had embraced her like that, and she was momentarily stunned.

'I'm so sorry, Anne,' he said, holding her close. 'I thought I'd lost you and I was so scared. Are you all right, daughter? Have you been hurt?'

'I'm fine, Father,' she whispered.

But a sob threatened to escape, and then she couldn't

hold it in any longer. It was as if his embrace had melted the ice on the winter hilltops, and suddenly her tears and pain were like unstoppable water, rushing down. He put his arm around her and began to lead her up the steps to go inside.

But just before she reached the door something made her turn back and look. She had to see him one last time.

And as she glanced over at the group of men who had seen her home, she saw Lord Stanton talking with Brand. He met her gaze over the other man's shoulder. Was he leaving and about to walk out of her life forever? Or were her father's men going to restrain him? Panic stirred in her chest. Either way, she knew she might never see him again, and that was the worst pain of all.

Chapter Twelve

Brand paced up and down in his room. He'd never slept in a castle before, and the room was impressive. Stanton had apologised, saying it was the best he could do at short notice, but Brand had been expecting nothing more than the servants' quarters.

He hated to admit it, but he liked the man. If the King had him in mind as a suitor for Anne, he knew he couldn't have chosen better himself, although the thought caused him pain.

Turning his attention back to the room—anything to try to rid his thoughts of her—he tried out the large bed for comfort, and then inspected some kind of barrel contraption up the corner. But the view was what made the room superb—of the rain-washed green and verdant pastures past the city walls. But although it was beautiful, the scene just served to remind him of the colour of Anne's beautiful eyes, so he was glad when finally it became cloaked in darkness.

He wasn't very good at being on Saxon territory, but

the King had requested a meeting with him the next morning. He hadn't been able to say no—after all, he was grateful he hadn't been thrown into the castle dungeon. He didn't expect that he could return the Princess to her home, after kidnapping her and fighting her betrothed, and be excused.

He wondered what would be said. If he'd been the King, after he'd taken one look at his battered and bruised daughter he would have rammed a sword through the man who was responsible. He should be dead by now, he thought. And if he was going to die he had just one regret. He should have made Anne his lover while he had the chance.

After his harsh treatment of her the night before she'd been true to her word and turned her back on him all day—right up until that last moment, when she'd given him a final glance over her shoulder as she'd entered the castle.

As he lay on the bed, staring up at the ceiling, he could hear Svea's voice ringing in his ears. 'If you take her back, they will be sure to kill you,' she'd said to him by the gates as he'd hugged her and said goodbye.

'It's something I have to do,' he'd told her. 'I have to make amends.'

And he had, in a way. He had seen Anne safely home, as he'd promised. And for Svea he had made sure Stanton had taken Crowe to the dungeon.

If he were to be set free from Termarth he would make things right with his people. He wondered how they would feel when they found out that he'd handed Anne back without earning a ransom for her.

He started when he heard a light knock at the door, and he swung off the bed and pulled it open.

A small, hooded figure stood in the doorway, and after looking from side to side along the corridor tilted her head up to face him.

Anne.

Anne had come to see him.

'Can I come in?'

He stepped back to allow her room to enter, and once she'd crossed the threshold he closed the door behind her. When she lowered her hood, his heart exploded in his chest. The bruise around her eye was beginning to turn a bluish yellow, but even so she was still the most exquisite woman he'd ever seen.

She had obviously just bathed—her glossy dark brown hair was still damp, although it had been braided into two immaculate plaits on either side of her head. She was dressed in a ruby silk gown that drew in her waist and had long flared sleeves and a full skirt. She looked every bit the pure and perfect Royal Princess and his mouth turned to dust.

'You shouldn't be here, Anne.'

'Neither should you,' she said. 'The Saxons won't like a Northman staying in the castle. They could hurt you. You may not be safe.'

He smiled wryly. 'Still worrying about me, Anne?' He shook his head. 'You know I don't wound easily. Whereas you... Your father—?'

'Is asleep. No one saw me come here.'

He released a breath and saw her swallow, watched

the pulse flicker at the base of her throat. What was she doing here?

'The King—was he pleased to see you?' he asked.

Brand was surprised to see her eyes swim with tears. 'Yes.' She nodded, smiling. 'He confessed that he had missed me. Can you believe it?'

He smiled. 'I can. I knew when I saw the size of that army that you might have misjudged the extent of his feelings for you.'

She wrung her hands. 'He apologised for his treatment of me since my mother died. Apparently, I remind him of her. He said that sometimes it's too painful for him to look at me. And after she passed away he became obsessed with wanting to protect me and keep me safe.'

'I can understand that,' he said, his lips twisting.

He thought perhaps he and the King might just have something in common. They would both go to great lengths to keep Anne safe.

'He has admitted he went the wrong way about it, though. He said he saw how the people cared for me when I was gone, and he has even asked me to be a part of his witan. He said I have such a loyal following he believes my opinions and ideas should be heard.'

Brand nodded. 'I am glad he has seen sense, Anne. But now you must too. You need to turn around and leave. You mustn't be seen here with me.' He motioned to their surroundings, hoping she'd understand what he meant.

'You can't give me orders any more, Brand. Not here.'

His brow furrowed. 'I'm thinking of you. Reputation is everything, surely?'

'To you. So much so that you let me believe you're some kind of barbarian,' she accused. 'And you did it again when we left Kald. Why did you let me think the worst of you, Brand? Why didn't you defend yourself? Lord Stanton told me… Why didn't *you* tell me you hadn't taken the gold my father offered?'

He ran a hand over his hair. So she knew the truth. She knew he had kept his word on that, at least.

'Everyone believes all kinds of things about me. It's not my job to set them straight.'

'Even me? After everything we've been through? I think you owe me a better explanation than that.'

He stood with his hands on his hips, his head bowed. 'I did promise my men a ransom for you, Anne. So I am all the things you believed. And I thought it would be easier saying goodbye to you if you still thought badly of me. But, no, the gold was never important to me.'

'If it wasn't the gold, what was it?' she asked, closing the gap between them. 'You could have killed Lord Crowe the night you came to Termarth if you had wanted to. Instead, you took me… If it wasn't for the ransom, why didn't you just leave me out of it?'

'And where would have been the fun in that?' He grinned, but his smile didn't quite reach his eyes. 'When I heard you were going to marry him, I guess all rational thought was lost. I wanted to hurt Crowe, and I knew I could get to him through you. But I'd be lying if I said I didn't take you for selfish reasons. I wanted to get to know you, Anne. You, the girl who helped me when I was at my lowest. I'd thought of you so often. And I'm ashamed to say I wanted to stop your wedding... But the more I got to know you, the more I realised *you* were the real treasure—not the gold or silver your father could offer.' He reached out to stroke her face. 'You really are priceless, Anne.'

Her eyes were swimming with tears again, and one slipped down her cheek. She turned her face into his palm and it felt so good to touch her again.

'My father says he and his witan will be speaking with you in the morning. I will talk to him, Brand. I will ask him to treat you well.'

Brand wondered what they would do to him. Would he be put to death, or would that be too good for him? Looking at Anne now, he didn't really care. Now he'd lost her, he had lost almost everything.

'Please. Don't worry about me, Anne,' he reassured her. 'I've made my peace with whatever happens now. I just want you to know I'm sorry. I hope what I have put you through hasn't caused you too much distress. I wanted to make it up to you and see you back home safely.'

Anne toyed with something in her hand, and he saw her swallow before taking a deep breath.

'Here,' she said, holding something out to him. 'This belongs to you.'

She placed a silver ring with a Y-like symbol on it into his open palm.

His head shot up. 'You kept it?' He shook his head. 'All these years you have kept it safe? Why did you even take it?'

'I heard the soldiers coming and I saw the rune on it. I realised you must be a Dane so I took it, hoping they wouldn't see it and…and finish you off.'

His eyebrows pulled together. 'My father gave it to me. It's the symbol of the elk. It offers protection. I thought you'd stolen it.'

Anne blanched. 'I would never—'

She had kept the ring safe in a little trinket box for years. She had often thought about that beautiful blue-eyed boy she'd met in the meadow. She'd just never put two and two together when she'd met Brand on the castle ramparts.

She knew that returning the ring to him wouldn't be enough to heal his hurt or fill the void of losing his parents, but now, standing here, she wondered, even hoped, if she could. Faced with his closeness, she realised she still wanted him. She loved him. And she wanted to heal his heart.

It was mad to think it had only been a week since they'd met. So much had happened…so much had changed. But the only thing that mattered was whether or not he still wanted her.

'Brand, I have to tell you something,' she began bravely, although she couldn't help but play with the tassels on her dress. 'In the hut with Torsten, I shut my eyes and wished to be somewhere else. I longed to be back on that boat with you, free from all this. All I could think about was you and whether I'd see you again.'

'Anne—' He shook his head, couldn't look her in

the eye. He knew what she was about to say, and he knew he should stop her now—before he did something reckless. Something insane.

'Brand, I know you blame yourself for what happened to me, just as you do with Svea, but you mustn't. I'm fine. You got to me in time.'

He closed his eyes briefly and Anne seized the moment to bravely step forward and wrap her hand around his beard, tugging him closer.

He inclined his head in that smouldering way she'd grown used to. 'Brand, I want you to kiss me.'

His eyes dipped to her lips. 'Here?'

'Yes.'

'Are you trying to get me killed?' he whispered, as he bent his head and his lips lightly touched hers. 'It would be worth it.'

His arms came around her waist and he kissed her slowly, trailing his tongue along her lips and stealing it into her mouth, stroking against hers in an intense, deep, sensual exploration. She sank against him, a melting sensation making her knees weak, forcing her to wrap her arms around his shoulders to stop herself from falling.

When he finally raised his head she was breathless. Their faces were so close she could see tiny flecks of gold in his dilated blue eyes. And his skin smelt of musk and the sea.

'Do you still want me, Brand?'

'More than I've ever wanted anything else in my life. But it would be wrong, Anne.'

'If it's wrong, why does it feel so right?' she asked,

as she raised herself onto her tiptoes and pressed her curves fully against him, as if she'd been starved of his touch.

He groaned. 'Anne...'

'Make love to me, Brand.'

He briefly closed his eyes, as if that was all he needed to hear, and then he drew her even closer to him, so their entire bodies were touching. And when he kissed her again she knew he'd made his decision. Because this kiss was different from any other. It was raw and unapologetic. And his tongue didn't hesitate to invade her lips in the most impassioned, frantic open-mouthed kiss...as if he was determined now to give them both what they wanted at last...as if he'd finally been given permission to take what was his.

The kiss detonated a fire in her stomach, sending a flame of butterflies soaring, but while her tentative, trembling hands stole over his cheekbones and into his hair, his confident, reassuring fingers travelled over her hips to grasp her bottom, moulding her to his intimate ridges. And she revelled in the feeling of being in his arms again, coming to life under his touch.

His large palms curved round her front, grazing up to cover her breasts, but the thick, expensive material of her dress was annoyingly in the way.

He nuzzled and nipped at her neck. 'You're wearing far too many clothes, Anne.' When he kissed her again, he tugged at the cords at the back of her gown to loosen it. 'Turn around,' he said.

On unsteady feet, she slowly spun, so that her back was to him and he could unlace the material, and it felt incredibly intimate. Her heart was in her mouth. The sleeves fell from her shoulders first, allowing him to place little kisses there, and then the gown dropped down her arms, loosening around her waist and sinking to her hips.

Brand used both hands to push it down over her bottom so it pooled at her feet. She heard his sharp intake of breath and swallowed in anticipation of his touch, tiny tingles rushing down her spine. She felt his breath on her neck first, and then one arm came around her waist, tugging her back towards him. She tipped her head to rest it in the curve of his shoulder, further exposing her bare upper body to him, and his handsome hands came up to play with her breasts.

He was gentle, but demanding, clearly desperate to feel every inch of her skin, hungry to roll her achingly hard nipples between his fingers as his lips moved over her collarbone.

She could feel his erection nudging between her buttocks and she wanted to explore him, as he was exploring her, so she roamed her hands down to feel the hard muscles of his thighs.

He growled and twisted her round to face him, pulling her into his large, muscular body. His fingers hooked beneath her undergarments, pushing them down to the floor to meet the rest of her clothes. Now she stood before him completely naked, and she felt so exposed under his heated gaze.

She shivered, and yet she felt incredibly hot at the same time. 'Brand...' she whispered, trying to cover herself up with her tiny hands.

He reached for her wrists and gently pressed them to her sides. 'I've never seen anyone or anything so beautiful in my whole life. Don't hide from me, Anne, let me look at you.'

He stepped back to rake his eyes all over her body and then dealt with his own clothes quickly, as if he couldn't wait now. He pulled his leather vest and his tunic over his head, tossing them to the floor, unfastened his belt, and she was transfixed by his body.

'Help me, Anne. Undress me.'

She reached out, fumbling with his trousers, fiercely tugging the cord and pushing them down so they bunched around his calves—and he laughed at her eagerness. And finally there was no material barrier between them and it was her turn to explore him. She ran her gaze and fingers over all the old and new scars on his torso. She wasn't shocked—she'd seen them before. Maybe she didn't have all the facts, but she had a vague idea. She determined to find out about the story behind every single one.

Her palms roamed down his back and over the firm globes of his bottom. And she allowed herself to luxuriate in exploring his warm, solid skin, which felt amazing pressed against the smoothness of her own. His fingers trailed over her thighs and up, reaching between her legs to find her secret heated places. She parted her thighs to allow him better access, but she wasn't sure she could stand up while he touched her. Her legs felt unsteady and her knees nearly gave way when his fingers stroked and delved inside her.

Throwing one arm around his neck for support, she

could feel his hard length pressing into her hip, and she mustered up the courage to move her other hand down between their bodies to take hold of him in her palm.

He groaned, resting his forehead against hers. She pushed him back against the wall and dropped to her knees to take him in her mouth. A string of expletives tore from his lips. With one hand braced on the wall, the other in her hair, he drew her head closer, over his length, and she knew he was going slowly out of his mind. *Good.* She wanted to torture him with pleasure, just as he had done to her the other night.

'Anne, stop!' he said, desperately tugging at her shoulders, trying to drag her back up towards him.

'Don't you like it?' she whispered. 'Am I doing something wrong?'

'It feels incredible,' he said, his wide blue eyes staring down at her. 'But I want you…and any more of that and you'll take me over the edge.'

He cupped her bottom and she wrapped her legs around his hips as he carried her over to the bed.

He laid her on the furs and came down beside her, kissing her slowly, his hands trailing up and down her back, as if he were giving her time to change her mind. He kissed her so tenderly she wondered how such a strong, fierce man could be so gentle. How could she and everyone else have got him so wrong? She wanted them to know what she knew. She wanted to shout it from the castle ramparts.

He caught her wrists between his hands again and pressed them to the bed above her head. And then he kissed and stroked his way over her lips, her heaving breasts and her taut stomach, and she knew he was preparing her for what was to come. Every stroke was making her hot with need. She wriggled closer, wanting to feel more of his silky hardness against her thigh. She wanted him inside her. She knew she was ready.

His palms drifted up her silky-smooth calves and he pulled her leg over his hip. Rolling on top of her, he pushed her thighs wide apart with his knee, holding them open as he reached between her legs to touch her again. He parted her intimate folds and slid his fingers inside her, and she gave a feminine growl of disbelief. Drawing them back out, he found her nub and teased it with his thumb, making her writhe with pleasure.

'This is your chance to change your mind, Anne. You can still leave… I'm not going to try to convince you that this is the right thing to do. We both know it isn't. But I'm no saint, Anne. I want you anyway.'

He was making her feel hot, feverish, needy. She was spiralling out of control, and she knew she must be making way too much noise as he gently put his hand over her mouth.

'Shh.' When he removed his hand he kissed her slowly, deeply, as he guided himself to her entrance. 'Are you sure, Anne?'

'Yes. Please, Brand, now.'

He thrust inside her and she tightened around him, her arms coming up to grasp his shoulders. He stilled, his forehead resting against hers for a second, giving her time to adapt to the feel of him. With the next thrust he breached her wall, edging deeper inside her, possessing her. And it felt so good, so right. He continued to kiss her and stroke her until her body began to relax around him.

He set the rhythm, every thrust allowing him a little deeper inside her tight body. Pure toe-curling pleasure shafted through her. And when she wrapped her legs around his hips, finally taking him all the way in, he groaned. She was totally impaled, pinned to the bed by his hips, which were thrusting faster and faster, his own urgency increasing.

'Oh, God, don't stop, Brand. Don't ever stop.'

Her hands were in a feral frenzy now, her nails tearing into his shoulders, down his back, gripping his bottom, pulling him into her. Their bodies were slick with sweat. She wanted him deeper, harder, faster.

And then her whole body tensed and shivered, and she screamed as her orgasm took her over. Brand felt every muscle in his body tighten. He thrust into her one last time and her name roared from his lips as the explosive rush of his climax pulsed powerfully inside her.

When Brand finally stirred, he realised he was still inside her. What the hell had just happened? Had he lost consciousness? He felt shaky, and didn't even have the strength to withdraw from her body. He wanted to stay like this, buried deep inside Anne, forever.

He felt her chest rise and fall—was she sleeping?— and violent emotions ricocheted through him. It had never, ever felt like that before. He'd never had such a fierce need to take someone so thoroughly, to possess her, make her his.

He had spent his life consumed with vengeance, and

in the space of a week Anne had torn down the fortress he'd built over the years… Now he was consumed with something else entirely. Was this love?

He was worried he was crushing Anne with his weight, so he gently rolled off her, pulling the curve of her back into his chest, his fingers lightly tracing over her stomach.

'You're awake,' she said, covering his hand with her own.

'I think I blacked out for a while.'

'Is it always like that?' she asked. 'So intense? So incredible?'

'It's never been like that for me before.' He planted little kisses along her shoulder.

'I guess you've never had sex in a castle before.' And then she giggled.

'You should know by now that I have expensive taste,' he said.

She laughed again. 'What else don't I know about you?'

He stroked his hands up to cup the weight of her breast, and she wriggled her bottom back against him. 'You're playing a dangerous game,' he warned. He stroked the soft skin of her chest and torso some more. And then, 'What's that over there in the corner?' he asked, nodding at the barrel, trying to distract her from torturing him further.

'Ah, now, that is how we like to bathe. We fill the barrel with hot water and get in it.'

He raised his eyebrows into her hair. 'Much more civilised than the sea, then.'

'Yes, I can't see you using one of those.' She laughed again, and it was infectious. 'You're much too wild.'

'I could be wild in that.'

She made that little movement against him again, as if to torment him, and he growled, rolling her onto her stomach and plunging all the way into her from behind. She gasped at the sudden intimacy. But he loved it when she raised her bottom to meet his next thrust, as if she wanted to feel him deep inside her again.

He lifted her smooth thighs up off the bed, so he could access her secret places with his hands as he rocked into her, and she cried out. Brand hushed her, whispering all the things he wanted to do to her into her ear. And she surprised him when she came up on her knees, pressing back against his chest, deepening their connection. She curled her arms back around his neck and he revelled in having full access to her body.

He squeezed her breasts with one hand, tugging at her hardened nipples, working his other hand between her legs.

'I told you I'd make you mine, Anne,' he whispered as he thrust deeper inside her, taking her with him into an excruciating spiral of pleasure he never wanted to end.

Chapter Thirteen

The next time Brand woke he saw that a shaft of daylight was streaming into the room. His limbs were heavy, yet relaxed, and his body felt sated at last. But when he turned his head towards Anne she wasn't there. He was alone in the bed.

He sat bolt upright. She wasn't even in the room. When had she left him?

He wondered if he might have dreamed everything that had happened, but then he realised he was naked, and he could smell her floral scent on the furs. Plus, he didn't think he could have dreamed something as amazing as the night they'd just had together.

He dressed, and waited to be taken before the King, like Stanton had said. He hoped the King was a man of his word and he wouldn't just be fetched and walked to the gallows, hung as the whole kingdom of Termarth looked on. Including Anne.

Now Anne had let him take her he felt more alive than ever, and he didn't think he was ready to die just yet.

It was the longest morning of his life, but the guards finally came to fetch him. His pulse picked up pace as they led him through long stone corridors and a large wooden door into a grand hall. The King sat in a wooden throne at the head of the ornate room, monopolising the attention of what looked to be his council. And at his side sat Anne, dressed in an elegant burgundy gown.

Brand felt a punch to his gut. Would his reaction to her always be like this? he wondered.

As he strode forward, with all eyes upon him, his senses were on high alert. He was aware of every movement. It was as if the witan had never set eyes on a Dane before. They all seemed to balk or cringe at the sight of him, turning their gaze away. And he couldn't blame them. They were looking at the man who had abducted their Princess and imprisoned the leader of their army.

When he reached the steps in front of the King on his raised platform Brand stopped. Nothing could have prevented him from taking another furtive glance at Anne as the all-too-familiar scent of her wrapped around him in a kind of warm embrace. She looked radiant this morning, her skin glowing, her eyes bright. Her robes were as beautiful as her personality. And yet she still had that blue bruise around her eye—a reminder to everyone in the room of her attack. Of him not being able to protect her.

He wiped his hands on his trousers.

'I sent for you, Brand Ivarsson of Kald, as I hoped to satisfy my curiosity in meeting you at last,' the King said.

'It is an honour to meet you, King Eallesborough.'

The King was a tallish man with a slight build, grey hair and a neatly trimmed moustache and beard. He had a calm demeanour and considered Brand with thoughtful green eyes.

'I have heard much about you and I am yet to decipher which parts are true. But tell me first—why did you take my daughter from me?'

Brand wasn't used to defending himself, or his actions, but right now he knew that he must. He owed it to Anne and her father.

'At first it was for revenge. It was my ambition to wound your ally, Lord Crowe.'

The King took a sideways glance at Anne. 'My daughter tells me Ealdorman Crowe hurt your family.'

'Yes. He killed my father and hurt my sister. He also desolated other Saxon villages, blaming the Northmen. I believe in order to send people your way and make more men willing to fight for you—against us. Where I come from, things cannot be put right until blood has been repaid. It is my right to take revenge.'

'Where you come from? And yet here you are in Termarth. Here, we do not take things into our own hands—things are not resolved this way. And you took my daughter as part of this feud?'

'Yes, King Eallesborough.'

He couldn't bring himself to look at Anne again. Did her father know he had taken her in every sense of the word? Brand had once hoped that after he'd had her he would grow bored and move past his desire, but now he knew that would never be possible. The infuriating, unrelenting longing for her was still there. Worse, even, because it wasn't just her body that he longed for. He wanted her by his side always. If he were ever to take a wife, she would be the only woman he could marry.

'But I realised it was wrong to have involved the Princess, so I have returned her safely to you.'

'That you have…but I see she is much changed.' The King glanced over at his daughter and his eyes softened. 'Why, I wonder, did you involve her at all?'

Brand felt a flicker of irritation in his jaw. What did the King want him to say? 'At first it was in the hope that you might pay a ransom for her. We had a bad harvest and a cold winter in Kald this year. And Saxons slaughtered our animals. Perhaps I wanted to earn back what had been taken from us.'

'But now?'

'I don't want your gold.'

The King's eyes narrowed on him. 'I wonder what it is that you do want?'

'I am willing to accept any punishment you see fit to bestow upon me for taking your daughter. But as for what I want… I wish to protect our land in Kald—and I want peace. We came here for a better life, hoping to farm, to trade…'

'Is that all?' asked the King wryly, and Brand had an inkling that he knew much more than he was letting on. 'And my daughter has helped you come to this conclusion?'

For the first time in his life Brand felt as if his emotions were being exposed—as if a blade had been brought down on his head to reveal all the deepest, darkest thoughts and feelings hidden beneath the surface.

Anne was toying with a tassel on a cushion and he tried to tear his eyes away from her beautiful fingers as they reminded him of how they had played with his body last night. But when his eyes moved up to her face, her lips, he remembered how she'd taken him in her mouth, those soft, full lips curling around him…

This was not helping. He needed to focus. Just being in the same room as her was torture—could anyone tell what he was thinking? Could anyone tell that he loved her?

'What else has my daughter changed your opinion on?' the King asked, but it must have been a rhetorical question as he then turned to his council. 'She seems to have a way of changing opinion. When you took her from us, there was uproar among the people here. I had never realised how much she meant to them. She seems to be a symbol of hope.'

Brand nodded—hadn't she been the same for him all these years?

'You took that hope away, and yet I am grateful that you have brought it back.' The King turned to his witan. 'My lords, Anne, you may now leave us. I would like to talk to Brand Ivarsson alone.'

'Father—' Anne began, rising to her feet.

She was wringing her hands in that way she did when she was nervous, or concerned. Was she worrying about him? Brand wondered.

'It's all right, Anne,' the King reassured her. 'We are just going to talk.'

Brand was almost relieved when Anne performed a little curtsy and reluctantly walked away, her skirts swishing behind her. He could breathe again…think clearly. When the last of the ealdormen had left the room, the King strolled over to a table and poured two goblets of red wine. He pulled out a chair and sat down, before motioning to Brand to take the seat next to him.

'Some of my witan believe I should have you killed for stealing the Princess.'

'It would be no more than I deserve.'

'Ah, but my daughter would be most displeased,' said King Eallesborough, his hands steepled in front of him. 'She tells me you treated her well—were kind to her. Even protected her.'

Brand swallowed. *Not very well.*

'It seems you have saved her from an unhappy marriage. And brought to my attention a thorn in my side in Crowe, for which I thank you. You are a boat builder, Brand Ivarsson?'

'I am.' Brand's brow furrowed. This was not going the way he had expected the conversation to progress. He had thought he'd be dragged in here and beaten, or beheaded. But instead Anne's father, the King, was talking of his beloved ships.

'Your boats can sail on the ocean as well as up rivers?'

'Yes.'

'I would like to see these ships. I have long believed boats are a necessity in protecting this island that we live on, and that they will also help with trade. I believe our river here in Termarth leads to the ocean, where your settlement is? These two sites, adjoined by water, are of strategic importance.' He picked up one of the goblets and handed it to Brand. 'I would like to talk about you building me some ships and setting up a trading route.'

Of all the things Brand had thought would happen, this was not one of them. This was his father's dream. *His* dream. Had Anne had some part to play in this?

'I would be honoured.'

'I am trying to work out, Brand Ivarsson, if you are a lion or a wolf. Which is it? My daughter has clearly made her decision... So, in atonement for all my past sins against my child, I will concede to her wishes and set you free. But we will come to an agreement. You will not invade our lands and we will not attack yours. And we shall seal this deal by me giving you a title. You shall be Ealdorman Brand Ivarsson of Kald.'

'I have no need of a title.'

'That is where you're wrong. You cannot marry my daughter unless you have land, wealth—and a title.'

Brand's head snapped up. 'You wish me to marry your daughter? But I am a Dane.' His brow furrowed. Was he still dreaming?

'At a price—and in return for your protection. I believe there is much to be gained from forming an alliance... calling a truce between Termarth and Kald. It would help to safeguard our lands and our power. My daughter has told me how your men would follow you into battle, and how you are not like the majority of your kind. We have seen the destruction and devastation that clans from the North and even our own Saxon neighbours have caused to villages across the land, and the threat grows greater every day. I seek order, peace and prosperity—just as you have told me you do. I can help with your food shortages, land and wealth. And in return you will provide me with warriors who will fight for me when I need it. And we will bind this deal with the hand of my daughter.'

Brand allowed himself a moment to let the King's words sink in. He agreed with all the points this seemingly wise and open-minded man had made, bar one. 'You have my loyalty, King Eallesborough, and you have my word that I will protect Termarth. I believe we have both come to realise that the greatest riches are here, inside these walls, and need to be kept safe. But, even so, I cannot marry your daughter.'

He couldn't believe what he was saying. Wasn't this everything that he wanted? But, no... All along he had wanted Anne to want to be with him. He wanted it to be her choice. He didn't want her to be sold in marriage, as she would have been to Crowe.

From the moment he'd met her he'd made bad decisions, over and over again. And even though he couldn't regret making love to her last night, he knew he must now do the right thing by her—even if he inflicted pain on himself.

'And why is that?'

'Because your daughter is a priceless treasure—not an object to be gifted to any man, to do his bidding. I believe she should be free to make her own choices to ensure her happiness.' He inclined his head towards the King. 'So I will accept your terms of peace, and I shall build your boats, but I implore you to allow the Princess to decide her own destiny.'

The King studied him for a long moment. 'You are, as my daughter has said, a surprising man, Brand Ivarsson. I would like to get to know you better. But for now, let us shake on this deal.'

King Eallesborough stood in his elegant red and gold velvet robes, his hand outstretched. And Brand rose to meet him, towering over him, and took his hand, sealing their alliance. Mutual admiration glimmered between them.

'I am very pleased. I only hope my daughter is as content with this accord.'

Anne was in the stables, grooming Rebel and feeding him carrots, when a shadow fell over the wooden shelter.

'You're spoiling him.'

She turned to see Brand leaning in the doorway, watching her, and her body almost sagged with relief and happiness. Her father had been true to his word. He had not hurt him.

The brush in her hand stopped mid-stroke. 'He deserves it.' She smiled, her heart thundering in her chest.

It had taken every shred of willpower to extract herself from his arms this morning, to leave his warm bed and get dressed. She had known she had to get back to her chamber before the household awoke, and yet leaving him had been torture. She'd had the best night of her life, and she didn't even mind the raw, aching feeling between her legs—it was a reminder of where he'd been and what they'd done together.

She had spoken with her father and begged him to show mercy to the Barbarian. And when Brand had stalked into the Great Hall her chest had almost imploded. She knew with every breath that she was helplessly, foolishly, in love with him. But she had no idea if he felt the same.

'How did you get along with my father?' she asked.

'He was far too lenient with me, if that's what you mean. I have not been punished enough for what I did, how I behaved. The King is different from how you described—as if he's learned the error of his ways. I hope he will be good to you now, Anne.'

He took a step towards her, tucking a wispy strand of hair behind her ears, and her breath hitched at his touch.

'He has asked me to build him a fleet of ships and to open up trade between our fortresses—I believe I have you to thank for that, and I'm grateful to you.'

She was delighted Brand and her father had come to an agreement. This was exactly what she had been hoping for—that Brand would build her father's boats and her father would in turn see the kind of man Brand really was…what she saw in him. But she didn't want Brand to be grateful. She wanted so much more from him…

Rebel nickered, as if to say *Keep brushing*, and Anne realised the brush was still suspended in mid-air.

Brand inclined his head, nodding to his faithful steed. 'Will you look after him for me when I'm gone? I think he should stay here. He likes you much more than me anyway.'

Pain lanced her, swift and hard, in the heart. 'You're leaving?'

She didn't know what she'd been hoping he would say, but it wasn't this. Never this. She shook her head a little, as if to say it couldn't be true, but when she looked up into Brand's eyes her stomach seemed to sink like one of his boats, landing with a thud at the bottom of the ocean. And she knew, instantly, that he meant to say goodbye.

He'd taken her to bed, made love to her, and now he was about to ride out of her life. How could he?

She felt the agony of a million arrows hitting her. She wanted to lash out at him, yell and beg him to stay, but her pride would never allow herself to do that.

'I must. I need to go home and make amends with my people…put things right.'

What about him making amends to *her*? She wanted him to start by taking her back to bed and making love to her all over again.

'But you only arrived here yesterday! I was hoping to show you the castle.'

She'd been hoping he'd stay a while. Forever. She had hoped he might get to know her father, win him round until the King accepted him as one of their own.

Until the King accepted him as suitable husband material…

But it had all been nothing more than an unrealistic hope. Of course Brand wouldn't stay. He wasn't the type of man to bow down to the rules of another, and he had his own lands and people to protect. She wouldn't want him to abandon them—and yet she couldn't bear it if he abandoned her either. She had been foolish to hope of having any kind of future with him. He had told her once he would never marry, so why had she begun to hope otherwise?

She didn't trust her voice to speak any more. A huge lump was growing in her throat. She had been mad to think that it could ever work between them. He was a Dane and she was a Saxon. They could never be together—her father would never allow it. Their people wouldn't like it. And yet she knew now it was what she wanted with every beat of her heart.

Brand gave her a cool smile. 'We have a harvest to focus on in Kald, and now new boats to build.'

He kissed her lightly on the lips, and it was almost her undoing. She nearly threw herself down onto her knees and begged him to stay. But she had too much dignity. So she just stood there, watching him saddle his stallion, watching him mount the horse.

'I wish I could go back and change what has happened. I really am sorry for everything. You'll always be my regret, Anne. I hope that you can one day forgive me.'

Her whole world was unravelling and yet she was rooted to the spot, nodding under his gaze.

'I do. I have.'

And then he inclined his head one last time, his blue gaze raking over every inch of her body, drinking her in as if to fix her in his memory, and then he was gone.

Chapter Fourteen

'Don't slouch, Anne.'

'Sorry,' she muttered.

Anne and her father were having dinner together in the Great Hall, but she wasn't very hungry. She had lost her appetite weeks ago and she wasn't sure it would ever return.

'Oh, for pity's sake, girl, is everything all right?'

'Yes.'

She offered her father a little smile, because that was what he expected. But it felt false, as if it had been carved across her face with her meat knife.

'You've been pushing that meat around your plate for the past God knows how long. If you don't want it, feed it to the dogs!'

'Don't curse, Father. I'm fine,' she reassured him, not wanting to talk about it. She saw no point in bringing up old wounds.

He sighed. 'You're lying to yourself and to me, Anne. You keep saying you're fine when you're clearly not.' He put down his own knife and sat back in his seat. 'When you returned from Kald with my men I was relieved. I had been so worried the Northmen had hurt you, or worse. I wanted to make amends. The people wanted their Princess back and I was desperate to have my daughter home, to make right all my wrongs over the years. But you are not my daughter! All I've got is a shell—a hollowed-out version of the girl she used to be!'

She stared across the table at him, her tears threatening to spill over. The summer had dragged on and on, and finally the leaves on the big oak trees outside the windows were beginning to fall. She felt bad upon hearing her father's words.

She'd been so pleased that he had wanted to make things up to her and get to know her properly. He'd been making such an effort. And she'd tried, she really had—throwing herself into tasks like reorganising his papers, or taking afternoon walks with him, going out riding together. She'd also thrown herself into studying the art of healing those in need. Finally, she felt needed, wanted…useful. She was no longer invisible to her father or his subjects.

She'd even made the King parade around his kingdom, meeting the farmers and traders to find out more about them, and they'd hosted a banquet in the Great Hall to reward the soldiers for her safe return. But it had all been with a false kind of enthusiasm. She'd hoped it would take her mind off what had happened, distract her from thinking about Brand, but it hadn't worked. Nothing worked. Her Danish warrior consumed her thoughts.

'If I'm not mistaken, you have not been yourself since Brand Ivarsson left to go home to Kald,' her father said.

Just the mention of Brand's name was enough to spur an onslaught of memories. She didn't want to talk about him. She couldn't. It hurt too much.

Watching him ride off into the distance had been awful. It was as if he'd ripped out her heart and taken it with him. She'd felt a terrible sense of loss and had sagged against the wall in the stables, sobbing. And it hadn't left her since. She hadn't been able to eat properly, and when she slept she dreamed of his voice rolling over her, like the gentle roar of the waves.

He had left her the shell he'd found for her in the ocean that day they'd been out on the boat, and she spent hours lying on her bed, its cool surface pressed up against her ear.

'I don't know what you mean,' she said.

'Don't you?' Her father leaned towards her. 'You've been shuffling through these halls with a vacant, lost look on your face for weeks. You don't eat, you don't sleep, but most of all, you don't smile, Anne. You don't know what to do with yourself!'

'That's not true... I've attended your witans, helped with the kingdom, and the banquet, and—'

'And you are always distracted!' He finished her sentence for her, throwing his hands up in despair. 'You're in love with the man, Anne. Admit it.'

'Father! How can you say such a thing?'

He sat back again, steepling his hands in front of him, as he always did when he was deep in thought or about to say something profound. 'I wasn't going to tell you this, but I think that now I must. I offered Brand Ivarsson your hand in marriage as part of our truce.'

'What?' Her knife slipped out of her hand and clattered down to the table.

'Not just because he can help to protect us, form an alliance, but because I could see what he meant to you. It was my way of making amends to you. You have to marry someone, Anne. And, yes, it should be someone with lands and a title, an ally to Termarth. But most of all it should be someone you love—and who loves you.'

'Wh-what did he say?' she gasped, not caring about letting her real feelings show now. She was too miserable to care. 'He must have declined.'

Her father took a gulp of his wine and swallowed it down. 'He said you shouldn't be any part of a deal between men. Instead, he made me promise that you'd be free to make your own choices, to marry who you wanted. And I agreed.'

Anne stared at her father in shock. She couldn't believe it. Brand had done that? Fought for her freedom? It was everything she had ever wanted... She was overwhelmed by what Brand had done. A man had put her needs before his own. She should be grateful to him. And yet none of this helped to make her feel any better.

'Why are you telling me this now?'

'I was selfish. I wanted to keep you to myself for a while before you left me again. Perhaps I had hoped you might take a shine to Lord Stanton. He is a good man, and he's a Saxon. But that was a fool's hope. I can see it now, as clear as day. You love the Barbarian and you won't be happy without him. And as our lands are now relatively safe—or as safe as they can ever be—you should be free to marry for love, Anne, not to bolster our kingdom's power.'

A tear slipped down Anne's cheek. It was everything she had ever wanted to hear. But there was one problem.

'He didn't want me,' she said, wiping the moisture away with the back of her hand.

Brand had given her a great gift, and yet she felt as if he'd taken something far greater from her at the same time.

Her father sat back in his chair. 'Surely you don't believe that? I certainly don't. I could have killed him for taking you from me, Anne. But when I saw how you felt about him I was willing to give him the benefit of the doubt. And then, when I met him, I saw a man standing before me who, in pursuit of revenge, had crossed his own moral boundary—and couldn't forgive himself. And in his determination to set things right he had to give up the thing he wanted most. You.'

She stared up into her father's wise eyes and stopped trying to wipe away the tears. She just let them roll freely.

'He had to set you free to make your own choices. I thought you might have told him what he meant to you, what you wanted, before he left...no?'

She shook her head, horrified. She hadn't even tried to stop him from getting on his horse and riding out of her life. She'd just let him leave without telling him how she truly felt.

'I loved your mother greatly, Anne. I know now that she might not have felt the same about me, and I would do anything to have another day with her, to try to win her heart. After she died, I was in so much pain. I couldn't bear to lose you as well. But I went about everything the wrong way.'

Hearing her father's words, she knew now that this was how Brand felt. She knew he blamed himself for his father's death and Svea's attack, and that he must feel he'd let Anne down too. Had he pushed her away to punish himself?

'Don't waste your life, Anne. I have caused you many unhappy years. Well, no more. Go after what you want, daughter, with no regrets.'

'What are you saying, Father?'

He put down his glass. 'I'm saying you have his horse, don't you? I'm sure it knows the way back to Kald. And I'm sure Lord Stanton would be happy to escort you there. I could even ask him to take you under the pretence of checking how my boats are doing. So, go, Anne. You have my blessing.'

The King had been right. Rebel hadn't forgotten the route to Kald and seemed happy to be heading back that way, his tail swishing freely as she and Lord Stanton and a number of the King's men galloped over the meadows and undulating hills.

If only Anne could borrow some of her loyal steed's confidence, all would be well.

She took in the vibrant, earthy tones of the countryside, signalling that autumn was almost here. The first fallen leaves crackled beneath the horses' hooves and the golden branches of the amber-coloured trees creaked in the cool afternoon breeze. The hedgerows were laden with delicious wild berries, but it seemed Anne was destined never to fully enjoy or appreciate this journey—her thoughts were always consumed by one thing...or rather one man.

The closer they got to the fortress, the more Anne's courage began to waver, and she started to doubt her decision about making this journey. It had been many weeks since Brand had walked out of her life, after convincing her father to set her free so she could choose her own path. And this was the path she had chosen to follow: this sunlit avenue through the forest and along the coast to Kald, back to her Barbarian.

She wondered what his reaction would be when he saw her. Would he curse softly in his deep, Danish tongue and pull her into his arms, telling her he'd missed her? Or would she blurt out how she felt about him, and then he'd tell her to stop babbling, before scooping her up and carrying her up to his room to make passionate love to her all night long?

She closed her eyes as if in silent prayer...

She wondered if the biggest battle she would face would be with his conscience—after all, that was what had kept them apart these past few weeks, wasn't it? What if his self-loathing for all he'd done wouldn't allow them to be together? Then she would have to soothe his worries and show him that they deserved to be happy.

But she was scared, shaking like the leaves rustling

around her in the trees. What if her father was wrong, and Brand didn't care for her at all? What if he'd simply wanted to bed her and then get away from her as fast as he could? If that was the truth, it would hurt like hell, but at least she would know and could return to Termarth and try to move on.

Her mind began to torture her, running through all the worst scenarios. What if she arrived and found him in the arms of another woman? Her heart screamed at the thought. What if he wasn't pleased to see her? Then she would have to be brave and put on a front, show an interest in seeing her father's boats and then make her excuses to leave.

But what if he was? Oh, what if he was?

When the small convoy left the forest and the ocean came into view, Anne began to feel better than she had in weeks. This was where she wanted to be—where she belonged. She took strength from the steady ebb and flow of the thrilling waves, and the trilling sound of the sea birds gliding overhead. The fiery autumn sun was beaming down on her, so full of promise, and just like the pretty little toadstools that were flourishing all around her in the undergrowth, hope mushroomed inside her.

It was a while longer before the high, imposing wooden walls of Kald came into view. She slipped down from the saddle and the men led the horses along a weed-strewn path and over the heath where Crowe's army of Saxon soldiers had gathered. Anne heard the horn signalling their arrival and felt as nervous as she had when she'd stood before Brand naked. Once again, she was about to lay herself bare.

Damn, she must have brushed against some stinging nettles. Her legs had begun to burn…

'Are you all right, Your Highness?' Lord Stanton asked.

'Yes, I think I've just landed in a mass of nettles. It's nothing—just a little prickle.'

There was no time to focus on that now. Approaching the tall wooden gates, she looked up to the parapet on the bridge and saw Kar staring down at her. He grinned, and she raised her hand in greeting. Her heart was in her mouth as the gates slowly opened, her entire body trembling.

As the convoy made their way into the settlement, many of the villagers rushed forward to greet them. Anne was pleased to see them all—especially Svea, Kar, and Ulf. Svea hugged her tight, and Anne instantly noticed a difference in her—she seemed free, happy…perhaps because she knew her attacker was locked away. Anne was glad. Ulf proudly showed her his battle scar.

'It's wonderful to see you. You're very welcome,' Svea said.

Anne scanned the central square, her eyes full of enquiry. *Where was he?* And then, out of the corner of her eye, she saw a tall, dark figure emerge from the doorway of the barn and her heart bloomed inside her chest.

Brand.

His towering presence was enough to make them all turn and stare, and Anne's reaction was the same as it had always been. Her heart took flight and she knew there was no point trying to contain it. He looked more dangerous, more formidable, more magnificent than she'd ever seen him as his steely gaze assessed the scene before him.

She struggled to work out what he was thinking. Those penetrating eyes she'd dreamed of every night since she'd last seen him regarded her coolly, and she realised this was not the welcome she had imagined or hoped for. And when he began to stalk towards them, all power and lithe legs, her carefully rehearsed words abandoned her.

'*Heil ok sæl.* Hello, Anne... Lord Stanton.' He inclined his head. 'This is a surprise.'

So much for scooping her up and spinning her round in his arms. She just nodded, revelling in seeing his face again and hearing his velvety voice. Since when had she ever been rendered mute?

'What are you doing here?' he asked.

'Lord Stanton and I have come to see how you are getting on with my father's boats,' she said, with a strained, overbright smile.

He didn't look pleased to see her. If anything, he looked angry. And he must know the King wouldn't have sent her—someone who didn't know the first thing about boats—all this way to check on his ships. It was a ridiculous excuse. She cringed and a blush burned her cheeks.

His icy gaze continued to rake over her, then lanced Lord Stanton.

'Perhaps you and the King's men would like a cup of ale and something to eat by the fire?' Svea asked.

Anne could have hugged the woman for cutting through the tension as Svea took her elbow and steered her in the direction of the longhouse, away from Brand's dark judgement.

But neither the fire nor the meal Svea served them helped to warm her up. Brand's glacial gaze had sent shivers through her, and a cold hand had reached into her chest, squeezing her heart. They were all seated around the large wooden table, but Brand was talking about ships with Lord Stanton, and even though Svea was asking her questions about Termarth, and her summer, Anne felt as if she had been cast adrift, totally and utterly miserable.

She knew that she'd made a mistake; she shouldn't have come. Brand didn't want her here.

'I am surprised you have made this long journey… King Eallesborough told me he didn't want the boats until the spring.' He was talking to Lord Stanton, but his gaze rested on Anne.

So he wanted to know why they were really here? They were here because she hadn't thought ahead, that was why! She'd thought only of her wants and desires, her hopes and dreams—not his. Hadn't he told her once he never wanted to marry? Why had she thought she could convince him otherwise?

When a pretty young serving girl topped up Brand's tankard, smiling at him, flushing scarlet when he thanked her, Anne's heart felt as if it was being trampled on. Had there been women since her? Why had she thought she was different and meant anything to him? He must take women to bed all the time—perhaps a different one every night. There was nothing stopping him.

Oh, God, why had she come? She'd just made the agony worse by seeing his fascinating face again.

She stole a look at him. His hair had grown even longer since the early summer, and it was tightly fastened with bonds at the back of his neck. His skin was a golden colour and she noticed he wore his father's silver ring. He looked fit and well—had he not missed her at all?

Her father had offered Brand her hand and he'd declined. The King had convinced her it was because Brand loved her, but that was just his opinion. How could she have come all this way on a whim, hoping he might feel the same? He was being so distant and aloof...surely she had her answer? He didn't.

And now she was trapped. She couldn't just leave; they'd travelled day and night to get here. Her Saxon men would at least want a good night's sleep before they returned home.

And then a thought struck her. Where would they sleep tonight? Where would the Danes put them? Would Brand send her to sleep in Svea's house while he took that serving girl up to his room? It was all too much to bear...

She shot to her feet, clumsily knocking over her drink.

'Is everything all right, Your Highness?' Lord Stanton asked. 'Is it the sting?'

'Sting?' Brand asked.

Anne waved her hand in the air. 'It's nothing—just a few nettles.' She'd almost forgotten about that; it was her heart that was hurting.

Brand's brow furrowed. 'Still putting yourself in danger at every turn, Princess?'

She sighed. 'Everything is quite well. I think I just need some air,' she said, seeing all eyes upon her. 'Please excuse me for a moment.'

She headed out of the hall and across the square, making her way down the grassy slope towards the boathouse. Whichever way she turned she was taunted by memories, and she realised she had fallen in love with this place—the purple heather covering the heath, the undulating farmland, the endless expanse of sand and the rollicking waves.

But she had fallen for Brand first.

When she reached the little jetty and saw the long-ship they'd sailed in weeks before still tied up and bobbing about on the water, she smiled wistfully. She carefully lowered herself into the hull and sat down on a bench, no longer concerned by the gentle rocking movement. She wished she could conjure herself away to that day when they'd sailed around the headland, right back to the moment when he'd asked her if she wanted to sail away with him...

'Planning on going somewhere?'

Brand. She whisked round to face him, and the boat toppled a little.

She shrugged, suddenly feeling more than a little

silly at being caught sitting in a moored boat. 'I was debating my next adventure. Are you following me?'

'It wouldn't be the first time,' he said darkly. 'I would have thought you'd done enough travelling for one day. And why are you roaming about the place on your own? You should know better than to do that.'

'Well, I'm not on my own, am I? You're here. But you can't always be there to protect me, Brand. I don't expect you to be.'

His eyes narrowed on her. 'Come on—get out of there. Show me your nettle sting, I have something for it.'

She stood up slowly and made her way towards him on the jetty. But she refused his offer of help. She didn't trust herself to touch him.

She lifted the hem of her dress to show him the red rash that had appeared on her shin.

He let out a gentle curse and busied himself on the bank, looking for something. A moment later he came back towards her, brandishing a leaf, and knelt down to cup the back of her leg in his palm.

She swallowed. 'I can do it.'

'It's fine,' he said, as he used his other hand to rub the leaf over her skin. 'I've done it now.'

He took a step back and crossed his arms over his broad chest. 'The rash should start to fade now.'

'It feels better already.' She tried to smile, but she couldn't quite manage it. She wanted him to always take care of her like this—and her him. 'Thank you.'

Although the leaf had cooled her skin, her leg was still tingling from his burning touch.

'You know, you shouldn't have made the journey to Kald on your own, Anne,' he said, his brow creasing again. 'It's dangerous. If you'd sent a messenger I would have ridden out to meet you.'

'I wasn't on my own. I was with Lord Stanton and—'

'Damn it, Anne, I don't want to hear about him,' he grated, stepping closer to her, ambushing her senses with the familiar spicy scent of him. And then she wondered— was he jealous? Just as she had been about the serving girl? Was that why he was being so cold? Was he hurting too?

He gripped her wrists with his hands and heat raced up her arms, as if he was binding her with red-hot bonds. She welcomed it. She longed to go back to being his.

'Now tell me what you're really doing here.'

He was staring down at her in such a heated, penetrating way, making her feel as if he knew what she was thinking. And she didn't mind. She didn't want to hide from him or her feelings any more. She wanted to risk her heart and tell him how she felt.

'Why did you refuse my hand in marriage, Brand?'

'What?'

She wondered if her question had come out like a silent wail—that was how it felt in her heart.

'My father told me all about your conversation. Your agreement. But why did you reject me when my father offered me as your wife?'

This wasn't the carefully crafted speech she'd learned on the way here. It was all coming out wrong. But she felt so wretched and miserable, she didn't care.

She just needed to know the truth. She needed to know if he felt a fraction of what she felt for him.

'You know why.'

She shook her head. 'I don't, Brand. I need you to explain it to me.'

A muscle flickered in his jaw. He was not a man of words—she knew that. He was a Northman and a man of action—a warrior, a beautiful boat builder and a farmer. A protector of his people. And her saviour.

But she needed to hear this, so he would have to try.

'Because you always said you didn't want to be treated like an object. Because you said you were sick of men making decisions for you. I knew you didn't want to be just another Saxon woman, offered in marriage to form an alliance or in exchange for peace. I wanted you to be free to make your own choices, Anne, not to have your father make another one for you just to suit him or me. And because...'

He stepped back a little.

'What?' She closed the gap between them again.

'Because I wasn't worthy of you, Anne. I was so single-minded in my vendetta against Crowe that I hurt you in the process, and I couldn't forgive myself for it.'

Her father had been right. Brand was punishing himself. He didn't think he deserved her. But that didn't mean he didn't want her.

Hope soared inside her. If she could just be brave enough to let him know how she felt... If she could make him see himself the way she saw him, they might just stand a chance.

'But I forgive you, Brand.'

She moved closer towards him and, emboldened by the way his thumbs were gently stroking over her wrists, tried to put into words just what he meant to her.

'My father didn't send me. I came here of my own accord because I wanted to see you. It doesn't have anything to do with the boats. But I think you knew that anyway.' She swallowed. 'I came to tell you that I can't live without you. That I never expected to fall in love with a Northman, but I did—from the moment I saw you on the ramparts that night. You stole me away, heart, body, and soul.'

'Anne—'

'Let me finish. I have no regrets about any of it— apart from not throwing myself down in front of your horse and stopping you from leaving Termarth. I didn't know then that you had fought for my freedom to choose my own future, but I do now, and I choose you, Brand. I don't care that you are a Dane and I'm a Saxon. All I care about is that I will be yours and you will be mine.'

He pulled her towards him so suddenly, so urgently, she gasped. And he held her so tight, as if his life depended on it. At one point in time she might have struggled, might have gasped for air at being so confined, but not now. This was where she wanted to be. In this man's arms forever.

'It broke my heart to leave you, Anne. The day I met you when I was a boy was the best and worst day of my life. You were a glimmer of light in a dark time. My hope. And I've dreamed about making you mine ever since. But after I'd taken you from Termarth I realised that wasn't enough. I wanted you to want me too. I came to Termarth that night with vengeance in my heart, but when I left it was filled with love. I didn't believe I deserved you, Anne. I'm still not sure I do... But I promise I'll spend the rest of my life making you happy, making sure that I am worthy of you. *Ek elska þik*. I love you, Anne.'

Anne stared up at him and brought her hand up to cup his cheek. 'Growing up, I heard all kinds of stories about you, Brand the Barbarian, but the man you have become surpasses all those tales. You're so much more than you think of yourself. You're everything to me. You're a Northman with a huge capacity to love. And you have my heart forever. I love you too.'

Epilogue

The happy noise from the wedding celebrations going on in the longhouse could be heard from where Brand was leading his beautiful bride up the stairs to his room, his hands covering her eyes. She looked more stunning than he'd ever seen her, with intricate braids and little wildflowers in her hair. But it was her glittering green eyes and her breathtaking smile that had made him feel so happy as she'd walked towards him up the aisle earlier today.

'What's going on?' Anne laughed.

'I have something for you,' he said. 'An extra wedding gift.'

It had been the best day of their lives. They'd held the wedding down on the beach, and under the bronze autumn sun they'd spoken their vows. It had been the first time in his life Brand had felt tears in his eyes. They'd given each other family swords—a symbol that both families and kingdoms would protect each other from now on—and they'd stuck to tradition and carried out the bride—running up the hill, where the Danes and Saxons had raced each other on foot to the longhouse.

The Danes had won, of course, so King Eallesborough, and Lord Stanton, and all their Saxon guests had had to serve them ale throughout the evening. It had all been done in good spirits.

Brand was glad they hadn't fought the Saxons in some great battle at Kald. He wanted his home to be a place of peace, not a place of bloodshed. And over the past few months Kald had thrived. There had been no more attacks on his people, and they had used the gold he'd been given for the boats to buy more crops.

His people were happy. They said he'd done them proud. They told him his father would have been proud too, and he finally believed it himself. He was glad his legacy wouldn't be the slaughter of hundreds of men. No, the greatest battle in his life had been over his wife's beautiful face and body—a battle he'd had with himself. But, looking at her now, he knew he'd been victorious.

They'd enjoyed a hog roast feast and then, while the festivities still continued, they'd slipped away to be alone.

Anne tripped on a step, laughing in her long white silk gown, unable to see where she was going, so Brand picked her up and carried her the rest of the way in his arms.

At the top, he took her over the threshold, then placed her down gently, putting his hands over her eyes again. 'Ready?'

She nodded.

As he lifted his hands away, and her eyes adjusted to the steam-filled room, they fell upon the beautifully carved wooden barrel under the smoke hole. It was filled with hot water and scattered with rose petals. It was big enough for two and their initials had been carved into the side.

She looked up at him in delight. 'Did you make this for me?'

'I did. I couldn't have my Princess going down to the sea to bathe in the freezing cold water, now, could I?'

'Oh, Brand, I love it,' she said, clasping her hands together over her heart. 'It's incredible. It must have taken you ages.'

'You're worth it.'

She flung her arms around him and kissed him. 'You'd better not show it to my father,' she said, with a glint in her eye. 'He'll wonder why you were making this for me rather than building his beloved boats—after all, you are his oath man now…'

He growled, pulling her towards him. He knew she was teasing him. Over the past few days, in the run-up to the wedding, they'd hosted the Saxons, and Brand and King Eallesborough had got on well. Anne had joked that she'd hardly seen him—that her father was monopolising him and she was jealous.

'The only person I will ever make an oath to is my wife. And that was only ever going to be you, Anne.' He kissed her deeply, savouring the feel of her tongue moving against his. 'I love you, Anne Ivarsson. Now, shall we try it out?'

She nodded. 'Actually, I have a surprise for you too. Sit down,' she said, ushering him to the bed.

She reached up to unfasten the straps around her neck, untying her wedding dress, and his throat constricted. So it was going to be that kind of present... He was already hard with anticipation.

She let the material fall down her chest, skimming it over the flare of her hips and her thighs and he watched it sink to the floor. She stood before him naked, chewing her bottom lip. 'I got this for you,' she said.

And through a lust-filled haze his eyes flickered to the small inked flower on the indentation of her left hip.

'It's a primrose,' she said. 'To remind us of our first kiss. But I know that the primrose also means "I can't live without you", and I thought how true that was of me and you.'

He took her arm and tugged her closer, so he could inspect it better.

'Do you like it?' she asked, and he realised she was holding her breath. 'If you don't—'

'Anne, stop babbling.' He pressed his lips gently against the ink on her skin, making her shiver. 'I love it. It's beautiful. Just like you...'

And then his lips began to stray downwards.

Soon they were both naked in the water, and he was holding her wet body in his arms, as he'd dreamed of doing when he'd first seen her bathing on the beach. He was sitting on the bench in the barrel, and he pulled her onto his lap, weightless in the water. He gently lifted her up and then lowered her down again, impaling her on his huge, hard length. He gave her a moment to accommodate him, their faces just a sigh apart, and then she began to move her hips. His hands were on her bottom, coaxing her to move harder, faster, and when she cried out her orgasm, burying her face into his neck, he soon came spiralling after her, knowing that all his dreams had come true.

Later, as they lay curled up together in the bed, with Anne stroking the ink on his chest, they talked of their first adventure together as man and wife. They hoped to make a least one journey before any much-wanted children came along.

Brand was planning to take her to one of the little islands south of here in the *Freyja*, to celebrate their marriage, and neither of them could wait to be out on the sea again alone. He was looking forward to showing her how to swim, and in return she'd promised to teach him how to read.

Rolling on top of her, pinning her beneath him, Brand lowered his mouth down on hers. 'Thank you for making me the happiest man in the world,' he whispered.

'I'm sorry you didn't get your gold as part of the marriage bargain...' She grinned, teasing him again.

'If I have you in my life I'm the richest man I know. All I ever wanted was to steal your heart, Anne.'

She wriggled beneath him, stirring his desire all over again. 'You can steal me away whenever you like.'

And he did—over and over again...

* * * * *